"MAYBE WE SHOULD KILL THIS STUPID AMERICAN!"

As the Chinese officer lifted his machine pistol, Bart Lasker's face was transformed from the mask of a bumbling tourist into a cunning grimace. He half crouched, his fingers trembled and bent into the Snow Lion claw attack. . . .

But it wasn't Lasker doing this; he was no longer in control of his body. This moment of danger had aroused the sleeping giant within him. The ancient warrior skills of his alter ego, Raspahloh, had been awakened. It had happened in the blink of an eye.

The Chinese officer gasped and stepped back, but it was too late. Lasker felt his body tense and then spring forward like the Snow Lion. He knew that Raspahloh's blood lust would soon be satisfied.

MYSTIC REBEL II

Ryder Syvertsen

THE DANCING DEAD

PINNACLE BOOKS
WINDSOR PUBLISHING CORP.

PINNACLE BOOKS

are published by

Windsor Publishing Corp.
475 Park Avenue South
New York, NY 10016

First printing: August, 1988

Printed in the United States of America

Foreword

Bart Lasker was an American bush pilot in Asia whose life was forever changed when he was forced to parachute down into the mountains of Tibet. There he became embroiled in the struggle between the brave Tibetan rebel tribesmen and the Chinese invaders. Caught in an avalanche, he was captured by the Bonpo Sorcerers and taken in a daze to the secret Shekar Dzong monastery high on Mount Kailas. There, he was recognized as a reincarnation of the Bonpo cult's evil fifteenth century assassin called Raspahloh.

A hideous mystic ceremony threatened to turn Bart Lasker into that powerful being Raspahloh once more, but he did not drink the blood of the sacrifice and remained partially in control of his fate. Lasker was trained in the Bonpo secret martial art, E-Kung, and used this art to affect a daring escape, pursued by hordes of bat-wing gliding Bonpo monks. He wandered back through the wilderness and was taken as a disciple by a ragged old hermit. Through this hermit-master, Lasker became the Mystic Rebel, heir to the knowledge and power of both the Bonpo and the ancient lost race known as the Cultivators.

Now Bart Lasker has pledged his loyalty to the Dalai Lama and serves the cause of free Tibet. His mission: restore the ancient Kingdom of Tibet so that it can serve as a sanctuary for mankind in the dark age to come.

But to accomplish that mission, the Mystic Rebel must not only do battle with mortal foes such as the mastermind of death, Dr. Woo, but also he must fight the insidious creeping evil of the Bonpo, who have vowed vengeance upon him.

And another enemy lurks in his own body; he must also control his powerful enemy/ally within, his alter ego, Raspahloh.

It is not an easy task set before him, but the outcome of his battles will determine the fate of the world.

Chapter 1

Hong Kong is a city of contrasts, a capitalistic bastion in the shadow of communist China, and ever-mindful of the clock, which ticks off the hours and days until the city will be turned over lock, stock and barrel in 1997 to the strange behemoth next to it. In its 23,000 acres, 30 million plus people of every nationality and economic situation pursue their collective and separate aspirations. Narrow lanes filled with peddlers' stalls and stately glass office towers abut one another, physically sharing the same streets of commerce. But the gulf between them otherwise is impassable; the difference between the life of a millionaire and a harbor junk dweller is awesome.

The richest inhabitants of Hong Kong literally live in ivory towers. And the most stately marble-clad palaces of the rich are on exclusive Victoria Peak. . . .

Perched on a steep cliff high above the teeming city shimmering in May heat stood the most sumptuous of all oriental mansions, The Palms. Seen like a vision through a veil of smog and haze from below, it glowed like a phantasm of the imagination, a veritable castle in the sky. The Palms' five collonaded stories were trimmed at each corner with gold-plated dragon-gargoyles. The mansion's manicured, lush green grounds were a veritable botanic garden of exotic blooms, giving up their perfumes to the air. Topiary hedges in the shapes of elephants and horses were being carefully trimmed by a group of efficient gardeners; the whole thirteen acres of expensive real estate was as close to perfection as money could buy.

All of this oppulence and splendor was, of course, well-protected. The Palms was patrolled by a small army of grey-uniformed guards, each trained in the martial arts, each carrying a mean-looking Uzi machine pistol. The exclusiveness and privacy denoted by the sheer thirteen-hundred-foot-high cliffs was assured in this manner. The only access to The Palms—aside from the mansion's roof heli-port—was a private tram.

The owner of the mansion, Dr. Woo, was ostensibly an international businessman. But in actuality, Woo was more than that. The cleanliness and esthetic serenity of The Palms was a veneer, his neat covering for a cancer on the world; a pleasant backdrop for the sinister activities that were planned and executed by those who were privileged to visit the mansion.

Dr. Woo was the enigmatic dark lord of the largest and most hidden of all criminal organizations: *The Jade Octagon.*

On the morning of May 29th, rising like a silver spider on a grey thread, a glistening single-car tram slowly ascended the sheer granite escarpment, heading to The Palms. In it, sitting in a leather chair in the car's living room-like interior, rode a single passenger—the young Chinese woman named Tse Ling. She was a vision of oriental loveliness. She was lithe and alluringly sinuous, like a jeweled snake, tempting as a goddess. Her long, streaming, silken black hair was shot with blue highlights in the morning light bouncing off the light-colored rocks. She wore a simple, almost severe, powder-blue silk cheong-som that was slit halfway up her smooth thigh. Her high cheekbones were flushed with the barest touch of expensive makeup. Tse Ling's slanted eyes were dark jade mysteries, an invitation to love—or to death. Alluring and repulsive.

The tram driver couldn't keep his eyes off her. She was, the driver estimated in his quick furtive glance, about thirty years of age. A person of education and privilege. Who could she be? Not a prostitute surely. Her bearing told the story of power and control. Of course, it was not his right to know. It would be dangerous to even appear interested in finding out. He knew little about his employer's business except that it involved vast amounts of money, that it was secret, and that to know more could be fatal. But he couldn't stop speculating about his passenger. Surely, she was a woman used to being deferred to, used to giving orders.

Tse Ling became aware of the driver's eyes looking in her direction. Her nostrils flared; her eyes glowered.

She snapped, "Do not stare at me, fool! Keep your eyes on your work."

The driver quickly looked away, his eyes directed back at the glistening track extending for another seventy yards up the steep incline. He felt as if his heart had been pierced with an ice bullet, so full of power and hatred was the beautiful woman's voice. He felt a constriction in his throat. He had been foolish, foolish to dare look at her—yet what man wouldn't?

Tse Ling lit a gold-tipped, pink cigarette and vacantly stared out at the steep rocks slowly passing by the steel tram car. It seemed somehow like the rock face of the cliff was time itself, a ceaseless passing of moments; and her mind's eye conjured an image. She saw not the irregular rock but the face of a man: the man who had possessed her briefly, but utterly, over a year ago in Tibet—the man they called the Mystic Rebel. He was the only man who had ruled her—ever. And there was pain, and desire.

A slight tremor—the slowing of the tram—drew her back to reality. She snapped, "Driver, why the delay? How long must this take?"

"Sorry, madam," the driver apologized, not daring a glance. "The automatic scanners are observing us. It is the routine security check. It will be over in just a moment."

She exhaled the last drag of her privately made cigarette through her nose, then crushed the butt in the silver ashtray next to the leather chair. She waited for a long moment and then felt the hum and saw the rocks moving by again.

Her heart was suddenly beating wildly in her chest with apprehension. After all, her future depended on this meeting, and she had no control of the outcome.

She had met Dr. Woo only one time before. That time, for the first time in her life, the Virgin Dragon, the Terror of Tibet, had *herself* been quite terrified. Yet that fateful meeting had worked out well enough. Dr. Woo, though apparently immune to her charms and unswayed by her beauty, had accepted her into the organization—accepted her as a Jade Octagon leader, duties unspecified. Immediately after that meeting, she had been tattoed—on her left thigh, just above the knee. Everyone in the organization wore the mark of the eight-sided green figure: A tangible symbol of fidelity, a recognition that there was no withdrawal from the organization, excepting death.

The cable car now glided to a halt; a crisply grey-uniformed guard opened the car door. The minute Tse Ling stood up and walked to the door to alight on the stone walk she noted it: a fetid odor that rose from the slums and polluted harbor. You could smell the city even up here. But the many rare blossoms lining the walkway wafted perfumed essence her way, covering the odor.

Bowing slightly, the muscular gurka guide said, "Dr. Woo welcomes you warmly." She nodded and the man led her along the stone path. It wound among tall rhododendron bushes alive with flowers, then cut across a manicured lawn. The white marble

11

mansion was now visible. She hadn't noted the fine filigree, gilded screens on the upper windows the last time—a new security measure? Probably.

It was hot. She wished to be quickly back in an air-conditioned environment. Her years in cold Tibet had made Tse Ling abhor extreme heat. As Tse Ling was guided down the rose-rimmed path to the grand entrance, she heard a dull thudding in the air. It was growing louder.

Shielding her eyes, she looked up into the azure sky. A sleek black helicopter with a gold crest on its side was arriving—that would be Dr. Woo. Was he perhaps taking this means to make his entrance grander than hers? The helicopter moved over the building and began descending. The craft's windows were opaque—no glimpse of the secretive man inside. She was disappointed. On her previous visit he had sat the entire time behind a filigree screen. Dr. Woo had been a shadow, no more.

She strode up the three red, carpeted steps. A set of doormen opened the doors, and an English butler bowed his head and said, "This way, madam." He took her down a long corridor which was lined with the priceless paintings the billionaire fancied—Fauvist, Impressionist—and then the butler opened the brass-handled, oak door of Woo's office. Tse Ling stepped in, and the door closed silently behind her.

It was the same office, the one with a magnificent panoramic view of the city and its busy harbor half lost in the haze. There were four upholstered chairs, all facing the same elaborately carved Chinese screen. A figure moved across it, casting a shadow over a counter or desk behind the screen. "Please sit down Tse Ling," a hoarse voice intoned.

She decided on the Queen Anne chair and sat down, crossed her legs and waited. There was a long silence that she didn't think fit to break. Was he watching her through the filigree of wood? She took out a cigarette from its silver case and lit it with her matching silver lighter.

"Please," the man behind the screen requested, "put the cigarette out in the ashtray to your right. I must insist that you do not smoke. My health, you understand, does not allow it."

She said, "Of course," and hiding her irritation did as he asked. Silhouetted by the window, the mysterious man behind the screen was in profile. All she could discern of his appearance was a sharp nose—not characteristically oriental.

In the last brief interview, Dr. Woo had mentioned his poor health; perhaps it was a bandage on his nose. Oh, it was so annoying not to face Woo directly. As long as this hiding game continued, Tse Ling was at a disadvantage because he probably couldn't see her any better than she saw him. Her feminine attributes—the power she had over men—were going to waste this way. Something would have to be done to give her an edge. She decided on a course of action.

"I would feel better if I could see you, Dr. Woo."

A muffled laugh. "You'd feel better?" Another stifled laugh. Then a studied silence.

Finally, she said, "Yes, if you could remove the screen."

"Very well, then—please come forward Tse Ling;

13

roll back the screen, if you wish. But I doubt it will satisfy you."

She stood up and pushed the screen. It was apparently on well-functioning castors and folded like an accordian to the left.

Tse Ling couldn't help gasping when she saw the man's figure revealed. It was like getting an electric shock. Dr. Woo was a small man wearing a blue business suit. His face was entirely covered, save for the sharp nose, by a pink plastic mask. The mask had small circular holes in it for both eyes and one hole for the mouth. One of the man's sleeves was pinned up—he had no left arm. His right hand was covered by a white glove.

"You see, I—have a disfigurement—no amount of plastic surgery will completely remedy, for it has been caused by radiation. You see, it does not heal. The mask provides—nutritional sustenance for my facial skin. Perhaps you wish to replace the screen?"

"No," Tse Ling said, and took her seat. When he took up a container with a glass straw from the desk top and sucked through it, there was a queasy feeling in her stomach. She maintained silence, composing herself. He stopped sucking and put the drink down.

"Oh, I'm sorry. Would you like a drink? Do you drink Perrier? If so, there is—"

She said, "No thank you, but you are most kind." She felt his brown eyes moving over her body now, pausing on her exposed thigh. Her advantage. But she wished he would draw the screen again. Everything about him had an air of sickness. His labored breathing was quite audible now, uneven and thick. And that mask. She half-shuddered as she wondered if she would have to sleep with him.

He put down the container. "Before we discuss your new responsibilities to the organization, I have news for you. Perhaps you will be interested to learn that certain information has reached my attention. Information which leads me to infer that the American agent that upset our nuclear material operations in Tibet is *not* dead, after all."

She controlled her surprise—and felt something like relief. "Is that so? Do you mean the C.I.A. man—or whatever he was—the one named Lasker? My sources in Tibet say he perished in the explosion of Smoke Mountain Facility." Tse Ling had long sensed, *felt* inside, that Lasker was alive. To hear her intuition confirmed was amazing. She yearned for it to be true, and feared it. Conflicting emotions.

"As long as he lives," Woo said gravely, "my astrologers, who are unerring, predict that Lasker will be a continuing danger to the Jade Octagon."

"I agree he is a threat," Tse Ling said cooly. "Lasker is unusually resourceful, and I told you about his power. He can read minds."

"That was no doubt a trick of drugs or hypnosis. In any case," Woo stated, "no one who has defied the Jade Octagon can be allowed to live. It sets—a bad example."

His white glove silently tapped on the desk's onyx surface—a sign of Woo's irritation. He again sipped the greenish liquid through the glass straw and swallowed loudly.

Tse Ling sorely wanted a cigarette, but she refrained. She steadied her breathing before asking, "Do you know where Lasker is?"

15

"Various sources have placed him in Bhutan and in India. Others of my informants say he is in Nepal. I suspect," Woo said hoarsely, "that they are all correct. I believe Lasker has come out of Tibet via Nepal and is now in central India." There was a trace of anxiety in his voice when Woo added, "I must now put out a search for the American and any of his associates. I will find and eliminate this threat."

"That might not be so easy. He is resourceful at escape. There have been stories. Some Tibetans say that when Lasker died he became the Mystic Rebel, some predicted a savior of Tibet. They say he can summon the demon protectors of Tibet to do his bidding."

"Bah," Woo said with disgust. "He is a mortal man. The myths that have arisen after the earthquake at Smoke Mountain are the result of the Tibetans being a superstitious lot. That the American somehow escaped the area alive is no more than happenstance. Yet the Tibetans made him a god! Such is the human weakness: to believe in what cannot be."

She nodded. But Tse Ling couldn't help but wonder how Woo could dismiss one set of superstitions and yet have utter faith in and depend so utterly on his Chinese astrologers.

Woo asked, "You still have contacts in Tibet, do you not, Tse Ling?"

"Yes," she said. "Certainly I do. If Lasker reappears there, I will soon know."

"Good. My men will search elsewhere—worldwide if need be. He's cost me dearly and made me abrogate a contract—something I am loathe to do.

My customers rely on me and now," Woo said pointedly, "must know I can depend on you, Tse Ling. I must know if you can be an esteemed member of the organization."

"I can be relied on," she said firmly. "I can command."

There was no reply. Tse Ling listened to the slow irregular breathing of the masked horror before her. A faint smell of carrion—rotted flesh—singed her nostrils; his dark brown eyes bore into her, undressing her. It was, she decided, not desire, but a look of appraisal. Then he hissed. "Yes . . . the matter at hand—your assignment." Woo opened a drawer and clumsily took up some papers with his one hand. He offered them to her, leaning over the desk with effort. "You will be in charge of the fourth side of the octagon. The previous leader of that part of my organization has proved unworthy—and therefore has been removed."

Tse Ling took the folder, sat back down and opened it. After a quick perusal, she looked up with alarm. "This is the worldwide prostitution ring. An unworthy assignment! I—"

"No," he insisted. "It is not unworthy. We do not handle street prostitution. This fourth side is an important part of my intelligence gathering, the key to the control of certain important officials and military men. That the organization makes a profit is good, but this is only a secondary factor."

"I would rather have another assignment," Tse Ling politely insisted.

"You will—in time," Woo comforted. "But prove yourself first, Tse Ling. Improve the fourth side of the Jade Octagon. Make us privy to more information; get more of the targeted individuals hooked on our narcotics. We must shape up this part of the grand plan. Of course, you should also pursue this Lasker matter."

"I . . ." she started, "would rather—"

He shouted—a strangely muffled frightening shot—and banged the desk. "Do you wish to go to Beijing? To face the Chinese government as a traitor? Do you have any choice? I have been unduly kind to you Tse Ling—considering your miserable efforts in Tibet. Now I warn you, take what I offer." He sat back down, sucking in air, his hand on the container with the glass straw. She was frightened. What would he do to her?

But the next time he spoke, Woo was calm once more. "I will make unlimited money available to you. My men will give you the keys to your own suite of apartments in the highest tower of the city as you leave. Take them. As I said, prove yourself with the fourth, and you can have—say, banking—or some other side of the octagon—in a year. What do you say?"

Tse Ling knew enough to say, "Thank you."

"You are beautiful, Tse Ling," Woo added.

"Thank you." Her eyes half lowered.

A deep sigh. "I am beyond such pleasures as men have, due to my illness. But I can appreciate—no matter." He paused. "I can arrange anything you want. What is it you want now, Tse Ling? Men? Drugs?"

"No. No men, no drugs!"

"*Good*. Your wish is simply for wealth, and

power? That is fitting for one of the eight. You may go, Tse Ling. I will be in touch. Please replace the screen."

She did so and left. Tse Ling walked carefully controlled, slowly back along the painting-lined hall. She was, however, in a rage. She didn't like being told to do anything, didn't like not having her own way. She had not defied the Beijing authorities, nor had she worked for Woo in the very dangerous Tibetan operation to simply run a chain of houses of prostitution!

She bit her lip as the butler met her at the door with the keys to her new tower-suite. She took them. After all, it could have been worse. She was lucky she was alive. Was it because, like all men, Woo coveted her? But he had made no demand. Surely he was impotent, or right now she would have been in bed with the monster. Would she have done it? To get another assignment?

Yes.

To survive, to be rich. There were worse things.

Chapter 2

Bart Lasker stared at his newly shaven face in the bathroom mirror. He still had trouble accepting how he looked: the white streaks in his dark-brown hair, the extra lines on his face, the crinkles around his eyes. He looked older—and yet somehow more vital—more rugged and alive since the events last year in Tibet. He noted the change in his brown eyes, eyes that had beheld another world, another dimension more evil and powerful than the everyday reality. He rubbed his jaw, which was unfamiliarly strong, then felt his broken and reset nose. Yet there were some signs of the old Bart Lasker: the gentleness of the lips, the very fact that he had to shave again.

He had been back in India for a year now, living here in the Tibetan exile community of Dhramsala, north of Delhi, recovering from the Tibetan ordeal that had changed him from mere man to the Mystic Rebel.

Since Bart's unexpected sojourn in Tibet, an adventure that had given him an unwelcome second-self, Bart had adjusted back to western ways. But he had also managed to keep up his E-Kung martial arts exercises, an hour every day, as well as continue to meditate as he had been taught in Tibet. He had hoped to strike and maintain a balance between East and West. But indulgence, made possible by Lasker's well-filled wallet—he had collected an overdue fee for his ill-starred flight into Tibet—was now threatening the balance. Deep inside himself, Bart could almost feel Raspahloh squirm. The mindset of the west was alien and threatening to his previous incarnation, the thing sharing Bart's body. To a fifteenth century assassin known as Raspahloh, such things were inimical.

Bart turned the light off over the mirror and glanced at his watch. Ten A.M. Whoever the hell he was, he had a class to attend—a class where he was the oldest pupil by about twenty years. He threw on his parka, opened the beam-wood door, looked around and shook his head in wonder.

Dhramsala—the seat of the Dalai Lamas exile Tibetan government. The town was not as spectacular as Lhasa, the spiritual capital of old Tibet; there was no Potala Palace looming over the city, but the other-worldly feeling of old Tibet was here. Despite the ceaseless industry of the refugees in rebuilding their culture, the cacophonous sounds of construction, he could hear the early morning call of conch-shell horns calling the monks in the nearby monasteries to devotions, the low rumble of the age-old meditation gongs. There was the feel of free Tibet here!

His house was part way up a hill, one of many slate-roof structures built of piled stones. Each house had a whitewash finish. The narrow, steep, winding road of gravel outside was suitable only for motor scooters and yaks—of which there were several he had to avoid. He began to walk uphill, nodding at people he knew. The air was cool and crisp. On bare hills seen over the rooftops, prayer flags fluttered over collections of thatch-roof cottages—the beginnings of monasteries being built to replace the ruined ones in Chinese-occupied Tibet.

He took deep breaths of fall air. Life was definitely improving. Slowly, through the assigned meditation and just being allowed to be, much of the nightmares and sudden nausea that had swept him since Tibet had disappeared. He had steadied and prospered. Now Bart was well into the more advanced medical classes, fascinated with his studies of the Aryuvedic health-system.

He walked on past the construction site of the new Johkang Temple. It would not be a tenth as large as the one in Lhasa, and it was being built of poured concrete. Nevertheless, it was another visible sign that Tibetan culture endured. A hundred child-monks would soon be moved there from the huts on the mountain to perform its daily rounds of ritual and learning. And the rebirth was continuing, Tibet's legacy for the world, the Way of Compassion and Knowledge—the dharma—would endure.

Lasker zipped his blue parka up. In autumn, the weather was crisp, after the monsoon—warm summer rains from the south—a relief. The winds were from the old land.

Lasker turned into an alleyway between the new temple's south wall and Shagh's vegetable stall, and passed Tranga's tattoo stall. He remembered too well the wild June night of drinking arak with two old acquaintances—Namgyal and Wangyal—that had resulted in the elaborate dragon tattoo on his right arm!

He had his choice of several routes to the Medical Institute but chose this way today to say hello to Yeshe, the wizened old Ngapa—weather creator—in monument square. He found Yeshe sitting bare-chested in the sun on an ochre wool blanket, spinning a copper prayer wheel. The crinkle-faced oldster stopped chanting and nodded to Lasker, who was already fishing into his pocket for a five rupee note.

"Yeshe," Lasker said, squatting next to his friend. "It's too cold, can you make it just a bit warmer?"

"Not today. Saving heat for crops next month," Yeshe apologized. "But I will make less wind for you later."

"Good." Lasker handed him the five rupee note.

Yeshe took it with both his long narow hands and put it under the blanket with some other crumpled money. He lifted a foot-long piece of broken slate from a pile on his left. Yeshe had carved a red-stained mantra on each of these mani stones. He handed it to Lasker. "Good day."

Lasker rose and went to the center of the small sunny square and circled clockwise the pile of thousands of like stones there and then added the stone to the pile. That was for luck today. Call it superstition, but Lasker had gotten into the customs of the people he lived among. People he had scarcely heard of a few years earlier! As he put the stone in

23

the pile, suddenly his mind flashed back. Lasker was in his burning plane, falling toward a glacier. He felt the jerk as the chute opened, then the blow of hitting the ground, waking up, stunned and bleeding. He had a flash-vision of staggering in the darkness in the terrible cold, finding such a mani pile as this and collapsing.

He looked back and smiled at Yeshe and continued on, nudging past mocha-skinned Tibetans in fox-fur hats, women with heavy turquoise stone necklaces. Lasker went on up the slope, and between Lama Youngden's house and the grain storehouse. When he made the turn, the Institute loomed before him, three whitewashed stories with red-painted, vertical wooden beams. There were a dozen shining, gold-painted points on the rooftop to draw cosmic energy: the Tibetan Medical and Astrological Institute's new building. Just a few years ago it had been only one crude wooden shack. The first Tibetan refugees to arrive here, on a grant from the Indian government, had been given this hillside to colonize. And the first thing they built among their tents was a small hut to begin the recreation of their destroyed medical college in Lhasa. Now it had become a three-story building with many rooms. More additions were under construction, thanks to generous contributions by people abroad. The contributions to the Institute had been increasing yearly—grateful patients donating money in thanks for the cures they had obtained at the center.

Today was special; today Lasker was to be shown how to make the Nahk pills. He was eager to see the arcane, the hitherto secret, process.

The door was open underneath the flickering rainbows of square, silk banners hanging down. Lasker brushed under them with his six-foot three-inch frame and entered. He went immediately to the main hall. There he saw that most if not all of the others had arrived. Lasker saw his best friends, Kaba, the sixteen-year-old with the crooked left leg, Leski and Gyaltsen sitting on their red cushions already, muttering the dedication prayers. There were other young monks gathered around the iron, pill-pressing machine. The plump Lama Drogang, the abbot of the Institute, was stirring an herbal concoction over boiling water. He turned and let his assistant take over. As Drogang came toward him, Lasker made the chenbu gesture, hands together before his chest. Lama Drogang smiled and shook hands. "Lasker-la," he said, "take a look at how the repaired press is working! I am so pleased."

The last of the tsosel mercury pills were being pressed, three young monks hanging off the huge metal handle adding their weight to the pressure of the iron mold. After a moment they dropped off and pushed the long handle up. There, in the many one-quarter-inch circular depressions of the press were thirty-three perfect brown pills. Drogang sprinkled some absorbic powder on them to soak up the bit of moisture, then told the boys to gather the pills and quickly wash down the raised part of the floor area for the precious lama who would visit. "The head of our Blue Hat Sect, Chupten Rimpoche, will come soon," Drogang said. "Lama Chupten is our foremost medical expert, the inheritor of the Nakh wisdom! But one must not forget," said Drogang, "that we must always acknowledge that were it not for the Sakyamuni Buddha's teachings, and the subsequent great ones, there would be no such effective medical system. Lasker-la, can you retell how the Buddha, when asked for the compassionate teaching of the way to help the sick, sent rays of multicolored light from his forehead into the disciples and imparted all the root knowledge of scientific medicine?"

"But, that would take too long. Chupten Rimpoche is coming! Anyway, I don't remember the story completely, just the nutshell version."

"Yes, you thought to give it 'in a nutshell.' But a medical practitioner cannot get by with just a nutshell of information! Why, friend, do you not know that in Tibet we memorized twenty thousand pages of text before we were allowed to study the preparation of pills?" Lama Drogang looked sad. "I have made it much too easy here. . . . Ah well, times change."

He patted Bart on his shoulder. "You are a good student. I mustn't be too hard. You should be proud, Lasker. You are the only foreigner rigorously trained by the medical lamas who made it across the border into India, of which I am the senior. But do not take these studies lightly. After all, there is no more traditional medicine being taught in occupied Tibet. As for the huge Lhasa medical college and its 333,000 medical-book library that was burned to the ground in the 1960s by the Red Guard, do you know the Chinese replaced the medical college with a tv station? One playing bad Chinese popular music and propaganda twenty-four hours a day! You must apply yourself; the knowledge must be saved!"

Lasker felt like two cents. The roly-poly Lama Drogang turned from him, cocking his head as if he heard something above the murmur of the young monks and the creak of the mop handles.

"Attention," Drogang announced loudly. "Today's visitor, Chupten Rimpoche, will come here in thirty minutes. Be presentable. He will show us how to prepare the Nahk. Try not to make a fool of yourselves when he comes! Keep your knees covered! In the meantime, there is work."

He turned back to Lasker. "And you, my friend, stop speculating on whether I am psychic or not and get to work! I knew Rimpoche was coming in thirty minutes because he is supposed to be here at eleven, and it is ten-thirty by the clock on the tower! I can see it from where I sit—through the window! Here, take this." He produced a note paper from his robe.

"What is it?"

"A prescription to fill. It is simple enough for even you. So go make up some of these cold tablets. The Blue Hat Monastery in your country's New Jersey has been hit with a flu; it has need of the Eagle-12 remedy."

Lasker took the paper and headed to the small work station at the north corner of the room, under the poster depicting the thousand-armed Aviloketshvara, lord of compassion. A mortar and pestle sat on the table, and some plastic bags with various medicinal vegetable matters in them were nearby. Lasker bent to his task.

Then Lasker suddenly realized he had just been

promoted, and smiled. Only first level students could make pills!

He looked over at Drogang, who winked back at him and laughed heartily, causing a series of tremors across the abdomen of his voluminous maroon robe.

Bart felt elated. He was being allowed for the first time to make a medicine himself and had not even realized it. He had responded not to the lama's words, but to the tone. A clever lesson to him to listen more carefully.

He mixed the black pulp of the Armorak plant with Brown Rock Fungus #5, crushed the mix with the pestle vigorously, and then sprinkled in the three coarse minerals. Then he added water and the dry bluish leaves of balang liverwort, which only grows in the Himalayas above sixteen thousand feet. A simple enough remedy for a simple flu. He felt rather self-conscious humming the mantra that would activate—so they said—the ingredients. But he did it; the mantra was after all a part of the age-old formula. Who was he to say it was useless?

The name on the prescription, he noted, was American: Dr. Sandy Marshak, New Brunswick, New Jersey. That wasn't uncommon. The medical clinic was increasingly concerned with providing medicines for far-flung colonies of Tibetans—and for some Westerners who had embraced the system.

Just as he had sealed the package of Eagle-12 pills for shipment, there was a sudden hush in the chamber.

Chapter 3

Chupten Rimpoche had arrived. Everyone froze in place and stuck out his tongue—the Tibetan greeting reserved for only highly respected lamas. Chupten was amazingly tall—nearly seven feet—and had very long arms. If the mustachioed man in the blue robe wasn't seventy plus years old and a bit shaky, he would have been a credit to any basketball team. He wore a peaked, foot-high blue hat which made him seem even more like a giant. He motioned slightly, was assisted to a cushion, and bowing and putting his hands together in chenbu, he sat down. He called them all to gather around him. Quickly, the students gathered up cushions and placed them in a semi-circle around the Rimpoche. Drogang placed all the many implements and the earthen mixing pots before Chupten. The Rimpoche adjusted his robe and made himself comfortable. Then he said in a very soft voice, "These Nahk pills I am about to make are to cure the new diseases. The cause, as you know, of the new diseases, like the old ones, is in the three poisons: ignorance, clinging and aggression. These root causes of mental karma create the situation wherein disease finds a home. Once a disease progresses, cutting the energy circulation of the body, it gradually cuts off life."

Lasker thought, That's the way I explained it once to Drogang!

Drogang winked at Lasker.

The Rimpoche took a scroll out of a pouch and opened it. He held up a diagram showing two rather fanciful trees, each with seven branches and seven leaves per branch.

"These diagrams," said the learned lama, "are the diagrams of illness and health. Each of you has studied these diagrams for a long time. But how many of you realize that by merely noting symptoms and reading across these diagrams, you can make a good quick estimate of the type and seriousness of a disease? You all know how to feel a person's right and left wrist and to feel for the various life pulses. You have been taught to sense the subtle pulse signs of the seven new plagues of the twentieth century. These are shown on the branch of the tree of illness on the stem labeled 'cutting off life.' Normally, there can be no cure for these disorders. But they *can* be cured by concoctions of the wish-fulfilling gems. The Nahk pills are to be made of the rare gems brought out of Tibet last year by our American friend Bart Lasker."

Lasker smiled self-consciously as all eyes for a moment turned to him.

Then the Rimpoche took a red cloth pouch out of his robe and opened its tie string and spilled out six sparkling gems of various colors and cuts. Some looked green, some red like rubies and others like sapphires. But they were more precious.

"Let us begin our Nahk lesson. Are we ready? Take notes as I demonstrate!"

Lasker actually felt saliva at the edge of his mouth. This was the moment he had waited for—the demonstration of the ancient ritual technique kept hidden and passed down from learned lama to disciple century after century. Now for the first time, a Westerner would partake of this medical secret.

The lama said, "As you see now, I first place an oblong red gem into the bowl of black paste made of the gamgon fungus. It will slowly dissolve. The residue—just the liquid—is what we are after for the first step."

Then there was a creaking of the floorboards by the chamber door. Lasker turned and made out a voluminous man in a three-piece, double-breasted, black pinstripe suit. The ghost of Sam Spade?

"Lasker, come with me." The fat man puffed half out of breath. "You must come!" It was Losang, Lasker's friend—or Harpie—depending on how one looked at it.

Chupten Rimpoche said, "Ah—we will pause here for a moment. Please go and confer with venerable Losang, Lasker."

"But—"

The Rimpoche smiled in understanding at Lasker's extreme annoyance. "Go. It is all right."

Bart got up and hastened to the doorway and whispered, "What the *hell* is it Losang?"

The round-faced, coffee-complexioned man said, "A message from His Holiness, for you." A hand with five silver rings clutched Lasker's shoulder.

31

"Not now! I've waited for a long—"

The Rimpoche had overheard Losang, and Lasker caught his expression. It meant: "You must go! A message from His Holiness is more important than anything!"

The admonition was all in his one raised left eyebrow.

Lasker nodded. "If I may be excused, your eminence . . ."

The Rimpoche nodded.

Drogang said, "Ngordal will take notes for Lasker." The youngest student seemed gleeful as he nodded vigorously. "I will surely do that," the nine-year-old promised. "Don't worry!"

Lasker groaning inwardly bade goodbye to the class with a chenbu gesture. Then he and Losang walked down the steps onto the pebbled walkway.

"What's up? I really don't see—"

"*Everything* is up, Lasker. Come into my office, and you will see! Perhaps it is time you leave Dhramsala—for the north!"

Lasker moaned. He had almost managed to forget his promise to His Holiness to go on a mission. Bart had somehow thought he could bask here in this Indian center of learning forever. "Ah well," he sighed, "first noble truth—suffering. No getting away from it. Losang, this is just another example of your bad timing," Lasker said. "Lead on!"

Losang took the lead. The many silver rings on his fat hands glinted in the bright sun; it was like following a blinking airport beacon truck.

Chapter 4

Losang's house was a slant-roof bungalow built of concrete blocks. There were long boxes with blossoms of every color in the windows on both sides of the red wooden door. He bid Lasker to go in. Lasker sat down on the leather recliner in the well-illuminated, American-style living room, and pushed the controls to lean back. Losang put his fat frame down on the paisley sofa. He picked up an envelope off the end table and took out a letter. "The Dalai Lama has sent this for you to read."

Lasker popped the seat back up and took it. It was typewritten and had the elaborate letterhead of the Tibet government-in-exile. It was addressed to him, had the black wax seal and was signed by the God-King leader of the Tibetan community. As Bart read it, Losang put a carved ivory cigarette holder in his mouth, inserted an Indian cigarette in it and lit up.

By the time Losang had finished his smoke, Lasker looked up.

"His Holiness is simply asking for me to look at certain old documents he says you have received. There's nothing about my going to Tibet."

"The inference is there, Lasker, if you read between the lines. You will understand what His Holiness wants, once you see the Terton documents. But before I take them out of their container for you—let us speak about your relationship to the cause."

Losang started off on a tangent, reminiscing. "You know," the man in the Bogart-suit said, "I can remember like it was yesterday that fateful day when you first walked into my office in New Delhi. You were *so* hesitant to go into Tibet then, so wary and reluctant. I wondered if you were really fated to be with us. I *still* wonder sometimes, though I'm pleased you've found something in our medical system to amuse yourself. I am not one of those—like Lama Youngden—who are disappointed in you for not taking holy vows. We don't need more monks. We need the Mystic Rebel! I am sorry you have refused the Boddhisattva vows that would make you a Mahayana Buddhist, but I understand that you are following your own spiritual master—this mysterious hermit of yours. You must do as your conscience dictates. . . ."

The Tibetan smiled, his tombstone-sized teeth glinting in the bright overhead track-lights. "Tell me, Bart, in your work you have translated many old Tibetan texts. Did you ever come across the story of the Tertons?"

"Tertons? Yes," Lasker said with impatience. He wanted Losang to get to the point. "They are mystics that wander in the mountains and by some sixth sense find buried documents of the ancient ones."

"Yes. Very good. Well, one Terton who recently arrived here from Tibet has brought with him a text which he unearthed in a bronze chest. It is a fascinating bit of eighth century writing, a clue to the location of the cave where the Great Guru Padmasambhava meditated. Up until now we did not have an inkling of the place's location."

"That's very interesting. Can I see the Tertons' text? Where is the chest?"

"You have only to use your eyes, Lasker. Look over by the fireplace!"

Bart had seen the bulky burlap bag in the corner. Now when he went to inspect it, he saw it had a hundred small black seals on its seams—seals of the Dalai Lama. "Is the—"

"Yes. The chest with the Tertons' text is in the bag." He folded his fat hands on his voluminous lap. "Go ahead, break the seals. I am interested, too."

Lasker's mouth fairly watered. "Well, okay. Here goes."

Lasker carefully broke the black seals and pulled the burlap open. He gasped as the corroded bronze box with gold embossing was revealed. It was rectangular, about two feet long by one foot high, the shape of most Tibetan wood-block print books.

Bart opened the rusty latches which were already broken. He carefully lifted the lid to expose the dry and bent wooden book cover, then the first crumbly page. He took it out and set it on the desk. Losang came over to peer over Bart's shoulder. Under the light of the goose-neck 1930's lamp, the barely visible words could be discerned. The title, as near as he could translate the arcane Tibetan words, was "A Guide to Finding His Holiness Padmasambhava's Holy Cave, Wherein the Ancient Secret Akashic Record Exists, in Perfect Form on Shambhala

Parchment's Timeproof Paper."

"What's Shambhala Parchment?" Lasker asked.

Losang said, "It is a kind of glistening, high-mineral content parchment that withstands the ravages of time perfectly. No one to my knowledge has ever seen it—it is only in myths! The paper is said to come from Shambhala itself!"

The very mention of Shambhala—the ancient source of the Tibetan secret teachings—made Lasker's heart pound. Shambhala was the mystic realm where superior beings living in perfect harmony spent their lives philosophizing and study-ing the universe. Some wise men said Shambhala was located west of Tibet, some said south. Some even claimed Shambhala was underground. This mythic perfect place of peace and enlightenment, wherever it was, had been providing Tibet with sacred teachings since the dawn of time. The Tibetans took Shambhala seriously; they even dated the beginning of their calendar from the day that a holy man first brought back from Shambhala a translation of the Kalachakra Tantra.

Lama Youngden believed, as Lasker did, that Shambhala was a world in another dimension, hence the difficulty of getting there. Only the greatest meditators, by slowing their earthly vibra-tions to a different pitch, could enter such a rare world in space-time. Or so his friend Lama Youngden said!

Lasker read the first page with Losang peering over his shoulder. It was an ancient form of the Sanskrit-derived Tibetan tongue, but Lasker, thanks to his peculiar state of having a fifteenth century alter-ego, was able to hesitantly translate.

Losang was amazed at this ability. It took an hour to read the twenty pages. Losang used a cassette recorder to tape Lasker's translation.

The text told that the cave contained prophecies of events leading to the Great Darkness to come, and gave rather vague, but voluminous directions to finding the cave. There was a crude map.

"Lasker, that cave is important! If the Akashic record is there, it must be obtained for His Holiness!"

"It sounds," Lasker said with awe in his voice, "like the book in the cave has something to do with our present time. Aren't we—according to the predictions—on the verge of the Dark Age?"

"Yes. Legend tells of a record of the future of earth, taken by Holy Padmasambhava from the all-knowing cosmic repository called the Akashic record."

"I don't follow you, Losang."

"Prophesies, Bardun Tharpa!" Losang exclaimed, using Lasker's Tibetan name. "Padmasambhava's cave has in it a long-missing text that contains the many prophesies that Padmasambhava derived by meditative power-mind. The holy man meant them as guidance for the future of mankind. We know that from other sources. You must know that the dark ages are already nearly upon earth; the seven new plagues are already here—and soon, the fall. But Tibet could be—will be—the light of the world in these dark times to come. If we can restore it. In order for that place of sustaining to exist, though, we need that text from Padmasambhava's cave. Tell me, Lasker," Losang asked softly, "do you understand, fully the importance of the cave's prophesy document? It is not that we want to just *know* the future—that is rather a bother, if one cannot do a thing about it!"

"Hmmmm. Well," Lasker offered, "If this missing book can fortell future events, perhaps it also tells what events can affect the future."

"Yes. You *do* understand. The Dalai Lama, with this text, can know the future and can change it."

"That isn't possible, is it? Can things, the future, be—altered?"

"Yes, Lasker. Time to come can be altered with this book. The Dalai Lama can guide events to a proper conclusion. You see, we know from the Kalachakra Tantra that there are certain—let us use the word, critical points—in time. Places where things can turn on a single event. A carefully considered action at these juncture points can keep the winds of karma from annihilating all! We can, with the knowledge in the missing text, keep the dark ages down to a few generations—and restore quickly the light of learning and civilization. It will be difficult, but not impossible. Surely, if it is the lost text that these crumbling pages speak of, it is written in an even more arcane form—Dakini writing. It must be brought out of Tibet to safety—and carried to a high lama of the Purple Hat Sect. Only they can read Dakini writing."

"You want me to be the one to go into Tibet and get it!" Lasker exclaimed.

"Yes. It won't be found unless you go find it, Lasker."

Lasker said, "Now I see what is so important that I had to miss the Nahk preparation. I will, of course, go."

38

Losang frowned. "I was afraid you would say that. But I must warn you. Listen a little more before making a final decision. Have some tea and we will discuss it."

"As you read, Lasker-la," Losang said, "this Terton text gives the path to the location of this cave. But the directions are from the Rong-lam obelisk, a landmark that probably no longer exists. In any case, no one knows where the obelisk is—someplace in North Tibet."

"I can find it. I have powers," Lasker insisted.

"Yes, I know. You are the Mystic Rebel. And I have heard that a map to Rong-lam obelisk can be obtained at Tsurphu Monastery in Tibet. That would be your first stop. But then—"

"What?" Lasker asked.

"There are—legends of deadly guardians at the Padmasambhava cave. Legend has it that in order to enter his cave and come out alive, one must defeat the Dancing Dead."

"Dancing Dead?"

"Yes. We don't know what form these guardians are, and perhaps they are just myth, or exaggeration. Perhaps not. Some say the dancing dead are powerful sub-earth beings—that they have been left there to destroy any infidel who might accidently stumble upon the cave's secret and try to remove it."

"I'm not an infidel. I'd be in the service of—"

"Yes. But you have a Bonpo part to your personality, do you not? Raspahloh is an unbeliever."

"I can do it. I control Raspahloh. I'm the man for

the job. You said yourself that no one else can get it. You can't send a high lama. You can't risk one. I am young, strong and—expendable!"

"Don't think of this quest that way, Lasker. If you are the best for the job, so be it. But the message from the Dalai Lama is, as I surmise, merely a feeler, an inquiry. Not a request."

"I will go." Lasker suddenly was not interested in Nahk pills and other peaceful endeavors. Tibet meant adventure, action and a fulfillment of his destiny as the Mystic Rebel—Guardian of the Kingdom. He stared at Losang for so long and so intensely that the rotund Tibetan had to look down, adjusting his wide paisley tie.

"Very well, go. I have confidence in you. We know you want to help us—and this is the way. We *need* Padmasambhava's prophesy book. You will, I think, be greatly undoing much of your bad Raspahloh karma, which used to kill Dalai Lamas, with this great endeavor." Losang plopped back down into an easy chair. "How far along are you in integrating the two of your personalities, Lasker?"

"Not very far." Lasker frowned. "We're basically enemies. And I have been trying to rid myself of Raspahloh."

There was a long silence as they both stared at the cherry-red fire coals in the log fireplace.

"Then, if you are not reconciled, I advise you not to accept this quest," Losang said gravely. "Think for a while. How will you fight off your enemies, the Bonpo? How will you conquer the danger the Chinese occupiers present if you are at war with yourself? Just ponder awhile."

40

Losang went over to his grand piano and lifted the cover on the keys. He began to play Bach's *St. Matthew's Passion.* He played it with such emotion and precision that Lasker, if he hadn't known who was playing, would have sworn it was Arthur Rubinstein, or some other piano master . . . not the fat-fingered Tibetan.

Perhaps it was the immense quality of the moment—the place, the strange sense of portent in the room—and not so much the fluidly rolling tones that made it sound so great.

Lasker stared into the red embers of the fireplace, seeing in the flashes his Tibetan lover Dorjee's lithe copper body, her dark doe-like eyes, her high-cheekboned, noble face, and then the Tibetan mountains, so tall and dangerous, glaciers glinting. He did know that he was not—whole—yet. But there was no better way for Lasker to serve the Tibetan cause. Lasker knew that he was but a single entity in life's stream coursing from beginningless time, just part of a wave, part of the great wheel of life. He had been presented a great task. It would be necessary to live with Raspahloh, work with him, share body and mind with the infidel alter-ego to accomplish it.

But the cause needed this power of Raspahloh's. He would tame his other self, use Raspahloh.

The flames flared up as a log snapped and collapsed. Losang rang out the last tremulous notes of the symphony, holding the pedals down so the notes vibrated and slowly, so slowly subsided.

Lasker was near tears with emotion as he broke the silence. "I will not change my mind. I'm going."

Chapter 5

Losang walked Lasker all of the way back to the Medical Institute. As they slowly wound their way up the hill in the bright sunshine, Lasker resigned himself to the fact that the Nahk pill lecture was over by now. Their "little talk" had taken two and a half hours.

Losang said, "Be careful in Tibet. You will be given protection as best we can there, I assure you. And you will not have such a hard time getting in. Arrangements will be made. Once you fly to Kathmandu, you will go into Tibet by land, on a Chinese sponsored tour, with proper papers.

"The Chinese have again shifted their policy to allow tourists in Tibet—what they now call China's Province of Xishang. Your first stop, once I give you all the instructions and documents tomorrow, will be Kathmandu."

As Lasker expected, when they got to the institute, the class was over. The door was, as a matter of fact, barred. A note pinned to the door stated "Dear Bart, Ngordal has your notes. Signed, Drogang."

Lasker bade, "So long," to Losang and headed back toward his own cottage. He had one other overpowering reason for going into Tibet besides the cause: his Tibetan lover. Perhaps he could track her down. That would be his reward for the dangerous undertaking. He would somehow find Dorjee, be with her, make love to her as before. Perhaps he would be able to take her out of Tibet to safety. One part of the mission for the Dalai Lama, the other for himself.

And if there was killing to be done—as there surely would be—that part could be aided by Raspahloh. Raspahloh and he had one thing in common—a distinct antipathy for the Chinese occupiers. Only Raspahloh's antipathy was more bloodthirsty. Bart focused his eyes on the mani pile again as he passed it. When he got into Tibet, his first stop would be at the cave of the hermit—his spiritual master, the inheritor of the Cultivators' power. The millions of piled stones, each with a prayer on it, reminded him that he needed the hermit's spiritual guidance.

The sky suddenly dimmed, a huge thunder cloud coming from the north. It was growing dark, but the sun was still glinting off the faraway Himalayan mountain peaks. Red and white and blue rays, like the Tibetan flag—a good omen?

Beyond those mountains were his Tibetan rebel friends—and many enemies, too, like the Bonpo priest magicians. He thought about the Bonpo as his boots crunched along the gravel path. Having once been prisoner in their evil realm on Mt. Kailas, perhaps in another space-time, he had no intention of getting anywhere near them! But if the Bonpo surmised he was back in Tibet, they would seek to reclaim him for their own—seek to vanquish Bart Lasker from the body they had reserved for Raspahloh, their champion.

He scratched again at the tingling on his arm where the dragon tattoo was emblazoned. He picked up the pace as hailstones started to pelt the town.

Once in his house, he began to pack. He would take only the essentials—one backpack full of compasses, maps, waterproof matches, high-energy food rations—and the U.S. government survival kit: space blanket, thermal mini-tent. As for weapons, the short Katama sword would be hidden in the frame of his special custom-made backpack—a bag of tricks that included a knife and a nunchaku-chain weapon.

He laid them out on the thick woolen mat that served as his bed and just stared at the equipment he had gathered for a year. This was a hell of a lot better than the half candy bar and book of matches that he had parachuted into Tibet with the last time! He'd also bring white khatags—home-spun white greeting scarves—a necessity of custom in Tibet. And he'd wear—for good luck—his V-shaped sky-object pendant.

He almost forgot something. He went to the cupboard and found two boxes of chocolate chip cookies—the hermit's one obsession.

He'd get a good night's sleep and wait for Losang to bring the travel documents and instructions at eight A.M. He looked at the clock on the wall—a little early in the day to begin his *Katas,* the dance of power. But he wanted to have an extra long workout, so he would begin now.

Bart went out onto the flagstone terrace he had built himself. The rapid moving clouds had passed, and it was sunny again; odd weather for this time of the year. The wind from the north was brisk, and a prayer flag fluttered and cast a shadow over the terrace from his roof.

He would not do the usual twenty minutes of E-Kung, but work-out as long as he was able, to strengthen himself further.

Bart began by stripping off every stitch of his clothing. The bushes around the terrace shielded him from the road, and though it was near freezing, he had grown used to the cold in Tibet. This temperature felt warm.

First, he as usual got down on the slates and spent five minutes in lotus position, legs crossed, each ankle up over the opposite thigh. He tightened every muscle of his hard-toned and deeply tanned body, feeling the icy air on his naked skin as a mere cool breeze. Bart's eyes focused on a spot twenty-eight inches from his nose, on the slate. Oh how *well* he knew that spot.

He now soared into a state of well-being and calm unknown to those who do not meditate.

By the time the terrace was entirely in shadow, he came back.

That was the pleasant, restful part. *Now* for the hard stuff! Lasker got up and assumed what a yogi of the Hindu School would recognize as one of the most difficult of all Asanas or meditative poses. There were sixteen warm-up Asanas to stimulate Chi energy in E-Kung practice. The E-Kung martial art drew power from these stances that stretched out every muscle and fiber of the body.

The first Asana was left ankle over the shoulder behind the head standing on the right leg alone for five minutes with arms extended forward. Then the really hard poses began, each five minutes long.

That part of the exercise routine took an hour. He didn't let up. Bart went on with the practices taught to him by the Bonpo magician priests in Tibet, when they were trying to reawaken his previous incarnation as Raspahloh. He went directly into bone-breathing.

Step one of bone-breathing was to again sit down in lotus position on the cold stones, then inhale and exhale the cold air as deeply and completely as possible.

Lasker concentrated on imagining that the air he breathed was coming in and out through his splayed fingertips. Soon it felt as if it really were. And then he went to step two of bone-breathing—bringing the Chi-breath energy up his arms and into his chest, and then his neck and head. Then he brought the Chi energy-breath to the crown of his head; the burst of Chi-air in his brain was exhilarating and tension reducing. He easily brought the Chi-breath down along his spine, which became an icy clean stream channel. Bart focused it into his thorax, abdomen. He felt like he could carry it farther today; he felt strong and confident. So, for the first time since his last training day in the Bonpo Monastery a year earlier, he went on with the daring exercise. He brought the Chi-power into his sexual organs and finally his legs.

He felt a numb sensation as his Chi-breath went right down his legs past his knees, unbunching the muscles there. Then it was in his ankles and his feet, finally exiting out his toes.

God it felt like he hadn't had a bit of circulation there for a century! Then he brought the power to his skin and muscles. He felt the muscles hardening, almost like armor. This was the Chi-barrier of a Bonpo mystic warrior. Yet there was no sensation of another presence, no feeling of being taken over. He had feared that if he went this far in the exercises, it would kindle the power of Raspahloh too much.

Then he reversed the process, expelling air over five minutes till his whole body felt air-conditioned —the only way to describe the feeling.

Bart stood up and shouted "AIII!!!" the cry of the warrior and pounded his chest until the chest thundered like a drum. It felt like his steel-hard blows were hitting not a human body but upon case-hardened steel. The Chi-belt protective layer had been built.

Then he experienced the mental thrust of power that connected his upper and lower body— separated by the waist—and mentally made an energy current like AC-DC between them, alternating faster and faster and faster. It was time to see what he could do!

He took one step and slammed his bare left foot down. The thick stone slates cracked like cheap cardboard. Bart repeated with the right. Again the stones cracked, and powder splayed upward. Lasker slashed at the air, his lightning, catlike gestures making whoosh sounds. He moved his fingers as if he were playing a harp—feeling the pure power.

Birds took flight from a nearby tree. They knew what was next. Lasker looked about him for something—anything—to destroy. *There!* He channeled the steel-like power to each of his internal organs, until his heart, liver, spleen, *everything* inside was wrapped in the Chi-energy.

He got into a crouch and started a rapid series of Kandak kicks, demolishing three potted plants in a fraction of a second. The pots' shards flew in pieces a hundred feet into the branches of the bushes that the birds had abandoned.

Lasker turned, imagining the arrival of some unseen and awesome enemy. He leapt high into the air and smashed out both his legs as he spun, delivering a one-two pair of roundhouse kicks with his bare feet, and landed jabbing a fast right-left with his knife-edged hands. He was too close to the house's cinderblock wall, and his right hand went right through it. Lasker felt no pain, and he leapt up and kicked downward. His left foot went through the marble top of the garden table like it was gauze.

"Ahem . . ."

Lasker was surprised to see a somewhat taken aback Ngordal holding forth some papers.

"If I am not disturbing you Lasker-la, here are your c-class notes from the Nahk demonstration," he said. "Perhaps I shouldn't walk right in? You were busy?"

Lasker realized that he should cover himself. He picked up his pants and rapidly got into them.

"Sorry," Lasker said. "I was meditating."

"That was meditation?" Ngordal asked. "It is a very interesting type."

Lasker took the notes and smiled. "Yeah, it was meditation. Bonpo style."

Bart put the papers down on the ground. "Thanks. I'll look these over tonight—er—would you like some tea?"

Ngordal demurred. "Oh, no thank you! I must go and do—something!"

"Well, some other time—when I am not in such a destructive mood."

"Yes. Fine." Ngordal backed off. "I'll let myself out. N-Nice seeing you!"

Bart felt very embarrassed. He should have locked the front door. It was probably doubly shocking for Ngordal to see such violence from a medical student. Lasker thought of trying to straighten up, and then decided not to, for his body started hurting—alot. He limped off into the house and turned on the shower. For nearly an hour he stood in the hot stream of water, and then when he got out, he sat on the deep pile rug, groaning. The tortured muscles that he had thought were in excellent shape evidently couldn't take the strain of a full Bonpo workout.

He got off the floor and sat in the stuffed chair, trying not to retch up his guts. Finally he threw himself onto the bedding. He lay there, every muscle throbbing with pain.

Well, he thought, I do remember my stuff, but my body is a little rusty!

Chapter 6

Lasker sat bolt upright when a loud hollow noise erupted. He realized someone was pounding on the door. A quick look at the red digital readout of the clock showed it was eight A.M. Great Buddha's Gong! He had slept for over fifteen hours. The pounding on the door must be Losang!

Lasker shouted, "Just a minute," slipped on his shirt and made sure his pants were zipped. He went into the bathroom, took a well needed piss and then splashed water onto his face. A glance in the mirror showed his eyes were bloodshot. His legs felt stiff. In general, though, he felt far better than when he had crashed out. Bart yelled out again for Losang to be patient, slipped his flip-flops on and went to the door and opened it.

Losang stepped in, breathing clouds of cold air saying, "It's about time!" After a glance at Bart he added, "Say, have you been drinking?"

"No, I er—exercised too much last night."

"Oh," Losang said dubiously. "That's not what I heard."

Lasker sat down on the bed. "What did you hear?"

"Word all over town is that you went crazy last night from drink and smashed up your patio furniture—even the walls!"

Lasker laughed. "That Ngordal is some tattle-tale! No. I wasn't drunk—or crazy. I was just doing a few martial arts exercises. I made a few errors—and some things got busted up. Have a seat, Losang. Rest your bones. Hey, what's the humongous briefcase for?"

"This," said Losang, "is filled with all the documents and information you need for the trip." Losang flopped on the sofa and put the valise down on the floor. "Have you some tea?"

"Just what I was thinking," Lasker said, stretching and yawning. As he moved to the small stove in the corner and put on the tea, Lasker noticed Losang's outfit. The pinstripe "Bogie suit" was gone, and in its place Losang wore a summer-season ice-cream suit—narrow lapelled white linen jacket and pants. No wonder he was shivering. He had a red tie with a white pine-cone motif, a gray and white striped shirt—Brooks Brothers no doubt. The Tibetan had added the final touch—wing-tip brown and white shoes. As he leaned back and the tight white suit opened up, Bart could see Losang wore wide, red firehouse suspenders. A gold pocket watch made the whole look like the 1920s. Losang, the chubby Beau Brummel of Dhramsala, had gone back another ten years!

In a short while the tea was piping, and some biscuits were placed on the foldout table. They both sat chewing and sipping, Lasker wolfing the Carr's tea wafers down as fast as the fat man.

51

Losang said, "The valise has your British passport; you are still Bruce Arthur as far as our English friends are concerned. We were able to supply a recent photo of you when we renewed it—through special channels."

"Great. That'll make a big difference. When I used the passport last year, it was hard to explain why my nose looked different than in the photo."

"The second passport says you are Charles Grant, also with recent photo. I have been up since dawn writing out all the instructions and finding out what tour you must book from Kathmandu."

"Can I see the stuff in the briefcase now?"

"No! You have to leave right away. Just wipe your mouth, grab your equipment and parka and pack a change of clothes. We're off to the airfield in my Ferrari. I trust that your airplane is in good working condition? If not, we can book a charter—"

"Good Baby II is fit to travel. But the pilot feels a bit rushed, though I don't mind flying. I haven't been up for months."

"Good! Then we have—" he pulled out his gold watch, looking a lot like the frantic white rabbit in *Alice and Wonderland*—"we must hurry . . . five minutes! Are you finished packing? No? Then hurry! You have to be in Kathmandu, and in the Chinese travel office, in seven hours. They close at four P.M. our time."

As Lasker threw his stuff together, he asked, "What about my flight plan? It has to be filed with Delhi control . . . and the charts?"

"All in the valise. We've been very busy while you slept."

In six minutes flat they left the house, and Losang pulled the fire-engine red Ferrari out into the main street, Michelin's squealing. They drove down the bumpy macadam road toward Darjeeling and the grass-strip airfield where Good Baby II was hangared. Losang, on the way, told Lasker to look over the contents of the briefcase once airborne, and that Lasker should call him from Kathmandu if anything was unclear.

Twenty minutes later, they pulled up in front of the gate. The weather was fine, Bart noted: a clear blue sky with just a few fleecy cirrus clouds. That was a bit of luck so close after a fall storm. Bart shook hands with Losang through the driver's window. Then he checked in with the man at the gate and walked rapidly toward the single big hangar and entered.

There she was, his silver-skinned Vickers P3a twin engine. Good Baby II. She looked tremendous and shiny and very impressive next to the half dozen Cessnas and old Pipers.

Lasker checked in with Alf, the pock-faced British mechanic and general all-around man of the small field. He flipped through the maintenance sheet with Alf, then he kicked the wood blocks out from under the wheels. Alf rolled the big doors wide open. Lasker climbed up the hatch and into the cabin. He popped into the worn cracked-leather seat and started checking overhead switches. He checked the list and instrument readouts, then hit the ignition. First the port and then the starboard props swung into action with a few kerosene coughs. It was go.

Bart pushed the wheel forward, and the sleek

plane rolled out of the hangar into the sun. He twisted the wheel and added some choke, taking her bouncing onto the single dirt runway, pointing toward the prevailing west wind.

A few minutes later the plane wobbled off the ground, and Bart put her in a gradual climb and banked to the north. Eight minutes later, he reached his cruising altitude—twelve thousand feet—and he set the stick on automatic. Only then did he turn to the co-pilot seat and snap open the locks on the expensive, brown leather valise Losang had provided. There were six zip-folders, each a different color. He whistled. "James Bond should be so lucky."

He took a deep breath and snapped the celophane tape seal on the first fat folder, labeled folder #1. It was three typed pages concerning the tour. The gist of it was that he must book the Thursday tour bus from Kathmandu to Lhasa—bus #60. The driver and guide aboard that Chinese bus had been bribed to let him feign illness to leave the tour at Tashi Lumpo Temple in Shigatse. There, a friend would help Bart slip away to start his trek to Tsurphu Monastery and pick up the map that gave directions to Rong-lam obelisk, the obelisk being the starting off point on the Terton map to Padmasambhava's cave.

What friend? he thought.

The second folder—the bulkiest—was a Xerox copy of the Terton map and the twenty pages of text Lasker had translated the previous day, plus a Yashika XE 35 mm camera and film.

The third folder was—thank God—clearances to

land in Kathmandu and the approved direct flight plan. He was already on the right one, having guessed correctly. The fourth folder containd three hundred-pound notes—he had wondered about that; tours cost money—plus some Chinese money, renminbao, and British Barclay's travelers' cheques. The fifth folder contained more information about the friend at Tashi Lumpo. Not his or her name, mind you, but just code word question and reply. Bart *must* memorize these words. *God!* Losang had read too many spy novels. "Give me a break!"

The green folder, six, was really an envelope. It contained his passport, visa, vaccination certificate, and other travel documents, along with Losang's final spy-stuff note: "Please memorize and burn contents of these folders, aside from needed travel documents."

Bart wasn't going to make a fire on the plane. He just tore the stuff up he didn't need and flushed it down the toilet. That would have to do.

Bart arrived at Kathmandu airport two hours later. After parking the plane, Nepali customs had a perfunctory look at his Bruce Arthur I.D.s and rifled through his backpack stuff, finding nothing suspicious. Then he was out and flagged down a taxi. The land-rover-come-cab jounced and bounced him onto the paved road and into the teeming, ancient caravan city that was the gateway to Tibet. He kept his backpack in the seat with him.

Bart had been in Kathmandu many times, but he never ceased to be impressed by its chaotic orderliness. Having accommodated all sorts of Western things—heavy traffic, camera-clicking tourists, name-brand glass and balcony type hotels and snack bars—Kathmandu yet remained wildly Asian and exotic.

He got out near the ornate twin-towered Gamhara Hindu Temple and walked across Victory Square's cobblestones toward a distinctively British Victorian-looking building: the Ashland, the only decent hotel here that Losang said had no Chinese trade-group, peace delegation, or visiting Beijing officials permanently booked in. He checked in at the desk, aware that he was being photographed by an Indian in a white tunic, Nehru hat and dhouti pants. Many eyes watched a newcomer in this city of intrigue, where half the tourists were one sort of spy or drug trafficker or other illegal type. Bart threw his stuff in his room and went out with the camera, without loading film, to do the typical thing: sightsee and take pictures.

He didn't want to appear hurried, but he was. It was five minutes past three. There was less than an hour to spare. He clicked along and wended his way to the Chinese tour office. He walked up the three steps and tried the door knob. Locked.

Can't be! He jiggled and banged. No answer.

A passerby, a British sort with a blue nylon backpack, told Lasker the Chinese tour office had closed early because some delegation from Beijing was at the Hilton and they went to a party with them.

"Don't worry," the Brit said. "They'll be back here at 8 A.M. sharp."

"Terrific," Bart mumbled as he went down the

steps, pushing through the hawkers and pedicabs and tourists toward a side street. Damn! The Chinese tourist office was closed already. An hour ahead of time! If he didn't catch bus #60, if he wasn't at the Tashi Lumpo Temple at Shigatse, one hundred miles into Tibet on Thursday, there would be big problems. Should he call Losang?

Angry at the stupid twist of fate that could abort the whole project—and a little superstitious; he didn't like things going wrong right away—he walked aimlessly.

Wait, he told himself. You never know. . . . This could be a fortunate turn of events. Suppose the delay means some sort of unfortunate event is avoided. In any case, it was his karma. Good or bad—it was his alone to deal with!

He continued being the tourist. He sat down and had some tea and hot spice mo-mo's—Tibetan fare—in an outdoor cafe. The place was ripe with German trekkers. He avoided conversations, feigning not to understand their very good English. Then he paid and went back to the Hotel Ashland. He sat on the floor and did deep Vipassna meditation for three solid hours. Feeling restored and calm, Bart went to the hotel restaurant bar and ate an English-style steak and potatoes supper. He had a Virgin Mary or two, and then went to bed early.

The next day at 8 A.M. he strolled down to the office of the Chinese Tour Bureau again. He was the second person in—the Brit he had met the day before was first. They both were told to wait, and they cooled their heels while the thin-lipped middle-aged Chinese official in a blue Mao jacket watered his fifty or so philodendrons. You could see that's what he was doing through the semi-frosted glass of the office door. Then the Brit was asked in, spent ten minutes and left. It was Bart's turn.

The starch-collared soldierly official asked, "Are you alone?"

"Yes," Bart said.

The Chinese made marks on a note pad. "And what is the purpose of your booking passage into Xishang Province? Are you a Buddhist?"

"No. I intend to photograph in Tibet. I am a freelance photographer. Say, is there a bus tour soon?" Lasker asked. "I can only stay there a few weeks."

The official said, "Maybe," extended his hand, and Lasker handed over his papers.

"How far do you wish to go?" He flipped through the passport.

"All the way to Lhasa."

"Hmmmm," the official said. "That is as far as the tour goes. It is a two-week tour." He leafed through his passport, feeling the pages and holding it briefly up to a little device on his desk—some sort of purple light.

"It's real," Bart said.

"Of course . . ." The Chinese official smiled. But it was a slight, crocodile smile. "There is one seat that has become available suddenly. An official of my government is unable to return to Xishang as early as planned. Had you come to my office yesterday, it would have been impossible to book you in for a month. Can you leave today? In a few hours?"

"That will be fine. I can make it." *Karma*.

He smiled. "Now, for photography—you are

58

aware that in addition to the usual tour charges, there are photography fees at the historic sites?"

"Er—I was told that they were nominal."

"So they are. But just so you are aware. It is ten to twenty dollars a picture inside the temples—for the restoration funds, of course. The People's Republic makes no profit."

He started working an abacus on the desk. "That will be twenty-one hundred pounds for the bus tour, hotel accommodations and food."

Of course Lasker knew from Losang's instructions what the tour would cost, and the bit about photography fees, but he knew he should appear as shocked as any free-lancer would be. Lasker gasped.

"English pounds?"

"Of course—and in cash."

"I had no idea it would be so much . . . but . . . can you accept Barclay's traveler's cheques?"

"Yes. No worry." His eyes gleamed. "They can be exchanged right in the building. You see, most of our travelers to Xishang are American or British. We are set up to cash traveler's checks," he said proudly. "Mr. Tzu, over there at the teller's window, can exchange your checks for pounds."

He went to the window. Thin-lips kept his passport.

Lasker thought Tzu looked a lot like the other officer—a cousin? A brother? This Chinese informed him there would be a ten percent charge to change checks into cash! He refused adamantly and shouted, "I'll be right back," to bastard number one and went to the bank ten minutes away. Then he came back looking pleased. Bart forked over the money to the tour booker.

The Chinese official smiled. "Ah, went to the bank and saved a few dollars?"

"I'm not Rockefeller," Lasker said.

"Of course not." The Chinese smiled. He put the money in a drawer. Lasker wondered how much would reach Beijing and how much was skimmed. "You are aware," the Chinese said, stamping Bart's passport, "there are *few* amenities until you reach Lhasa. But we expect you will enjoy your sojourn in Xishang. If you can endure some discomfort, it is a wonderful scenic province."

Bart took his visa-stamped passport and thanked him. As he put it in his parka pocket, thin-lips added, "I have taken the trip myself. You will enjoy. There are the quite spectacular vistas of the Himalayas and many ruins of the superstitious past in the area! We will call you when the bus is ready. There is no exact timetable for its arrival—due to road construction. We will call you at your hotel."

"When?"

"I cannot say exactly. If you are not in your room, we will leave a message. You must appear for the bus at the appointed hour. Otherwise it will leave without you. It departs from the Ganjung Temple. Have a nice trip!"

Lasker left. Twenty-five hundred pounds, and they wouldn't wait for him if he was a bit late!

Chapter 7

Meanwhile, a thousand miles to the south in Dhramsala, a skinny young man with long, dirty blond hair and a scraggly beard, wearing a fleece-lined blue jeans jacket and lots of junk necklaces, was asking questions about Lasker. The Tibetans immediately dubbed him Jerry the hippie. Jerry was soon directed to the Tibet Medical Institute, where the earnest hippie hung around for hours trying to get Lasker's address from the monks, who in their own way avoided telling. Perhaps, just because he was *too* anxious to see Lasker.

Drogang, cornered by the young American and asked the same question, didn't like the feeling from the man. But he didn't know if there was anything wrong, aside from the American's great ignorance of manners.

"Bart Lasker is a friend of mine," Jerry the hippie insisted. "He wrote me about this great place, and I wanted to surprise him."

"He left," Drogang said.

"When did he leave? Where'd he go?"

Drogang was about to answer, and then he shut

his mouth. Something had flared red in the hippie's energy aura, and the lama knew there was not just ignorance in Jerry—but evil as well.

He realized that he should not speak of Lasker and particularly not about the Mystic Rebel's sudden departure for Kathmandu.

One of the student monks was standing alongside, though, and started to say, "Lasker left yesterday for K—"

Drogang shushed him by saying, "Get to work inside and talk less!"

The student ran off, feeling chastised.

Drogang now calmed himself with his mantra and by visualizing his patron Yidam protector over the crown of his head. Then he looked into Jerry's soul through his clear blue eyes and saw cleverness and great danger. Drogang decided to reverse the situation and question Jerry the hippie. He said, "I can tell you more, but I must go inside. There are pill-liquids to stir. They will cake up if I don't go—"

Jerry volunteered, "Can I help? Oh wow, I always wanted to do that. My friend Lasker told me all about this cool far out place, man!"

"Then come inside," Drogang said, like a spider inviting a fly to his web.

They went inside and immediately to the large iron cauldron, in which a vat of steaming brown fluid was beginning to separate.

"Here," Drogang said, handing the scrawny blond youth a ladle the size of a Polynesian war paddle, "stir with me."

"Sure man," the hippie replied, and started to lean in opposite Drogang, stirring vigorously.

Drogang watched Jerry's eyes and his red aura. He noticed the fact that despite Jerry's energetic stirring, the liquid to make the Eagle-17 pills wasn't breaking and softening up the way it always did. Drogang assumed it was because of that evil red aura of the man disturbing the highly sensitive process. "That will be all," he said. "I will do the rest."

Jerry handed Drogang the paddle. "You said you would tell me about my friend, Bart Lasker—"

Drogang said, "He went to Kalimpoor to do some shopping. He'll be back at his home at eight tonight."

The hippie looked at his watch and smiled. "Great. He'll be glad to see me. Where does he live? I'll surprise him!" Again, the high lama through use of his "third eye" psychic ability was able to see the American's normally invisible aura flare.

"Lasker lives on Drepung Street—opposite the temple under construction. There is a blue-doored house next to the butter lamp shop; that's his," Drogang lied. It was actually a bolted-shut storehouse for lama robes.

"Thanks a lot!" Jerry left.

Now Drogang called Pelemu, the young monk he had scolded, and told the student, "Sorry I snapped at you. There was an evil influence here. That American means neither Lasker nor this community any good. We must dump this batch of liquid out now. Tell him nothing about Lasker—spread the word everywhere to beware, or we will place this whole community in great danger."

Hastily they lifted the caldron together, lugged it

to the rear window and poured it out. "Bah! Hours of work wasted," Drogang muttered under his breath.

While the young monk went off to spread the news about Jerry the hippie, Drogang put on his orange-down vest—it was getting cold—and walked rapidly to Losang's house and knocked.

Losang, upon hearing Drogang's evaluation, decided Jerry would have to be bound from causing harm by a special severe ceremony that had to be performed right away.

The two of them made the *torma* (butter and dough) images for the *puja*. Five minutes later, they were seated on Losang's rug and started banging the human-skin invocation drums. It wouldn't be a pleasant thing that would happen to Jerry, Drogang realized, but measures had to be taken.

Jerry was sitting in front of what he thought was Lasker's door, waiting to kill Lasker with the .38 he was holding in his jacket pocket. He felt funny. His hand twitched, and Jerry let go of the gun. He jerked upright, standing up involuntarily. *What the hell?* Jerry tried to talk—to shout. Just garble and drool came out of his mouth. He couldn't remember now what he was doing. He didn't know where he was.

Jerry, jerking like a crazed puppet, wandered out into Dhramsala's market street and sat down on his haunches on the roadside, drooling up green liquid.

A fat man who came by gave him a cup. A monk came along and put a coin in it. Soon the drooling idiot Jerry had a cup half full of coins from passersby. He was hungry and got up to buy himself some rice and began the jerky walk toward a store stall.

"W-w-want f-f-food!" he repeated, so he would remember. Thinking was *hard*.

It would be months before Jerry would come to himself; in the meantime, he would be just another ragged beggar at the village roadside. Drogang watched the assassin stagger along. Perhaps people would think his mind had been blown on hashish like so many druggy Westerners who wandered down from Nepal, and take pity and give him a few rupees. A pity indeed, Drogang thought, but Jerry was evil, and had to be bound.

At least this way he would not stain his soul with bad Karmic actions.

Chapter 8

In three hours and twenty minutes the man at the Chinese Tour Bureau called. "Your bus is ready, Mr. Arthur. Please go immediately to the Ganjung Temple to board it. Have a nice stay in Xishang Province."

Lasker said, "Thanks, I will," and put down the receiver.

The British man who had been ahead of Lasker at the tour service was there, and so were a few dozen other hardy-looking souls. All appeared eager and excited.

Lasker was concerned he couldn't see the right number on the bus—it had to be #60, the one whose crew had been bribed. But where was the number? Then he saw it—a peeling, faint marking by the door—#60. He handed the crew-cut, broody-looking Tibetan guide the ticket and his passport. Their eyes met like electric shocks; this was the right man, the bribed guide. He looked very afraid of Lasker. Lasker looked away and climbed in the bus.

The driver wasn't at the wheel. Bart walked down the aisle, finally found a seat, and stowed his backpack in the overhead. A young blond woman sat down next to him in the icy-cold leather seat, extended her hand for a shake and said, "I am B.J. Landers—and you are?"

"Bruce Arthur."

"British?"

"Yes, though I've been away a lot."

She nodded. "I'm from the colonies—ha ha—America, get it?" She then asked, "Been to Tibet before?"

He said, "No, but I've been everywhere else: Bhutan, Sikkim—all the border states."

"I *thought* you'd travelled a lot. It's your face." She blushed, aware that it could be considered an insult. "Well, what I really mean is that your face is fine, of course, but it looks like you've done a bit of trekking. Oh I'm sorry! It's a perfectly good face. Oh! I'm making a mess of this."

"No, you're quite right," Lasker said. "I'm a nature photographer—and have travelled a lot off-road in Asia—hence my weathered look. Lots of hiking, climbing. You are very perceptive."

She smiled. "I was sure you had been in Asia awhile! Your accent is not quite Oxford—if you know what I mean."

"Yes. I have been all over. And I spent a lot of time in Canada." Damn, *why was she so talkative?* Was she a spy or—just attracted to him?

"Oh, Canada! That explains it," B.J. went on. "You almost sound like an American." She gave a quick smile and then turned to the window to watch

67

as her suitcases were loaded on.

"You have to watch these Tibetans," she said. "The Chinese are more organized, and they wouldn't steal a thing. Why, I was in Beijing last year, and I lost my wallet on a subway; and you can't imagine how many people made an effort to get it back to me. They're so kind and efficient, not like the rather— savage Tibetans. Don't you think?"

Lasker smiled. "So I've heard." He had experienced a different kind of Chinese than she had! An occupying army oppressing a sullen, hostile population. He had experienced them, not as a Western tourist but as a Tibetan would. Bart wondered again about Miss B.J. Landers. Was she trying to get him to criticize the Chinese? Was she a spy for the Chinese? or for—Woo?

He watched the rest of the passengers settling in. Buddhist monks—six of them—each with a single, fat carpetbag. Then some hippie climber types, all blond—must be Germans—scruffy and well equipped with camping gear, though this was not a camping tour. Now they were talking—yes Germans—talking about being booked into the Lhasa Hilton.

The six monks looked a bit ersatz—too well fed and orderly. But they were real Tibetans; he could tell that. He wondered, though, if they were real monks. Most monks didn't get to come and go to Tibet. Some official delegation perhaps, or monks in name only. That kind of monk was appearing every place in Tibet, Bart had heard. The Chinese trained young Tibetans in Marxist camps and then sent them to monasteries and temples to spy on the others.

The bus started up and pulled out to the cheers of its passengers. Soon it was traveling up a gravel road toward the mountains. Lasker nodded once in a while as B.J. kept rapping. He watched the back of the heads of the guide and the short Chinese driver. Somehow he could feel their tension. How much had they been bribed to let him "disappear" en route? Was it enough?

Were they going to betray him? Was she?

He tried to relax; eventually B.J. shut up. He leaned back and closed his eyes.

The engine sounded good. It was a nice, new German bus, not a Chinese model, thank God. He didn't want to be tumbling down an abyss tonight. He had things to do, things that could mean the salvation of all mankind.

Chapter 9

They were two hours out of Kathmandu. Lasker saw a small roadsign "Entering Xishang." No border guards, no fences. *Yeah*. Phoney openness. The sunset was spectacular—and mostly behind them. The snow-capped peaks were yellow, then red, then a somber purple. Then darkness reigned. Not a sliver of moon.

The Germans moaned about the darkness, complaining they were missing some of the most spectacular scenery in Asia: the approach to the Tibetan Plateau. Lasker wondered if the bus hadn't delayed its arrival—and thus its departure—on purpose. The Chinese military might have a lot of troops moving around here, or be building new fortifications—whatever. The bus, of course, would have been cleared to zip along where any other vehicle would have been blasted by an RPG. Thus giving us tourists, Lasker mused, the impression that Tibet is virtually unguarded. How wrong an impression that was! Chinese troops were poised to push into India if the call came.

The road was bumpy now; the driver swung the wheel around curves only he could see. B.J. Landers began more inane but earnest conversation. Bart mumbled affirmations and looked around at the passengers. The bus had interesting "trail" people and intellectuals, too. Most of them had the small overhead lights on and were reading books. He glanced at the guide slumbering in the seat opposite the driver. The guide knew that Bruce Arthur was someone who would slip away—and had been bribed to ignore it. He and the Chinese driver were on his side—if they were the right ones, of course. Lasker had no idea what side the other passengers were on. If any. Probably none. Just curious people with dough.

Lasker got B.J. to stop talking by no longer nodding when she said things. Eventually she dozed. She didn't read—did that mean she was a spy? He sat back and watched his reflection in the glass. Gradually there appeared a quarter moon, and the mountains seemed to glow. Everyone clicked off the lights and just gawked. No place like Tibet for scenery.

They travelled all night, the headlights cutting a swath through the crisp, thin Himalayan air, the well-built road clear of rockfalls. A fast, safe, comfortable ride. So far!

Lasker managed to relax, and he actually got some shut-eye, confident of the throaty thrust of the engine, the smooth shifting of the Borg-Warner gears and the deft piloting of the Chinese driver.

"Lamdrung," the guide shouted. "First stop."

They got out. It was four A.M. Kathmandu time, but the driver shouted in accented English and then German, "Please adjust your watches. It is nine A.M. China time. All China has the same time zone as Beijing, the Capital."

Groans. It was barely getting light, there were still stars in the sky.

"Some time system," B.J. waxed ecstatically, "but it keeps the nation together." Since it was nine A.M. now, it was time for breakfast in the square quonset hutlike shed called the "Lamdrung Quick-Eat."

"God it's cold," some female muttered.

It was bitterly cold, but very dry. "Don't worry," said the guide, "the temperature is low at night in Xishang, but in an hour it will be hot enough for you to remove your down jackets."

They filed inside the hut. The breakfast in the hut was pried-open cans of pork and some hot water sold in bottles.

Everyone complained. One German woman didn't want to go on. Someone with a cassette recorder kept playing a Beatle recording, "Roll up, roll up for the mystery tour—the magical mystery tour . . ." A laugh. True. How true. And it had only begun.

After some grumbling, they all got back on the bus, after the Americans aboard left scraps of polaroid pullouts all over the mountainside, clicking off pics of the red sunrise on the snow peaks. Just before the second stop, the driver pointed out with loving detail the scene below the steep sharp turn. They paused while everyone took pictures of the wreckage of a bus that hadn't made it the month before. "Many died, oh so many," the diminutive driver laughed, "but that was bad old Indian bus. This is good German bus." Lasker wondered if the driver knew his parted-in-the-middle, slick-oiled hair made him look like Mo of the Three Stooges!

The Germans applauded, shouting "Mercedes! Mercedes!"

When they again started up a pale B.J. said, "He needn't have dwelled on the wreck so much, don't you think . . ."

Lasker nodded, feeling for the first time that B.J. perhaps was just another tourist after all. He could tell by the slight clouding of her eyes that she was disappointed that this wasn't going to be a budding bus romance after all. Something was wrong, she had realized, with this virile and rugged-looking male companion of hers. Bart had to half smile as he saw her lean back, starting to carefully look over the other passengers for her next-best prospect. He saw her eyes zero in on a professional looking fiftyish German. A professor?

The guide said, "We are approaching scenic stop two." Most of the passengers had their coats off. The sun was blazing.

"It must be ninety-one degrees," an American woman gasped.

"No, thirty-nine," the driver said.

"That's all?"

"Celsius," Lasker explained.

The bus screeched to a halt. "This overlook is the last stop before Shigatse."

B.J. exclaimed. "Look at that big map on the side

73

of the road. It says you can see the ruins of an ancient lamasery from here!"

It was an awesome vista indeed: saw-tooth mountains, and on one sheer slope miles away, high across a green misty valley, a vast ruin. The Tonke-Gompo, a Red Hat Sect, thirteenth Century monastery—over one hundred buildings now picturesque half-eroded walls. . . .

Lasker took out his 345mm Yashika, changed lenses for no good reason, remembering that he was supposed to be a professional photographer, put on a filter, and clicked pictures like mad. The film was still in his bag.

"Please save your film. Supplies are sporadic," said the Tibetan guide. The Chinese driver tried to be polite and posed with many of the tourists. No one told him about the hair. Then right on cue, some very clean, colorful and well-fed Tibetan local men in fox hats and women in elaborate gold-threaded chubas and turquoise and amber-laden headdresses, appeared for the photo session.

Lasker thought that they were extremely well-dressed, and their costumes were atypical of southern Tibet. They were here for show.

Several Chinese soldiers working on a pipeline installation stopped work and came over, too—all casual, smiling—no guns showing. The new image. Then the officer among them, a cool colonel, went around and carefully checked the bus riders' passports. Lasker could tell the officer's rank by the five-star lapel cluster, despite the absence of stripes. By the steely-edged look he gave each one of the visitors, he was K-5. Border elite patrol.

He paused at Lasker the longest, evidently not liking the weathered, rugged face—the face of a fighter. But the colonel nodded and smiled civilly. "Have a good time in Xishang Province." He moved on.

This had been the *real* border.

Sure, Lasker thought as the officer left him. We'll all visit Xishang and spend lots of money and tell everyone back home that this "part of China" is nice.

They drove on, down toward the place where he'd get lost—Shigatse—once the Capital of Tibet in Kubla Khan's day.

Lasker hadn't seen the ancient Sakya Capital on his last foray into Tibet. He wished he could explore all its exotic sites: the eternal hot springs, the crying goddess waterfalls, the many exquisite small shrines and stupas scattered in its environs. But there wasn't time.

There it was, Tashi Lumpo Temple, in the green valley ahead, the place arranged for Bruce Arthur to slip away, and for the Mystic Rebel to be reborn!

Chapter 10

The bus descended wildly toward the town of Shigatse, which appeared from Lasker's steep angle to be a city of small whitewashed houses with flat rooftops. There were doors—as was the habit with Tibetans—on every roof. The doors of Tibet are roof holes with ladder entrances.

Off to the side, entirely surrounded by a high wall with several gates in it was the sprawling Tashi Lumpo Temple and monastery, a collection of three- and four-story ornate buildings painted red or white, with stubby spires on their roof edges. The town had grown up, like most towns in Tibet, because of the temple.

But there was an intrusion.

Smack in the middle of the ancient temple grounds was a new five-story, blue, glass and brick government building, the Chinese contribution to destroying the sacredness of the place in one fell swoop!

The driver, overly anxious perhaps for a beer, drove like a devil down the sheer winding incline. Lasker had seen him sipping from a flask secretly

76

at every stop—maybe his nerves were giving out—and a drunken accomplice was not something Bart savored.

"Stopover is four hours," announced the Tibetan guide, avoiding Lasker's eyes. "There is running hot water in the main building where the bus stops, along with a snack shed, a cinema, and even a bar. If any of you tire of the quaint and primitive religious sites, you can take liquor there. There is also a post office across from the Tashi Lumpo Temple, where you may post letters you wish to send."

"How about postcards?" the English woman who had complained earlier about the heat asked.

"How about a shower," someone else complained.

"There is a souvenir shop in the temple—where cards may be purchased. The Tashi Lumpo Temple is a must see. It is one of the grandest temples in the world, carefully maintained and improved by the generosity of the central Beijing government." The guide went on, in rote, extolling the Chinese improvements to the old city, especially the glass tower.

Lasker felt his pulse quickening and his blood boil. The temple was partially destroyed in the 1960s by frantic Red Guards. And a dozen other mad officials since the occupation began, including Tse Ling, had tried to make it into some sort of military fort—sans artwork and monks. Only the intervention of the Tibetan people and passive resistance by the monks had kept it standing.

The bus leveled off and barrelled down a narrow dusty street, blowing its horn, scattering Tibetan children and chickens, and roared through the open gate of Tashi Lumpo in a cloud of impenetrable road dust.

Lasker looked around. The central area of the temple grounds didn't look much like a Tibetan place: all Chinese signs, some soldiers with rifles slung on their shoulders, a bar with a flashing neon sign. Neither did the surrounding hillside looming over the buildings, scattered with tin shacks and truck motor pools. Shigatse always had a vast population—the third largest city in Tibet—but mostly transients, pilgrims and strangers. Now the Chinese had moved in big—and permanently. A moderation of Chinese aims here didn't mean they'd leave! If there was a fanatic shift in Beijing again, all of Tibet, including Shigatse, could disappear in a week to be replaced by drab concrete blockhouses.

The guide gathered them on the steps of the glass-front administrative building and started his spiel:

"Rigaze was the traditional seat of the Pachen Lama, recognized by the fifth Dalai Lama as the Amitabha, Buddha of limitless light. In late 1960, the seventh Pachen Lama was in Peiking giving a speech when the monks, stirred up by the C.I.A., caused a disturbance here. Central government troops surrounded the Tashi Lumpo Monastery—which was set afire by the monks but saved by the soldiers. The Pachen Lama denounced the C.I.A.-Dalai Lama conspiracy. The soldiers seized all four hundred monks as counter-revolutionaries. But only the ringleaders were punished. Many instigators unfortunately committed suicide."

"Why?" B.J. asked. "Were they going to be punished?"

"Oh, no. The central government always gives the opportunity for thought reform. No, the Tibetans believe in reincarnation, so they thought it was better to reincarnate than face mild reprimand. We tell you about these disturbances because some reactionary Tibetans here might tell you false stories. You are free to sightsee on your own or follow me in a tour. I recommend you stick close and avoid the confidence men trying to sell false relics and exchange money illegally."

Lasker wished he could be one of those reactionaries and tell the tour now that the monks at Tashi Lumpo had committed suicide rather than face a lifetime at hard labor and endless brainwashing sessions. Those that didn't kill themselves were taken for "forever servitude at hard labor for the people." Only two hundred young novice monks were allowed to remain. The Pachen Lama, who had tried to be friendly to the Chinese people despite what had been happening—in the hope of mitigating the worst abuses—changed tactics. He hadn't denounced the C.I.A. They had nothing to do with the insurrection. He supported the Dalai Lama openly, and then the Pachen Lama himself was placed under house arrest as a result. He was forbidden to speak in public. Over the years he was again and again asked to denounce the Dalai Lama as the instigator of counter-revolutionary bloodshed. In 1964, the Chinese gathered four thousand people at a prayer ritual in Lhasa and thought the Pachen would denounce the Dalai Lama. Instead of denouncing the God-King, the Pachen Lama delivered a stunning speech of support. He was promptly re-arrested and beaten into signing confessions of malfeasance. He "disappeared" until 1978. Then, when the corrupt dictatorship of Mao was slowly being dismantled, he reappeared. The winds of change in Beijing had brought him out of years of torture in prison, and the Pachen Lama was given some minor desk job in Beijing, as advisor on the Xishang region. That was the reactionary truth!

Everyone without exception followed Gerlum the guide for the official tour; if not because of his warning, then because the place was like a maze on the poor map of the temple they were each handed. Lasker kept his backpack on, claiming he needed its photo equipment.

The Tashi Lumpo Temple was a town in itself, surrounded by ancient ochre walls. They huddled together to walk to the main temple and for the first time saw saffron-robed shaven-headed monks coming and going. Many had sort of half-monk, half worker outfits.

"The monks no longer," the Tibetan guide said, "exploit the people for their indulgent life-style of the past. They have to work as well as be monks now, or they wouldn't be allowed to live here! One of the many improvements put in effect by the central government!"

They came to a statue in a cobblestone-block square between paint-peeling buildings.

"This is a statue of the so-called previous incarnation of the Pachen Lama. The people, though reviling the Dalai Lama," the guide lied, "have some respect for the Pachen and have not removed it."

Yeah sure, Lasker thought. Gerlum should have said the Chinese hadn't destroyed this statue because the Pachen no longer made strong pro-Dalai statements and went through some motions of support for the Chinese. Now, under the "liberal" Chinese reforms in Beijing, the Pachen's liberty to make controlled tours of Tibet to bless the people was supposed to be an example for the Dalai to return here—to forego his opposition to the Chinese occupation and accept the same sort of role for himself. The Pachen was still revered, *that* was true. The Tibetan people knew what had happened to him, and that he was yet unbroken.

They now came to a small bushy park before the main four-story temple. It was being repainted, and scaffolds covered its face. Stonework was being repaired. Several ragged townspeople trying to get in to worship were being turned away because they didn't have admission money. Lasker perhaps was the only one who could understand the quiet argument at the temple door.

"But this is our place of worship," one said. "Perhaps just one of us, my wife, could go in—just for a moment," the old man pleaded.

"Sorry." The old monk guarding the doorway seemed concerned. "Everyplace is the Buddha," he whispered. The old man and his bent-over wife brightened up and took his blessing and left quickly now, seeing the tourists coming.

The tourists—Bruce Arthur included—paid the seven renminbao admission, eight U.S. dollars, and approached the temple's vast timeless interior.

The old monk who had spoken so kindly to the poor townspeople volunteered to guide a special tour, and Gerlum agreed. Lasker looked him over, thinking of the quick blessing he had bestowed on the aged couple. Was he for real?

They walked through the fortresslike building of creme-colored stones and entered the Maitreya Hall, where they beheld the Buddha of the Future, the many-armed magnificent gold image.

The old monk said, "He is called Champa. When all are delivered from suffering, this Buddha will return to earth to rule."

"Sounds like Christ," someone said.

"Yes." The monk grinned. "He is your Christ, too."

The official guide quickly added, "This magnificent statue is twenty-seven meters high—about 80 feet. It is made of bronze with gold plating. The Maitreya is depicted on the traditional lotus seat and bears marks of divine wisdom in his forehead. The hand gestures of the many arms indicate the giving of dharma."

"What's that?"

"The dharma is the way," the old monk said, and then added hastily, "so superstition states."

"It is worth seven dollars!" a woman gasped, and started flashing her Polaroid. Everyone clicked madly. They spread out around the large candle-lit chamber to look at all the small shrines and ceremonial objects sealed museum-style behind glass cases. They were led to a stall in the hallway to buy things: reproductions and posters and of course expensive postcards.

Lasker took the opportunity to drift away, to find his contact. He was not far down a side hall lined with plaster reproductions of Bodhisatvas yet unpainted when the Chinese bus driver, eyes red from drinking, drew him into a dark corner. He showed a machine pistol and jabbed it into Lasker's ribs. "If this is where you get off, I want more money. If you do not give to me"—he cocked the mean-looking thing—"you die!"

Chapter 11

Lasker, in a lightning E-Kung move twisted left so that the pistol faced the wall, not his chest, and at the same time bent back the hand holding it, nearly snapping the driver's wrist. The man screamed in pain, but the scream was stifled by Lasker's cupped right hand. The pistol clattered to the stone flooring.

"Now," Lasker grunted, "you *obey* me! There will be no more money! Any betrayal and I will tear your heart out—" He clawed his fingers and pressed them deep enough in under the man's ribcage to nearly burst his flesh. "Understand?"

The bus driver gasped out, "Y-yes. Please!"

He collapsed retching to the floor when let go.

"Remember what I said! I'm not alone! Someone will be watching your every move after I leave, to make sure I'm not betrayed. Stick to the story. Say that I became ill and had to stay over in Shigatse."

The driver nodded vigorously as Lasker hauled him to his feet by his jacket collar. Thus chastized, he was allowed to have his pistol and he left post-haste.

The guide monk Dergay came up to Lasker shortly after. He grinned. "You are, I am sure, interested in seeing a bit more of the temple than the usual tourists."

Lasker looked in his eyes. Was this Dergay the mysterious monk he was to contact? If so, perhaps he hadn't given the code words because they had always been in view of the others.

"Ah—yes, I would like that."

"Come then. It won't take long. You won't be late for your bus ride. I can show you some remarkable things perhaps."

They went out between two buildings into a narrow courtyard. "Is this an interesting place?" Lasker asked in Tibetan.

"Ah! You speak excellent Tibetan," Dergay said, still not giving out the right code words.

Lasker was worried but said, "Lead on."

"Your eyes are unusual," the old monk said when they were at the center of the empty yard. They were standing by a small trickling fountain.

Lasker was amazed. At last . . . those were the code words. Lasker said his words, "They are unusual because I am a Migyu."

"I am glad to meet a friend of Tibet," the monk said in an excited whisper. "Is His Holiness well? Is he safe?"

"Yes on both accounts," Lasker replied, adding, "He sends his greetings and thanks you for meeting me."

"*Lha gyal lo,*" the monk said, prostrating himself at Lasker's feet.

Lasker pulled him up. "Thanks, but no time."

He and Lasker touched foreheads. "I was surprised it was you. I expected that the German with the handlebar mustache was our agent! But I am not disappointed. I saw you handle that Chinese dog driver. You are a powerful ally!" The monk's face brightened. "Tell me—how is Losang?"

"He is well, too. But look, Dergay, I am sorry. I have to go quickly. Can you take me to the way out, the way where I won't be seen leaving?"

"Of course. We must go through the medical library—behind the great statue."

"Are the others—real monks?" Lasker asked.

Dergay sighed. "In various degrees. Some are sincere, some are spies, some are what I call half-monks. Every young man, before he comes here to study the Dharma, has to pass a socialism test. And each has to do well on the test and become a young communist party member."

"But how can they be any kind of real Buddhist and a party member at the same time?"

"Not easy," Dergay said, taking Lasker through a narrow alley between rusting steel drums and piles of scrap wood. Rats ran helter-skelter to avoid their feet. "Many, despite all the brainwashing, really suspect the truth," Dergay continued. "They can see with their own eyes that communist freedom is a lie."

At the end of rat alley, he opened a weathered wooden door that creaked loudly. They came into a dark, dusty, small chamber.

"No tourists, *hee hee,* get to see this," he said.

There were loud noises and shouts in Tibetan behind the wall. They stumbled over some garbage, and Dergay opened a corroded brass door to a brightly lit large room. Swirling steam and the smell of rotten vegetables assailed Bart's nostrils. There were dozens of bald, nude men rushing around with huge spoons.

"Ah—the aroma! We call this hell's kitchen," the monk said. Lasker was amazed. There were giant copper cauldrons and the unmistakable smell of a million boiling mo-mos—Tibetan dumplings.

"We have added many tofu dishes. The Chinese have been good for one thing at least: Suggesting many healthy vegetarian dishes, and we use less meat every year. That is meritorious."

The sweating naked cooks ignored their presence and continued running around carrying pots or stirring or just shouting for others to do the same. A bedlam kitchen!

"Come through this way." He led Bart between two men on a tall ladder who were stirring a giant pot of evil-smelling greens. They climbed through a low doorway and entered into yet another dark room—no, there was light, just a shaft of sun coming through a high slit window. Lasker's eyes adjusted, and in the light of dozens of butter lamps, he saw a giant old statue, the old image of the Sakyamuni Buddha, the Buddha for this epoch in time. It was exquisite and radiated a soft but powerful feeling of other-worldliness.

"This is the true monastery, not the tourist part!" Dergay stated. "Most of the sincere monks, monks we are sure of, meet here for prayers. See—there are immense *thankas,* scroll paintings of the conquerer deities. Still safe! Very old!"

Lasker wondered if anyone except the monks here ever saw these magnificent things. The old monk seemed to read his mind.

"The *thankas* are taken out in Shigatse's streets for festivals. The last time was when the Pachen Lama stopped here in 1985."

"I met the Pachen once—or rather saw him," Lasker said, touching the brocaded silk border of one *thanka* depicting Chenresig, god of compassion, reverently.

"Really?"

"Yes," Bart said. "He helped me out of a jam, just his presence . . ."

"Yes," the monk agreed. "He has the power. Go around the back of this Buddha statue. Bend down, don't bang your head."

Dergay opened an old wooden storage chest in the secret room and bent to get something. He handed Lasker a typical nomad outfit to put on: Chinese work pants and old yak hide boots. Lasker put the boots on first—a bit loose—better than tight.

"You can wear your maroon parka—it's Chinese, isn't it?"

"Yes," Lasker said. "And it's warm. I'd hate to give it up."

It was hard to change in the cramped space, but Lasker managed. They then crawled along for about ten feet, and the monk pushed away some wood boards.

Lasker saw mountains. They were staring out the back of the monastery through a hole in the rear wall. Dergay squatted next to Lasker in the opening and pulled a circular box about six inches wide out of his robe. "Here's some Chinese shoe polish," he said. "Black. Better do something to your hair if you want to look Tibetan when you walk up the hillside." Lasker dabbed the polish in his hair until Dergay was satisfied.

There was a purple riot of flowers on the nearby rocks, which were twenty yards beyond a bare swath of land.

"Is that all fucsia?" asked Lasker. "It's beautiful."

"They are local flowers—always grew here. We call them *dampalis."*

"Really?" Lasker said. "They come from South America."

The monk said, "Then perhaps that is why the Chinese spray to kill them all the time. The Tibetan people are not a Chinese race. Perhaps these flowers indicate to them once again that we Tibetans are related to Peru and the Inca civilization! Good-bye, Lasker," Dergay said, squeezing his hand tightly. "Take care jumping down. There is soft earth, but it is twenty feet high!"

Lasker said, *"Lha gyal lo,"*—victory to the Buddha—and jumped down. Picking himself up like a jungle cat, he hurried toward the shadow of the great snow-capped mountain. The sky was already turning a dark cobalt blue. Soon it would be night.

He scrambled up the fucsia-covered slope into the glimmer of a star cluster called the Pleiades. All Bart had to do now was hike the sixty miles through what promised to be a bitter cold night to Tsurphu, his next stop on his mission. The thought occurred to Bart to pick up the well-trodden caravan path. It was already marked on the geological map in his backpack. No, that was just laziness. He'd keep to his plan of avoiding the easy way, keep to the high ground. That way he was sure to avoid motorized

Chinese patrols. If he did run across the Chinese, well he had the short sword and the nunchaku. He had timed how long it would take to pull apart the backpack and put together these two deadly anti-assailants: eighteen seconds. So, if there *was* trouble, he'd better see it coming.

He wished to hell he could take the pack apart now, but it was full of supplies: the food, his maps and aluminum space-blanket, some climbing picks, and a length of good rope. He girded himself for the long, cold night's walk, determined to conquer the miles of rough-and-tumble terrain with no more than an hour or two's sleep. He had a lot of experience trekking in the Tibetan mountains. He would make it.

Lasker paused at the top of a rise to look back in the gibbous moon's light at the town of Shigatse. It looked no more real than a painting; the temple complex completely hid the ugly Chinese flats from his view. He saw the smoke curling up from the western-style chimneys, warding off the night's bitter temperatures. He sighed and kept walking.

The temperature was dropping by the minute. His silk underwear and the down parka would have to serve him well. If he didn't get lost—or caught—or freeze to death, he would be at Tsurphu by tomorrow's dusk.

At a barren, lunar-looking place called Red Mud Valley, one hundred twenty miles north of Lhasa, one of the many looking for Lasker hit paydirt. The seeker, disguised as a wandering Tibetan pilgrim named Namghee, kicked the dirt clogs off his boots and stepped into the "Inn of the Mirror God," a ramshackle caravan stop in the midst of the dry valley.

Namghee merged into the hard-drinking crowd inside, drinking carefully and spreading juicy Lhasa gossip. He had a fluid tongue, and the inn crowded with caravaners spending this bleak, cold night in the comfort of the inn's roaring hearth, were starved for conversation; for any news that Namghee could provide. Namghee roamed among the coarse, rugged drinkers until he could sidle up to the drunken innkeeper, one called Telmez. Though constantly warned by the monks at the Mahaka Monastery not to talk about their comely guest in the nearby muontain aerie, Telmez forgot the admonition. Plied with gifts of his own arak and compliments for his pathetic establishment by the newcomer, he told Namghee his interesting tale. He told the travelling pilgrim of the beautiful woman staying at the temple twelve miles to the east. "She is not an ordinary person," he bragged. "No ordinary person stays here in this sacred area, in the powerful domain of the Mirror God."

"Mirror God?" asked the pilgrim.

"Oh, yes! Have you not heard of Mahaka? This valley and inn are blessed places! Oh, you may not think so by the appearance of this place, but our *fung shi* (geographic placement amongst water and hills), is excellent, and the nearby monastery's Lord Mahaka protects and blesses us every day. That is why caravans stop here, making me a good living! That is why I have two good sisters as wives, one very pretty, the other a strong housekeeper and child bearer!" There was a great swelling of his chest as Telmez continued, full of himself and his importance. "This place is not just a place of boot-sucking red mud. It is not just a few caravan stopover bunks—oh no. I run not simply an ignorant nomad's way station! Indeed," he boasted, "I am an innkeeper blessed to be below the sacred Mahaka Monastery."

"You mentioned a great beauty—a secret female guest among the monks at Mahaka. Who is she?" The pilgrim poured out more arak.

The innkeeper drank and leaned close. "The monastery holds not just a beautiful woman, but in fact," he whispered, "she is the lover of the great one called the Mystic Rebel himself. Have you heard of him?"

"I think—the name sounds familiar." Namghee's heart beat wildly. "Tell me more."

"Ah, he is the Westerner that leads our Tibetan freedom-fighters against oppressors."

The traveller nodded. "Yes, I have heard a bit about such a man." He poured out some Mou Tai. The Chinese liqueur's sickening smell was like flowers to the innkeeper, and he drank it down, and slurred out, "The Mystic Rebel is all powerful, imbued with the power of the ancient's magic! Why, it was he who called forth the dead at Smoke Mountain prison camp to free the captives there. And his lover and powerful consort, Dorgee, lives under the protection of the Mahaka monks, until he returns."

"Is that so," said the traveller. He looked pained

and excused himself to take a leak. Instead, Namghee went out a side door into the night. He went immediately to his horse, which had several bulging saddlebags on it. The bags were making strange cooing noises. He opened the straps on one and took out a small cage containing a homing pigeon. Namghee scribbled a message with his little Chinese pen and, taking the pigeon from its cage, put the tiny message into a little container on the left leg. Then he let the pigeon fly.

The innkeeper came out—to take a well-needed piss—at that instant. "Why do you let fly a pigeon?"

The pilgrim just stared at the innkeeper. Finally he said, "It got free by accident. I normally sell them to the religious people in the markets. They free them to gain good karma."

"You lie," sneered the innkeeper, all the while unbuttoning his pants. "I think you are a Chinese agent! Wait till I tell—"

He never finished his words. A throwing knife whooshed through the air and stuck deep in Telmez's heart.

The traveller got on his horse and said, "I will send off another pigeon with a prayer for you, and for *your* good karma."

He whipped his horse savagely with the reins, and he rode off into the night.

Chapter 12

After several hours, Bart checked his luminous watch's dial, only to find it had stopped. He had always worn the kind you wind, and Bart had forgotten! He figured he was about four hours out from Shigatse. It must be near midnight Tibetan time. So far so good. He had kept a steady pace. The going had been cold but uneventful. Now, however, there was a strange prolonged howl in the distance: Was it one of Tibet's fabled snow lions, or a migyu—the dreaded abominable snowman of the Himalyas? No, it sounded canine, like one of the wild black mastiffs that followed the caravans. In any case, his skin crawled at the sound. It was not repeated.

He walked on a bit more slowly, and with the moon partly obscured by a peak, Bart soon found he could barely see where to walk. Once, a long time ago, he had been able to tap into some mysterious inner power and actually illuminate his way by light of his own life-energy aura. But *that* Mystic Rebel trick he had never been able to repeat.

Bart wondered just how much of the Mystic Rebel he still was. Another indication that he was, after all, a mere mortal soon became evident: He was nearly exhausted. He walked for another hour in the near total darkness of the shadow of Mt. Kikanar—or at least he hoped it was that mountain—and then he slipped on a few round stones. For a heart-stopping second he was not touching anything. Then his shoulder hit, and he rolled down a gravelly slope. He had to take a chance and click on his penlight to grope his way back up to the yak trail. It was covered with small rock debris.

He'd find a place and set up the survivor's tent till dawn. The sky was becoming thickly overcast, and he didn't even have starlight now, anyway.

He found a rock overhang. His boot hit something that clunked. A flick of the light showed some old Australian Foster Beer cans, and a broken brown bottle labeled Tsing Tao—Chinese beer.

Lasker wasn't the first traveller to stop here. But he'd be neater than they had been.

He carefully unpacked his supplies, piled them against the cliff's rocks, and then stripped apart the pack and set up the crawl tent. He pulled the survival blankets over him and closed his eyes. He fell asleep instantly.

The next morning he woke up way after sunrise—bitterly cold and coughing. He slipped off his boots and rubbed his frozen feet for ten minutes, then put on a second pair of thermal socks, bringing circulation back to his limbs, packed, and started walking.

The sun's intense yellow beams quickly made the temperature bearable; the sky was indigo blue. After an hour of trekking, he even shucked his parka. The sun beat down so hard that Lasker put the flaps of his Tibetan hat over his forehead, peering between them to see where he was going. He'd lost some time, but felt he had made the right decision not to try and negotiate the rock-strewn and nearly invisible caravan trail last night. Why was it in such disrepair? When he had last been in Tibet, the many caravaners plying their ancient routes through the mountains would always pause to clear the debris whenever possible.

Speaking of caravans . . . did Bart's ears deceive him, or was that the tinkle of bells? A familiar sound to his ears. Then he heard rough talk in Tibetan. The words, "Get on, you lazy no good yaks!"

It *was* a caravan—just around the bend, coming along the same route toward Bart. He kept walking. Soon he saw the heavily laden yaks and a group of squat resin-faced goat-skin-coated men and women with well-worn chubas of faded colors.

Lasker recognized their dust-coated outfits as Kongpo dress, a people of the far west of Tibet. Lasker decided for the time being to keep pretending to be Bruce Arthur, and in English he shouted out, "Oh hello! Say, are you chaps Tibetans?"

The caravaners looked at him strolling up to them and fumbling with his camera. He clicked away. Bart's mad picture taking was watched without a hint of shyness. The Kongpo were curious at this action, that was all. Surely then, he reasoned, they were real Tibetans from Kongpo, an area so isolated that these people honestly didn't know what the hell he was doing. They hadn't a clue what a camera was, or that he was taking their pictures.

The rather gaunt and stringy women all wore the ordinary Tibetan chuba—a robelike garment prevalent all over the ancient kingdom. But these chubas were of a coarse homespun.

Why were the men wearing their coats in such hot weather? Were they hiding weapons? Were they sick? The goat-skin coats were made with the fleece facing inward. Hot!

Lasker saw one man's coat pop open, revealing that this Kongpo had a leather belt, with copper coins sewn into it, cinching his waist. A valuable belt, probably generations old. Mystery solved. Hidden wealth. Kongpo women usually wore round caps edged with gold brocade, but these had no hat or any jewelry. No doubt they, too, were being careful, hiding the elaborate turquoise earrings Kongpo women usually wore, fearing bandits—or the Chinese.

In any case, all of their feet were encased in new, multicolored boots, the kind made by monks as trade items. Perhaps the Kongpo had stopped to trade barley or butter in a monastery.

One larger man near the front of the group stepped forward and smiled. He said some words in his difficult dialect, but Bart understood well enough:

"Where are you going? Where are you from?" the caravan leader inquired.

He replied in Tibetan. Lasker said he was a British hiker making pictures, headed for Tsurphu. The caravaner, already pleased at Lasker's Tibetan language skill, now was doubly pleased to accept a

97

white khatag scarf. The leader smiled a set of gold teeth at him and asked if he might wish a cup of tea. Lasker produced a plastic cup and said, "Sure." Tibetans assume you have your own cup and utensils when they offer you their fare. It is very bad manners to expect to use the host's dishes.

Lasker sat down with the head guy on a blanket on the roadside. A teapot was heated on a yak-chip fire. The tea was made rapidly, the women using some tinder from their bags to heighten the fire under the kettle.

Soon Lasker sat cross-legged, facing the chief sipping the strong black tea—and conversing. It was all rather formal: polite inquiries as to the health of each of their friends and families and so on; but then there was a shocker! The man said that perhaps Bruce Arthur might wish to avoid the road ahead.

"Why?" Bart asked.

"Because," the man said, "the Chinese are just three li farther along the road toward Tsurphu, checking everyone's papers. They are asking if we have seen any Europeans, a man named Bruce, they said."

That was *him*—damn! The driver must have squealed after all. Bart realized he'd have to abandon the easy caravan path and head higher to avoid the Chinese. He thanked the caravaner for his tea and the kind mention about the danger ahead, and then set out perpendicular to the caravan route—heading up a steep slope.

A thousand feet higher than the well-trodden trail, he found a narrow path that was more suitable for mountain goats than yaks and humans. But

Tibetans had walked along here. There were little bits of snuff—the Tibetan vice—every so often along the path. It would have to do! It paralleled the lower route—or so he thought. But within a few hours, Lasker felt all twisted around, and by mid-afternoon he had to admit it—he was lost. Lost in Tibet.

That usually meant death by exposure or starvation within forty-eight hours. Bart climbed upon a particularly tall boulder lying on its side and surveyed the landscape. To the south he could see for miles all the way to a sliver of green valley, but to the west there was a huge range of granite cliffs. Either, he decided, they were the mountains marked M-34 and M-35 on the geological map—or they weren't. He needed another far-off point of reference. Perhaps if he got up high enough he could see Kichenjunga in Sikkim. Bart would have to climb the nearby peak to make sure. He got back off the boulder and opened the backpack. Unfolding the geological survey map, he figured that Kichenjunga should be slightly to the right of M-34, and directly southwest if he was where he thought. An hour's tiring climb revealed that to be the case. The well-worn face of Kichenjunga was a beacon of new hope.

Still, this meant he was miles off his intended route. He climbed down, walked on confident of direction, feeling exhilarated.

Gradually, despite the hardships of the trek toward Tsurphu, just being back in Tibet again filled Bart with an unparalleled exhilaration. The awesome vistas, dotted with the weathered chess-pawn shaped *stupas,* the exquisite memory of Tashi Lumpo Monastery, reached into his soul and reassured its longing for the ultimate, for the spiritual side of being alive. And there was an almost magnetic feel to the rock-strewn hills and verdant valleys, the rapid rivers and roaring cascades. The snow-capped mountains and glistening glaciers, too, had that holy quality. It was as if the whole forbidden land was a living entity, renewing and restoring faith that mankind is not alone, not just an accident, but rather a part of a grand plan. . . .

Suddenly, a group of blue-furred mountain goats, startled by his presence, bolted. They jumped right over him—a dozen of them. One nearly knocked him senseless with its rear hoofs, and then Bart had to run like hell from the rock slide that followed.

Stunned, he sat down on his haunches one hundred yards on. He'd better keep a straighter head on and stay alert, or he would be run over by a wild yak next.

So much for daydreaming!

Chapter 13

Keeping alert, Bart moved on with the determination to be at Tsurphu Monastery before dark. But the high trail was barely passable at times, and he couldn't keep up the pace necessary.

With a sense of gloom, he watched the warm sun creep lower and go behind the saw-toothed ridges ahead. There was soon a flickering series of red and yellow beams, and the sky's cobalt blue changed to a magenta, and then deep purple. The stars began to appear.

Lasker was high up, and had a headache from the altitude. On the Tibetan plains you start out at eighteen thousand feet. Any mountain adds to that. He sucked on a few Indian rock candies—sugar always helped. But he was breathing hard and had to go even slower. He would spend another night out in the open; that was for sure.

He decided to take a chance on there being no nearby patrols and use the penlight to walk on for a while, to find an out-of-the-wind place to make camp.

Now that night was falling Lasker felt great

loneliness, a feeling of being so insignificant amidst nature's majestic panorama. He yearned to see someone, anyone. He wanted to gaze into the doe-eyes of Dorgee. He had a stronger, more desperate yearning for her than he'd had in a long time. He almost sobbed from the sheer loneliness as he walked down toward a mountain pass, following the glow of his flashlight toward the cut in the mountains.

He caught a glimpse of the still sun-lit Mt. Kailas far, far away. On that snowy peak, blood-red in the sunset, was the dwelling of the evil Bonpo priest magicians and the hidden realm that had changed Lasker from mere mortal into someone whose destiny became wrapped up with the ordeal of Tibet. They had made him into a dual-man, against his will.

He couldn't, of course, see the ruin of Shekar Dzong, the hidden realm where he had been transformed, nor the high walls from which he had managed his death-defying escape.

He shivered from the very thought of the green-eyed, corpselike Bonpo leader Zompahlok and his rituals of death worship.

And now over Mt. Kailas the red faded, and there came a greenish miasmatic glow. It grew and brightened.

Bart stood still, transfixed. Was it some trick of the failing light? No, Mt. Kailas was glowing green, and worse, that greenness seemed to be coming his way, like some sort of spreading ray or . . . the clawed hands of the Bonpo demongod Yamantalai!

It was like a sickly colored aurora—spreading a twisting swirling arm of green hate across the miles.

What manner of phenomenon was this? Was he hallucinating from the altitude? Or could this green vapor be some evil power of the Bonpo seeking him out? Bart dreaded to walk on into its eerie light. And the ray, illusion or not, had spread across the way he was headed. He noticed that something was happening to the sky; it, too, was streaked with that evanescent green. Clouds formed out of empty air and boiled like they were being thrown around by great winds.

And speaking of winds, sudden howling gusts snapped at Bart. The temperature plummeted by the second.

It had to be just a freak weather occurrence, not the Bonpo, he told himself. With great trepidation and something more—a dread—he moved on into the greenish light across his path. The minute he was bathed in the swirling, flickering green glow, Bart knew that it was not a natural phenomenon, but something otherworldly. A nausea swept over him, from his toes to the crown of his head. He found it difficult to breathe. He tried to turn and retreat, but the greenness was drawing Bart on—deeper into its occult grasp.

There was no doubt about it—the green swirling light cast from Mt. Kailas was an attack by the Bonpo!

Unable to turn, dizzy and retching, sucking in the cold air with great difficulty, Lasker headed on toward something—different—ahead.

Yes, a shape on the nearby slope. It was rectangular, low; perhaps it was a hut. Even if it were a rock pile, he could hope to get out of the green death rays by hiding behind it!

By the time he staggered up the rock-strewn slope to the site, Bart was exhausted. He was being pelted with pebbles torn from the slopes by the ever increasing wind. Then there was a bone-shaking thunderclap, and golf-ball-sized hailstones started to fall.

He plunged into the protection offered by the weathered ruins that the rock pile turned out to be. He crawled along, past a row of broken vertical columns. There were a pair of tumbled obelisks with carvings to make them appear to be *linghams*—male sex organs. The green-tinted lightning flashes showed no good place of shelter. He still gasped for air; the green hail stones pounded him like great fists. Bart despaired, for indeed, this ruin was more open to the wind than the hillside he had foregone.

There was no time for exploration. The ground was ankle high in green hailstones, and Lasker was being pummeled to death. In the lightning strokes, he groped among the tumbled ancient stones, and he found a hole. A small room—its lintel was big enough to crawl under. The shelter was merely a few feet deep, and he could barely force his body in. Still, it was shelter from the pelting death. He squeezed in and pulled a nearby heavy flat slate over the hole.

He found he could breath more easily once inside. Rubbing his hands together, reciting the protective *Om Mani Padme Hum* mantra, he tried to keep warm and regain some of his wits.

Lasker's heart was beating wildly, and his breathing was too rapid. He steadied both with sheer willpower and put himself into a deep meditative state. He spent several hours in that trance state, the wind howling outside his tiny shelter. At times, the gusts seemed determined to tear the slate protection away from the hole, but failed.

As the hours went by, he was dimly aware of the wind dying down, the greenish glow around the edge of the slate fading to black. And then, utterly exhausted, Lasker drifted from meditative trance to sleep.

Dreams . . . voices: "You—are an intruder in the realm!"

Green glowing slit eyes . . . a thousand echoing voices, swirling like the green snow. "It is not Lasker's body. This is Raspahloh's . . . Raspahloh's body. Don't stay—go away—you are not welcome in this body, Lasker! Die! Die!" Zompahlok's twisted dry lips intoned.

Bart mumbled and twisted in the confined crawl-hole, and suddenly he was not in the small cold shelter in the mountain ruins. Instead, he was in the foul-smelling temple of Shekar Dzong—the hidden realm of the hideous Bonpo. He was standing naked, shivering before the three-story-high demon Yamantalai, whose claws dripped blood . . . a shimmering immense figure with three heads, its many metal arms writhing, its steel penises impaling three terrified, young human female sacrifices. He heard the twisted screams of the sacrifice victims as their bodies were slashed to pieces with a dozen ritual daggers.

Zompahlok handed Lasker a bowl to drink from.

105

It was blood.

"No, no, no . . ." Lasker turned his head side to side. "I don't want to be Raspahloh! Let me stay myself!"

Laughter.

And then the dreaded one, the green-robed, chief demon worshipper Zompahlok again came closer to Lasker and leaned over him. "You escaped once, but you are back with us! Well, that is good. Welcome to eternal darkness. Your body, your soul shall be reclaimed for our cause."

"No," Bart mumbled. ". . . not real . . . I . . . dream!"

"Oh yes. . . . We have found you Lasker—and forced you with our powerful magic into our dream world. You have taken our precious wish-fulfilling gems, you stole our E-Kung fighting power, but now you are ours. And you have no will, for this is a dream. Yamantalai controls your dream. See . . . see how his lips drool for your soul . . . see how he awaits your drinking of the elixir of death? Your body shall be ours, you shall be ours, Raspahloh—"

"No! Zompahlok," Bart shouted. But his voice was barely audible as if the words were being sucked away into a void. "The Shekar Dzong Temple is destroyed . . . you are dead, Zompahlok," the Mystic Rebel tried to say, but his words seemed breathless.

Mad laughter erupted as several green-robed guardian monks dragged Bart forward toward the towering statue of Yamantalai. The statue was animated, the demon of many horrors was real!

Forcibly, the Bonpo guardian monks set him on

an altar of skulls, raised their axes and poised them over him. They were ready to strike down, but then they saw the sky-object Bart wore around his neck. It glowed and sent blinding white rays into their green eyes of evil. Screaming in agony, they rushed away from Lasker, and he lifted himself off the skull altar and went spinning away into infinite space.

Where was he? In a coffin? He tried to stand and bonked his head, gasping for air in the darkness.

He remembered. He had sought refuge from the green lights in a ruin and found a crawl-space.

All right. Hold it; calm down. The voices were dreams. The events in the Bonpo temple were nothing but phantasms. Bart pushed aside the heavy slate door and shimmied himself out into the bright morning sun.

He was thirsty and took a swig from the canteen. Better. Lasker heard the pleasant sound of birds chirping. In the glaring sunlight, the snow was melting. He stood up sore and stiff, then yawned. Aches and pains everywhere. Bart looked around, squinting. There were ochre paintings on the temple stones—strange garish figures. This ruin was no benevolent, Buddhist hill retreat. The place he had stayed the night was indeed a Bonpo dream-place. These pictographs of Yamantalai devouring and crushing humans, drinking cups of blood . . . Bart had to leave!

He gathered his pack and stepped away from the evil stones, knowing that he had not just had a nightmare of unparalleled proportions, but that indeed he had been close to soul death last night. As he dog trotted away, the pictographs were still vivid. The rock inscriptions had graphically shown scenes from his dream, spoken of horror, of obedience to Yamantalai.

He then remembered the Bonpo tenzan axes that had been raised over his body to cut out his soul—and the life-saving protecting glow of his sky-object necklace.

Bart fumbled to open his sweat-stained parka and frantically felt about. He found the cold metal of the sky-object and took it out. It was no longer shiny. It was brown and pitted with rust as if its smooth substance had aged thousands of years in one single night.

He felt the burn on the skin under it. Was that burn from the white fire it had sent forth to save him? What was dream and what was real?

He had to move on out of these mountains before it was again dark. The Bonpo had power in this evil-permeated place.

Chapter 14

Six hours later, Bart climbed a rise and beheld the Tsurphu Monastery, the seat of all the sixteen incarnations of the Holy Karmapas, the leaders of the Kagyu Sect of Tibetan Buddhism. It was a series of immaculately painted, red and whitewashed structures that seemed to glow in the sun. Beyond the cluster of what were sparkling new buildings, higher on the slope was situated a tiny village. A single road led to a dozen more buildings, totally in ruins, the buildings not yet reconstructed in the twenty years since their destruction by the Red Guard fanatics.

The whole scene glowed. And, as Lasker looked at the ruins, though he had no idea of the actual extensions of the old architecture, self-forming images of what once was arose like ghost buildings. The famous illusion-structures of Tsurphu. One of the great mystic sites of Tibet!

He could hear a thousand faint horns and gongs. He rubbed his eyes and looked again. The images and sounds were gone.

The whole place was silent. No one stirred.

There was one truck—with a Chinese communist red star on its door—at the entrance arch to the main temple's courtyard. That modern intrusion was no ghost. Were the Chinese at Tsurphu looking for him? With such a grim reality in mind, he surveyed the scene for an hour.

Finally, a group of Chinese soldiers left the courtyard through the arch and climbed into that truck. They started up and left in the direction of Lhasa. He could hear them joking about good food and some Mao Tai. Bart waited a while, and then, in the gathering darkness, headed down the slope.

Though the whole area around the town was barren, this hillside, and all the other ones facing Tsurphu Monastery were alive with a hundred varities of wild flowers. There were small, dark-green bushes with berries on them, with chattering birds in them, too. Insects buzzed and chirped in the twilight.

It was as if the monastery was giving out some life-force, energizing the nearby terrain.

And there was a pleasant feeling—past life remembrance?—in his gut, as if he had been here before. A long, long time ago. Perhaps in some distant past incarnation, Bart had been a monk here. That thought pleased him. That would have been one of his more pleasant past lives. Having been the fifteenth century assassin Raspahloh in another past life was one of the more unpleasant!

He was to make contact with a lama named Narang, according to Losang's instructions, and convince him to give Bart the ancient map that showed the way to Rong-lam obelisk, the mysterious start-off point on the Tertons' map to

Padmasambhava's cave.

Lasker moved rapidly across the Chinese-built road to the new monastery's high wall. He hung around outside the wall. Now and then a few uneasy monks stared down from above. He bided his time, silently muttering *Om Mani Padme Hum,* when a slit opened in a small window high above him.

"Who stands out there? Whoever you are, go away."

"Call Narang. I've come to see him."

"No. Go away," the voice said.

He stood his ground. Eventually he heard the man's voice again.

"I am not some young Chela, I am the Abbot Kenpo Kemung. What manner of person—or demon—are you to come here and bother us? How do you know the High Lama Narang?"

Lasker could only see the shape of the abbot's round bald-shaven head above. He shouted, "I don't know Lama Narang, but he will want to see me!"

"Oh really, now! What is your name?" the abbot asked mockingly, "and who sent you?"

"I am known as Satan Rimpoche."

"Satan Rimpoche? I never heard of—"

"I was sent by Losang in India."

"Really?" There was a long pause. Finally the abbot decided, "Then you must be weary! You are welcome, great Lama Satan. Wait, I will come down and open the gate!"

When he got the huge gate open a crack, the round-headed abbot, squinting his bespectacled eyes in the dark, held a lantern toward Lasker.

"You are a Westerner! Is this a joke? Who are you?"

Lasker looked up at the old wizened eyes. "Losang in India sent me."

The gate opened a crack more. "You are crazy," the abbot said. "There are spies here—even here! Come! Come quickly to my room and tell me enough to confirm what you say! Then we will see about awakening the great lama!"

Once they crossed the sandy courtyard and went inside, they rushed down a long bare hallway with newly patched plaster walls; the abbot opened a door.

"Come—this is my room," he whispered.

There was a thin shaven-headed boy in a burgundy wool robe tending a small coal fire. The room was lit by a set of seven butter lamps set before a small golden Buddha.

"Sit down—"

Lasker sat down on a pillow.

"What is it you want?" The lantern cast orange highlights on the abbot's face: orange nose and eyebrows, the rest lost in inky black.

Lasker began an abbreviated cautious version of his tale. "Losang in Dhramsala arranged for my visit to Tibet, and for my leaving the tour bus I was traveling on . . ."

Lasker explained little more except to say Losang sent him for the map to Rong-lam.

"Say no more," said the abbot. He ordered the boy to go inform Lama Narang he had a visitor of importance!

Lasker accepted some fresh mo-mo's, and the abbot poured out some tea for him. They drank in silence a short while, then the young monk returned.

"Lama Narang will see him."

"Please," the abbot said, "finish your tea—and then follow Dewap."

Lasker put his half-empty cup down and said, "That's all right—let's go, Dewap."

Dewap led him through a maze of rooms, some on different levels connected by ladders. Lasker soon heard low sonorous chanting rising and falling and the tingle of cymbals somewhere in the butter-lamp-lit complex. Evening *puja* (rituals) were starting. Lasker recognized the beautiful Chenresig recitation.

Dewap knocked on a very elaborately carved oaken door: a motif of flowers and dharma wheels. The door opened silently.

"I am Lama Narang," a tall, gangly man in a saffron-colored robe said. He had a bit of short-cropped grey hair, black horn-rimmed glasses, and a wispy grey goatee. "Please come in."

An oil lamp revealed a room full of *thankas* and other religious relics: a huge prayer cylinder, crystal globes. . . .

Lasker sat down at Narang's bidding and told of the reason he had come to Tsurphu—in detail. Nrang listened attentively.

Then the lama frowned. "You came for the map to Rong-lam obelisk? That will not be so easy!"

"Why is that?"

"You realize that the map you speak of was here, along with many other precious relics, for centuries. But like the entire Tsurphu Monastery, the map, too, was destroyed in the years following the occupation of Tibet by the Chinese."

"Destroyed? Then I have come all this way in vain!" Lasker said sadly.

"Not necessarily." Narang grinned slyly, taking off his horn-rims and wiping the sooty lenses on the fold in his robe.

"What? Is there a copy somewhere?" Lasker brightened up.

"There is *no* copy—yet. But there *can* be! There *will* be."

"How?"

"We had no plans, no pictures even, of the Tsurphu Monastery. Even the plans were destroyed by the Chinese in the 1960s. But this sacred place was always the home of powerful Karmapas. Since the time of Kublai Khan. The buildings and their contents were destroyed, yet when we Kagyu-pa monks were allowed to return here, we could *see* the buildings! There are ghostly images where they stood. In the spiritual realm, they still exist. So we began to rebuild according to those images. Do you believe me?"

"Yes, I do. But only because I saw the ghostly images from the mountain," Lasker said.

Narang nodded. "Then that proves you once were one of us—in another life. That is the only way you could have seen them. I thought as much, friend."

"How does this get me the map I need?" Lasker continued, avoiding a desire to sidetrack with questions about reincarnation.

"We will do *puja*. If we are earnest, the map should reform."

Narang took Lasker down the hallway and into a

wide chamber of several stories in height. There stood a magnificent statue of Lord Buddha, shown quietly meditating, its bronze eyes half-closed. The floor was covered with thick rugs with elaborate snow lion and dragon depictions. There were hundreds of statues of lesser gods and Kagyu-pa Sect holy men on a series of descending shelves around the giant image, all lit by a thousand flickering butter lamps. The smell of sandlewood incense was strong.

No one else was in the chamber. "I was," Narang admitted, "feeling quite ill—my arthritis—and I called off the customary calling-the-dead service here. Now, I understand that this was not misfortune, but good fortune. You and I will have this holy place to work in, uninterrupted."

"But—what can I do?"

"Chant with me, Lasker-la. You *will* remember the words. The map will appear."

"How can you be so sure?"

"In the none-thing is the seed of all things."

Lasker chewed on that awhile as he sat down before the great statue in lotus position. The lama took a large silver bowl from a drawer in one of the shelves beneath the statue and placed it before Lasker. "Now," he said softly, "chant with me. The map could appear in the bowl."

"Could?"

"Potentiality always exists where there is nothing. Or else nothing would ever be." The high lama sat down on a round pillow next to Lasker, adjusted his robe, took off and folded his glasses, put them down beside the pillow, and began chanting. He went on

115

and on, and after a few minutes Lasker felt himself relaxing for the first time since he left India. Then an odd thing happened. Lasker, his eyes half-closed, joined in with the lama. He was reciting the long ancient mantra even though he had never heard it! The mantra of potentiality.

His tongue rolled with the thousands of words, his mind filled with images of a life long ago—his life—spent here at Tsurphu in the time of Marco Polo: a life of devotion and meditation; decades of placing fresh sacrifices before this same quiescent Buddha image; sacrifices of flower blossoms and sculpted butter cakes, not the sacrifices of flesh the Bonpo used—not torn human body parts!

After a long while, as they chanted on and on, there was a hissing sound. The silver bowl before Lasker was filling with a faint milky cloudiness. Then, in that gathering white mist, a parchment ever-so-slowly appeared.

The map to Rong-lam.

Lasker stayed the night, sleeping on the mat in Narang's room, snug in the thick yak-hide covers provided him.

In the faint light of dawn, he was shaken awake. "We have saddled a good horse for you, friend," Narang whispered. "Take the map and go quickly before the Chinese patrols return. Go next to the hermit, your master, and seek his advice."

Lasker did as he was asked. With the miraculous apparently *new* map to Rong-lam in his saddlebag, he rode into a sky brilliant with the multicolored rays of a Tibetan dawn.

Chapter 15

The horse Narang had provided was sturdy and sure footed. Bart made good progress, putting distance quickly between himself and Tsurphu. He was almost dizzy with an exhilaration, a triumphant feeling caused by his map, proof that matter, earthly substance, was not all there was to the universe. There was a realm beyond, which was an integral part of everyday life.

He was halfway to Gayarong Mountain, home of his hermit master, when he heard a shot. He reined up the black stallion and got off, tethering its reins on a scrub bush. Bart scrambled over a tumulus of fallen rock toward the place the shot had come from.

Now he heard what sounded like a woman whimpering. Bart crawled up to peer between two upright rocks. One hundred yards down on a narrow cliff road were several Chinese vehicles: two trucks and a covered jeep. He counted an officer and seven soldiers with SMGs slung over their shoulders. Except for the officer with the banana-clipped weapon—he had his weapon out. One look convinced Bart that they were hard-bitten Chinese mountain troops—the kind that summarily shot any would-be escapees from the wonderful People's Province of Xishang.

He observed them for a while, and overheard their conversation. The soldiers, he saw, had caught three ragged monks and an old woman. The monks were admitting that they were trying to get to the border. They offered what they had in their small carpetbags to the officer if they and the woman would be let go. The Chinese officer had them empty their few small bags and took what they had—a few amber prayer beads and some renminbao—and laughed. "Not enough!"

The utter gloom of the Tibetan victims was as palpable as the happiness of the Chinese officer. He said to the monks and the old woman, "Say your prayers to your non-existent gods—for you are about to die! One minute!"

Bart smiled. The officer was counting his chickens before they'd hatched, if the Mystic Rebel had anything to say about this!

The monks began chanting mantras, the woman whimpered again and the Chinese soldiers pushed them all against a cliff. They were getting lined up, facing the victims—a firing squad. One monk got on his knees to beg. Not for himself, but with his hands in chenbu gesture he pleaded, "Please do not stain your karma by cruelty to us. Your acts will in future lives and this one bring destruction upon yourselves!"

"Shut up," the officer snapped. He stepped back, and the soldiers raised their weapons. The officer said, "Ready . . ."

The Chinese were about to shoot. Bart would have to act fast, but to have a chance without a gun against eight armed men, he'd have to get much closer.

As quietly as possible, Bart rapidly disassembled the backpack's metal frame and snapped together the blade and handle, hiding them in his parka. Then Lasker bounded down the mountain, loosening much gravel in the process. The soldiers' SMGs turned toward him, but Bart deliberately slipping and sliding awkwardly down appeared to be such a clumsy intruder that they held their fire.

Bart shouted, *"Nihoma!"* ("hello" in Chinese) and "I'm a lost tourist," in English.

He sensed by their half-amused smirks and wry comments that they saw him as no threat. Right enough, the scar-cheeked officer told the soldiers to lower their rifles. They did so and waited for Bart's ungainly arrival. He virtually fell at the officer's feet, his tumble presenting his protruding backside close to the man. The officer poked him away with his SMG's barrel.

Lasker squawked, "You needn't be so brutish," jerking up to his feet.

The officer laughed and commented to the soldiers in Chinese, "This foreigner is no threat. Point your weapons back at the escapees!" He scowled, then shook his finger at Lasker. "And you, shut up, foreign dog!" he spoke in English. "What are you doing here? Are you English?"

Bart kept playing a hysterical Britisher.

"Well, I wouldn't be speaking bloody English if I weren't English, would I?" Bart snapped in return.

119

The officer appeared angered by Bart's evasion. "I said, what are you doing here? Are you alone?" scarface snapped.

"No! I'm not bloody alone," Bart shouted, picking himself up. "I was on a bloody fucking Chinese bus, you rotter! The damned thing went over a cliff. I'm the only one that can bloody walk! There are many injured and some dead—we need help. I've been scrambling over these god-forsaken mountains for a whole day, bloody freezing my balls off and—"

"Papers please!"

He fumbled in his pockets. "Papers? At a time like this? You're bloody lucky that I have them on me. I insist you send for help. You must have a radio!"

The suddenly sullen officer took Bart's Charles Grant I.D.s and carefully looked over them. He even held them to the sun to see if there were any water marks or erasures.

Lasker continued to grumble and talk rapidly. "I absolutely insist you help me. There is a woman pinned; several children with broken limbs. If you cannot understand me, then radio your base. You have a radio? Radio? Yes? Talkee-talkee on radio?"

"No radio," the Chinese snapped in good English. "Just keep quiet!"

Bart continued, flush-faced, to rant on. As long as he talked, the Chinese soldiers were distracted from their victims.

"I shall report you if you do not help. There are, you know," Bart whined on, "also Chinese on that bus! If you bloody won't help foreigners, think of your own people."

The Chinese officer was befuddled. He evidently

didn't know how to handle it, though by now he had a distinct preference! He looked quickly over at the detainees and his men. He muttered in Chinese: "Maybe no one will care if we kill this stupid Englishman, too!"

The soldiers chuckled and laughed. Some joke!

Lasker had heard what he needed to know. No radio. He had noted the lack of any whip antenna on the vehicles. But to have the fact of no radio verified was reassuring. It was just him against the eight of them. Getting to the vehicles first to disable any radio wasn't necessary, and that made it easier.

As the Chinese officer stood there deciding whether to kill him, too, Lasker's E-Kung steeled his well-muscled legs, preparing for a leap. His face transformed from a mask of confusion and desperate ineffectiveness into a cunning grimace.

But suddenly something other than preparation for combat was happening to Lasker. His heart was pounding wildly; the whole scene became as if bathed in a red color. It was an anti-Chinese anger pouring out of his hidden Raspahloh soul. This danger, this moment of intense necessity to fight like a demon, like a warrior of old, in order to survive, was bringing forth Raspahloh, his alter-ego.

As Bart half-crouched, his lips curled into a cruel sneer. The fingers of his hands trembled and bent into the snow lion claw attack angle. It wasn't Lasker doing all of this. The imminence of mortal combat had powerfully aroused the sleeping giant within him. Raspahloh was awakened. All of this seemed to happen in extreme slow motion, but in actuality it was in the blink of an eye.

121

Perhaps the Chinese officer, when his and Lasker's eyes met again, was surprised at the immense change. Lasker had transformed from the bumbling British tourist into something evil and deadly. Perhaps the officer had a fraction of an instant to realize he was staring at a supernatural horror. Perhaps he recognized that his own death was coming, signalled by the cruel grimace and the strange red glow that the "Englishman" had now in his narrowing eyes.

He gasped and instinctively started to back off, lifting his machine pistol.

Chapter 16

A sense of death, a sadness. Bart Lasker struggled to keep his own body but to no avail. Without control, without an iota of power, Lasker was in agony. He watched his opponent raise the weapon, unable to move his own hands, unable to bring his martial arts skills to bear. But replacing that human skill was something more powerful. Lasker, as he diminished, felt the rising strength and ancient, murderous skill. The power of Raspahloh.

Raspahloh's blood-lust knew no bounds. He didn't want to just kill these Chinese, he wanted to annihilate, to disassemble them. Bart felt the body he no longer controlled tense and shift to meet the challenge, in a way that only a mountain snow lion could possibly move.

Then Lasker-Raspahloh, screaming out a blood curdling challenge, lept high, slamming a devastating drop-kick into the chin of the Chinese officer.

The scar-faced officer's head snapped back, and he was thrown twenty feet. He was dead before he hit the dirt, his upper spine snapped.

Lasker felt himself tumble, and then Raspahloh

jerked his body up to his feet again. Dripping saliva from his lips, hunched over, he faced the seven remaining soldiers. He was Raspahloh, assassin, killer. Evil energy coursed through his muscles; his sinews rippled with cruel power. As the soldiers split up—two raising their SMGs, the others turning to run—Raspahloh screamed a banshee cry that made the two soldiers fumble as they pointed their guns.

Even the Tibetan detainees, who moments before faced the hostile Chinese guns, trembled and whitened with fear at the transformation they had observed. Lasker had assumed the countenance of a rock ogre, an immensely violent ancient menace.

"Bonpo!" one of the monks cried, diving over the edge of the trail and rolling a dozen feet down the mountainside. The others made tracks, too, scattering in all directions.

The Chinese soldiers, now that their bully leader had been so handily erased, were at a complete loss. The frighteningly changed Englisher advanced so boldly into the teeth of their fire, that these tough thugs couldn't hold their weapons on line. As their bullets fell on fallow ground and the strange opponent closed, he seemed invincible . . . impervious to death.

That awesome pair of hate-filled eyes bore into the shooters, thoroughly throwing off their aim!

Their weapons emptied, the Chinese soldiers turned and made tracks for the truck which stood idling nearby. They jerked and clutched the thing into gear, did a quick three-point turn on the narrow mountain roadway, and accelerated, hell-bent, directly at the transformed devil in their wake.

"Run him down!" screamed the man riding shotgun, holding onto his hat as the truck bounced and bounded down the rutted road toward Lasker-Raspahloh. "Splatter the running dog's guts."

"Don't worry," seethed the spooked driver, bearing down on the wheel like a demon himself, shifting to a higher gear as the truck's wheels bit deeper into the gravel. Huge pearls of sweat beaded on the men's brows as they approached their target. Closing, they winced at the point of impact, and missed seeing Raspahloh's sudden sidestep-skip, which brought him up comfortably onto the running board along the driver's side.

He reached his iron grip through the window, grasped the driver's face, and began pounding the man's skull against the back wall of the cab. The passenger dove from the racing truck in a panic as Raspahloh made a bloody mush out of the man's head, then swung the door open and let the battered corpse tumble to the ground.

Raspahloh situated himself behind the wheel and slammed the door shut. He stared at the wheel, then the controls. He *knew* this, because Lasker knew! Raspahloh braked the truck to a stop, reversed direction, and with a sinister laugh, began his own attack, twentieth century style!

In a moment he had the former passenger in his sights. The soldier, just barely recovering from his fall from the truck, lay prone in the road as the roar of the truck closed on him, enveloped in a cloud of dust.

"No . . . no . . . NAIEEEEE!" he screamed when he realized that now *he* was the prey. He stumbled to

125

his feet and began loping up the road, but there was no escape except over the edge—certain death. Even that would have been preferable to the fate that overtook him. The truck ran up his heels and swallowed him, gnarling and gnashing his body into a code-ten nightmare. Raspahloh felt the impact with glee, the sullen "chunk" of the body as it was hit by the machine, the flesh and bone ground into carrion by the wheels. Better than his ways! He liked the modern madness!

As he sped back up the hill, Raspahloh saw that the squad of Chinese soldiers had been reinforced. Another ten men must have been on patrol nearby and heard the gunfire. They had taken up a good position behind a collection of boulders at a place where the roadway widened briefly into two lanes. They poured SMG fire into the advancing vehicle.

Raspahloh ducked as the windshield shattered and shells ricocheted off the hood and around the cab. Still he poured forward, hard heel hitting the floor with the accelerator.

As the truck approached the redoubt, Raspahloh bailed out and let it rush violently into the rocks where it exploded in a fireball, consuming three of the enemy in flames. Good! Good screams! He was proud.

Raspahloh, energized by the thrill of combat, found his backpack hakama and plunged into the fray amid the confusion and tumult swinging the blade at any flesh that moved.

The Chinese had scattered and taken up separate positions among the nearby rocks, making perfect picking for the killing skills of the reincarnated assassin, and for one another's bullets! Misaimed shots rang out at shadows as Raspahloh crept stealthily on his hunt, hidden by the black smoke. He came upon the first of his prey as the man peered away in the opposite direction, calling to his friends.

"Have you seen him?" he cried out. "What is he?"

"Quiet!" came the reply. "Stay covered. He's not armed. We'll get him, whoever or whatever he is!"

"Just let the bastard show his face," the man replied. "Show your face, you coward!"

Just then, Raspahloh's chilling grip fell on the man's shoulder from nowhere, sending a charge of pain through his body. The Chinese soldier dropped his gun and crumbled to his knees as the clawed fingers dug into his flesh, bursting vessels. When he felt the man had suffered sufficiently, Raspahloh raised his hakama sword and sliced it neatly into the man's neck with a delicate twisting motion, releasing the soldier's Adam's apple in a bloody geyser. His death squeal was drowned in fresh blood.

Raspahloh stared at the man's strange stick-weapon. AK-47? "Yes!" He picked it up and checked the clip. Full!

As the killing spree continued, Raspahloh gained strength from each ghastly encounter. One by one the soldiers could hear the death screams of their comrades. One by one, each man met his own particular death: sword slice or burst of bullets. All in all, a fine feast of death for the ancient killer.

Not being able to stand the screams any longer, the last Chinese alive put his own rifle barrel in his mouth and pulled the trigger.

Wiping the bloody sword on the last head-shattered soldier's uniform, Raspahloh returned it to his scabbard. He looked around. The refugees were nowhere to be found, but he scented their fear. Raspahloh hated Buddhists nearly as much as he hated Chinese. And with Lasker somewhere deep inside him, still protesting ineffectively, Raspahloh went after the scent of fear, intending to continue his bloody rampage.

He rushed between the two remaining vehicles and saw the four Tibetans cringing in fear. "Now you die, too," Raspahloh intoned, "but slowly. I will wrap your intestines around one another's throats! Bonpo rule! No Buddhists!"

But Lasker suddenly felt himself returning to power in his own body. The danger was over, and with it left the adrenaline that had tipped the transformation! He felt his heart rate slow and his red-eyed view of the world return to normal color.

Lasker softly asked the refugees to come out. Slowly they obeyed him. There was, after all, no place to run, anyway.

"Please, mountain demon," the older of the three monks pleaded. "Return to your lair and leave us poor refugees!" He repeated an elaborate protective mantra against rock devils.

"Don't worry," Lasker said gently. "It is over."

The monks and the *anni-la*—Tibetan for "mother"—had evidently seen only the beginning of the fight. So when they came out from behind the truck they were aghast and petrified with fright. They beheld a bloodstained two acres strewn with body parts.

The monks found their stolen prayer beads in the

charnel ground, then started chanting out pleas for their attackers' souls. They were feeling guilty for having brought out such carnage. Even these sixteen Chinese killers' lives were sacred to the compassionate Buddhists! They fell to the ground, fingering their amber mala beads, reciting mantra to Tara, begging for forgiveness for causing these deaths.

"Not your stain," said Lasker in perfect Tibetan. "Pray for these evil men's souls instead, and for mine!"

In wonder they stared at him. He told the woman and the monks to pick up their things and move onward to the south. Still terrified out of their wits, they did as the mountain demon commanded, thanking him for sparing them.

Once he gathered the bodies into a pile, Lasker rolled rocks on top of them. The blood would be covered over by the next snowfall.

The soldiers would of course be missed. He had to make distance quickly.

His senses reeled. The essence of Tibetan Buddhism was nonviolence. Yet he had killed in cold blood. That contradiction—not wanting to kill and yet being forced to kill again haunted him. This episode had proven one thing: Violence, the threat, weakened Lasker and gave power to his kill-crazed alter ego, Raspahloh.

He hadn't realized how close to the surface, how close to permanent control of his body, that evil alter ego was.

If this kept up, it would be Raspahloh, not Lasker, who reached the cave of the Dancing Dead!

Chapter 17

In Hong Kong, Tse Ling was sitting on the terrace of her luxurious apartment high above the electric-lit city. She sighed, adjusted her black satin gown strewn with real diamond dust, and stuck out her bare right foot, the first foot having been completed.

Ming Star, her Burmese servant girl, began applying pink sparkle nail polish to Tse Ling's toes. The sparkle there, too, was from real powdered diamonds. The nail polish cost a king's ransom, but such luxury, such trivial ostentation, was the world of Tse Ling now. The Jade Octagon had taken care of her; she was snug in its black velvet womb. There was nothing she couldn't have—or do, except leave.

The phone rang. A gentle "ting-ting."

"Shall I—" the servant girl asked softly.

"Of course!" Tse Ling said and pushed Ming Star's nose with her drying toenails. The girl exclaimed and then shut up. She got up quickly and ran to pick up the receiver. Only then, when she entered the suite's well-lit interior, was it obvious that the patterned multicolored dragons on the servant girl's body were not smooth tight clothing, but an elaborate, total tattoo reading from toes to neck.

She was naked, and yet clothed—forever. That had been Tse Ling's whim: make her look like an object, for Tse Ling treated her as such.

Frantically the tattooed girl picked up the phone. She listened and then turned to the terrace. "Mistress, it—it is Wang Dzo."

"My agent in Tibet? Very well, I will talk to him." Tse Ling, remaining barefoot, walked across the black carpet and took the receiver.

"What is it Wang? Where are you?"

Heavy static. "Lhasa—I have news about the rare flower we spoke about."

"Where are you calling from? Is it secure?" Tse Ling shouted.

"As you suggested, I am calling from the office of Lieutenant Tang—"

"So speak normally, you fool. Dispense with the allegory. Lieutenant Tang's phone is equipped with a scrambler. No one can tap into us. If they do, they hear but a garble."

"Yes madam! Forgive my ignorance of such things. I am happy to report a lead on finding Bart Lasker."

"Where is he?"

"I do not know, but my agent Namghee north of here has tracked down his lover. He sent the message only yesterday by pigeon. It arrived just now. She is named Dorjee and is the very same Dorjee who is sole survivor of er—the sanitizing operation in the village of Tsok—"

"Where is she? Quickly, Wang, there must be action; plans have to be made!"

"She is at the Mahaka Monastery, a remote place above a valley called the Red Mud Valley." He gave the location in latitude and longitude. "It is just thirty li north of the great steaming lake of Tonkam Sath."

"Good work. I know the place! You will receive the envelope at the usual drop—with a bonus. Go there Wang—watch to see that this Dorjee doesn't leave the Mahaka Monastery until my forces arrive! Is Tang there?"

"No, he is on patrol. I believe he is expected back soon."

"Make sure he calls me the minute he returns!"

She put down the jade-handled phone receiver.

Tang called back twenty minutes later. By then Tse Ling had formulated a devious plan.

"Lieutenant Tang," she ordered, "you are to inform your superiors in Beijing that you have uncovered a nest of traitorous monks who are about to receive a visit by a high-level C.I.A. agent at the Mahaka Monastery—Wang Dzo will give you its location.

"You will not wait for any reply, but say you are proceeding directly there with sufficient manpower to secure the monastery and wait to trap the agent— Bart Lasker. You must emphasize to Beijing that your informants revealed that the monastery in question is part of a planned insurrection soon to come."

"But—"

"You have your orders. Do not defy the Octagon! When Lasker arrives, seize him, torture him to find out, record what he knows of us, then kill him! Send the tape to me!"

132

She hung up with a wry smile. Tse Ling was considered an enemy of Beijing, yet she still controlled many military men in Tibet! Such was the power of the Jade Octagon!

She returned to her terrace for a manicure, sipped a daiquiri—so much better than Mou Tai—as the tattooed servant girl worked. It was good all this luxury, but Tse Ling had had a strange floating ennui these past weeks. She thought of this Mystic Rebel, of the time Lasker took her carnally, and her loins burned at the thought; burned with desire. She swallowed down her eighth drink. Perhaps she had to indulge, to satisfy a woman's needs. There were ways to satisfy that need without a man!

She reached over and pulled the nail polish jar from the servant girl. Ming Star, trembling, let herself be pulled up to face the woman she served and feared. Tse Ling squeezed the servant's ripe left nipple. Men were not necessary; she had her servant to deliver service of any sort. Tse Ling moaned softly and widened her legs. The servant girl understood and leaned forward, touched lips to cool skin and slowly slid her lips down Tse Ling's thigh toward her hot desire!

Later Tse Ling rode the elevator to her private, heated, kidney-shaped pool on the roof of her luxury high rise. She felt better, satisfied. Yet . . . the servant's ministrations had not been enough. It did not bring the exhaustion of sexual release.

Tse Ling's figure was partly the result of her strenuous exercises as a young athlete in Beijing's central school. She had been the southern division's district swimming champ, and her body was taut and hard. Yet even the gift of beauty given by nature to her was enhanced by rigorous exercise.

She dove gracefully in, hit the pool's blue water and swam to touch the bottom.

When she gasped air at the surface twenty-five seconds later, she had shaken her unease. Tse Ling did a fast breast stroke to the edge and pulled herself up.

"Ming Star! Come, before I shiver!"

Tse Ling took the wide, soft towel from her girl and wrapped it around herself. Lasker would come to his lover, this crude peasant girl Dorjee, and then Tse Ling would have him tortured slowly, have his skin torn from his body.

But there was yet one thing to arrange. Lasker must know that Dorjee was in danger. Tse Ling had to get word to Lasker of Dorjee's plight. But how could she do that if she didn't even know where Lasker was? All the information the Octagon had indicated Lasker was in southern Tibet.

The Snow Lions. Tse Ling had learned that Lasker had run with that band of Tibetan nomad rebels. If he got in touch with them—sooner or later he would—she could plant with them a tale of Dorjee in danger.

She would arrange it. Soon she would hear Lasker's recorded screams.

Tse Ling looked at the lithe tattooed Burmese girl who had given her the towel. "I need you again."

The girl's lips quivered; her eyes were downcast. She said, "As you wish. . . ."

Chapter 18

For two days after the bloody encounter with the Chinese patrol, Lasker rode onward toward Gayarong Pass. The midnight-black stallion was energetic and surefooted enough to manage the difficult high altitude trails that Lasker had to take.

There were no overflights by Chinese spotter planes, no swarming troops in the valley below. Evidently the Chinese had thought their patrol was wiped out by an avalanche—a frequent occurrence in these shifting escarpments; especially in the fall, when plummeting temperatures froze the water in cracks and could send whole monasterys tumbling!

Lasker was crossing the highest point between Tsurphu and Gayarong Pass at five in the afternoon —Tibet time—by the watch he faithfully wound. It was 19,500 feet up, and he breathed heavily and had a splitting headache. Lasker chewed on the sweet candies from his pack. Sugar consumption was a simple cure for the thin air's effect on the brain. Gradually, as the sugar hit his bloodstream, and as he slowly descended the slope toward the green valley below Gayarong's twin peaks, the headache diminished.

There was a layer of mist floating above the valley on the far side, hiding his immediate destination—the rock crevice entrance to the hermit's cave.

Bart decided to avoid the small trading village of Yarang and to approach the cave of the hermit from the other side of the mountain, via a slaggy but negotiable spur.

Bart soon arrived in the valley and began his ascent. His heart raced at the prospect of seeing his master—emotions surprisingly strong. He loved the strange old hermit and was proud to call him his spiritual master. His throat felt tight, and Bart realized he was all choked up. Why not? The hermit had saved his life; he taught Bart almost all he knew of the deeper reality beyond the everyday world's screen of illusion. And he had, above all, been a friend and counselor.

Bart was weary of the trail and felt sorry for the horse. "Poor fellow, we'll soon be there." He petted its sweaty neck. The horse seemed to understand and poured on a last bit of energy to come up to the dark cave entrance in the granite face of the mountain.

Lasker got off and unsaddled the horse, then fed him the last Tsurphu garden's carrot. He loosely tethered the horse at a clump of green grass and went unhesitatingly into the darkness of the crevice. He found the rock that he had to roll aside to enter and, using all his strength, edged it over enough to effect passage into the cool chamber of the cave.

There was light—a single flickering butter lamp on the cavern floor, dully illuminating the chair-height, glistening, blue quartz crystal in the center of the rock-hewn room.

He carefully examined the rather plain chamber. There was a layer of dust on the floor, no footprints in it. But that didn't mean the hermit wasn't there. Lasker was fully aware that the mystic hermit might be able to walk and yet leave no prints!

What should he do now? The usual thing, summon the hermit! Lasker found a dusty meditation pillow in a corner, drew it over to the crystal and sat down. He started to meditate as medical Lama Cheojey once had taught him. Breathe out, breathe in . . . let go of all thought. When a thought arises, let it slip from your mind. Be clear . . . clear.

For hours he sat there, spine erect, eyes half-closed, thinking no thought, dropping any connection to the harsh, beautiful and brutal world outside. Eventually, the crystal seemed to start to glow. He opened his eyes more fully and saw on the crystals multifaceted faces. There appeared twisting, swirling patterns of light. A rainbow of incandescent colors. In the space between the entrance rock and the mountain's granite, the moon slid up into the black velvet sky like a huge magnet pulling at his body. The world was so different when one was calm. . . . Time moves . . . it was night already.

The light of the full moon shone through the crack upon the crystal and seemed to be activating it. From behind the crystal stepped a white-bearded scrawny old man with a broom, in a ragged turquoise robe. He started sweeping up the dust.

Lasker jumped to his feet and exclaimed, "It's you!"

"Of course it's me!" the hermit snapped. "I live here!" The hermit lifted his broom over his head, ready to bring it down hard on the intruder. "Who may I ask are you, and what are you doing here?" He squinted at Lasker in the semi-darkness. "Lasker? Is that you?"

"Yes master," Bart said, all choked up.

"Goodness!" the hermit exclaimed, dropping his broom. "You scared me out of my wits, Lasker—"

"*I* scared *you,* master of many worlds?"

"Yes! Don't ever do that to an old man again! But—I am glad to see you. I thought you were dead."

After Lasker explained about coming back to Tibet to find Padmasambhava's prophesy text in a remote cave, the hermit nodded. "I see. A very important and dangerous task you have gotten yourself into. And I assume you didn't come back here to me for just a visit?"

Lasker looked sheepish. "Well—"

"No, I thought not! You want something from me! You want help, teachings—and I suppose that again you didn't bring me anything as a present!"

Lasker smiled. "Oh, but I did remember!" Bart opened his pack and took out the two boxes of chocolate chip cookies.

"Cookies! Thank heaven for little things! I haven't had a cookie in years!" His sunken round eyes rolled in ecstasy.

As the hermit munched on the cookies, he asked Lasker, "Now tell me Lasker-la, what is it? What immense metaphysical act must I perform for you in exchange for these few crumbs of processed wheat and sugar? Here—sit down, and I will sit down facing you; and we can eat the cookies together."

Lasker took a pillow and sat down. "I need advice and your help," Lasker said, "in general."

"You need more than general help," the hermit said. "You need miracles!"

Chapter 19

Lasker felt the hermit's bony, dirt-encrusted hand placed on his knee. The hermit's dark unfathomable eyes bore into his. "Lasker . . . I missed you. Why didn't you let me know where you were? Why all these months without even a single word? I didn't even know if you were alive or dead! Do you think I didn't care?"

"Sorry—I—Say! How could I have sent word? You were here in a cave. You always stay here, or in the other cave. I was in India—"

"You could have sent a psychic postcard!" The hermit explained: "One can send a symbol psychically. It is easy. First, generate a clearness in the mind by meditation, then form a sharp image. Perhaps an image of a dawn of say—red streaks; or better yet, something I would associate with you— perhaps a bird! Yes that is good. You could have sent a bird image just to let me know you were alive. A bird is a good symbol because I trained you last time you were here to project your consciousness into a bird. You could have formed that image in your mind in far off India and then thought of me—

and I would have received. You know how a mother hen worries about her chicks. So I worry about you, my son. But karma brings us together again."

"Karma? No—I came here—"

"It is mere chance that I came here tonight. You could have sat before the blue crystal on other nights, Lasker-la, and it would not have glowed. The astral passage through the crystal between this cave and the Cultivators' cave would not have opened. Tell me: Why didn't you come to see me at the Peaceful Deity's cave? That is where I usually stay."

"I doubt I could find it, really. I hoped if I came here, and sat—you would appear. You have been doing that for years, coming here every full moon."

"Everything changes, Lasker-la. I gave up all that advice-giving business. Even the Rimpoches don't come here anymore to see me. Only people seeking predictions on when they should marry and such nonsense. So, I spend my time in the Cultivators' cave, at my studies. I am here merely by whim. I just decided to put down my book and do a little cleaning, and I knew this place would need it. Or perhaps I was picking up your telepathic summons."

"I'm not telepathic. I can't send thought."

"Don't you remember what I told you? *Everyone* is telepathic—a bit. In any case, let's get out of here," the hermit insisted. "This cave is quite cold and dusty; let us go to my home and have tea!"

Lasker's heart pounded. "You mean through the crystal?"

"Got any other idea how to get five hundred miles without a jet? Now come, time to get out of this draft! Just hold on to my robe. It's a new one you

141

notice! It should not tear so easily. Now that I don't have to play the holy hermit to visitors, I've decided to spruce myself up a bit."

Lasker got hold of the hermit's robe and they started walking in circles about the cave. They went round and round the central blue crystal, faster and faster, until Lasker felt his feet leave the floor. Then they went straight toward the glowing blue crystal. Lasker had a momentary feeling of discorporeality. He experienced, as if from someplace else, his own body and the hermit's body fading. There was a wrenching nauseous feeling, then a milky wholeness surrounded them. They were moving at a great velocity without moving.

He closed his eyes, just hung on to the robe, trying not to get sick. It seemed mere minutes, but who knew, before his feet plopped against stone.

"You can open your eyes now. We've arrived at the Cultivators' cave."

Lasker was surprised that the place looked different. Instead of a natural cave illuminated by flaming torches, there were smooth metallic grey walls, and everywhere a diffuse light; white, but with a hint of red softness in it. The glow was coming from all the walls, and yet he couldn't see any bulbs or source. And there was a new floor covering of cut tiles.

"Is this the same place?"

"Yes, Lasker-la. I just found out how to turn the Cultivators' lights on, after twenty years of studying the space peoples' manuals. The floor covering I put in myself. I'm quite handy, and I'm getting into comfort in my old age. Sit down on the floor, and you will find another improvement."

Lasker sat.

"You don't feel a difference?"

"No. I don't . . . it's hard. But—wait a second—it's becoming warm."

"Yes, the floor is heated. That's better for the old man's bones. The Cultivators have a heating system for this place; it was inactive till I found the switch."

"And how about the lighting? I can't make out where the lights are coming from."

The hermit laughed. "There are a million dot-sized lights—all recessed in the apparently not solid as it looked rock. What do you think of the cave's new look?"

"It's beautiful."

"Now come to the statue of the Peaceful Deity. We will put some incense before him in honor of our meeting again. Then I'm sure you will want to ply me with questions. Did I say questions? *Demands* for powerful magic more likely."

They went down a long, snaking rock corridor from the newly improved reception cave to the holy-of-holies of the hermit's solitary world, and Lasker beheld the tall, elongated green-granite statue of the Peaceful Deity. The fist-sized diamond between its eyes, half-closed in contemplation, glinted in the light of the hundred candles set before it. All around the circular chamber were smaller statues of like beings. Lasker had learned on his last visit to Tibet that these caverns had been occupied hundreds of centuries ago by a race from outer space: a race of humanlike six-fingered beings known as the Cultivators. Bart's spiritual master, the hermit, had lived in these environs for decades, studying their strange translucent books. The hermit had learned of the Cultivators' civil war on earth, and also of their religion of peace, taught to them by the being whose statue reigned over this cave. He had learned of the Cultivators' power to create—and destroy—at will. The hermit was heir to that power, or that part of it he could comprehend.

Lasker lit some incense and stuck it in the sand bowl before the diamond-foreheaded figure. The hermit reverently placed one of the cookies before the statue. Then the hermit picked up his amber mala beads from the cupped hands of the stone-hewn deity and limped over to the cushion. He said, "I will insist now that we meditate for a while. You are still shaken by our little trip through the blue crystal, son. I will let you know when it is time to talk."

The hermit started reciting an elaborate unintelligible mantra. It soon lulled Lasker, and it sent him quickly into a calm state of soft oblivion. In what seemed to be just moments, a little ping rang out. The hermit's meditation-ending bell. "Time to have tea."

Lasker opened his eyes and stood up. His knees were stiff. He was very thirsty. Timeless meditation. Hours were seconds.

The old man went behind the statue to heat tea on the stove there. "Come, Lasker-la, help strain the tea."

As usual, every cooking utensil and the stove were burnt black and dirty.

"It's a wonder you don't have roaches," Lasker complained.

"Hmmmph" was the only reply.

The tea was readied and poured into cracked cups. They went back to the cave and sat down on cushions at the small, red lacquer table.

Lasker sipped slowly. "Jasmine tea?"

"Yes, I ran out of Tibetan black tea. You know, it's terrible what's happening to Tibet. The few offerings to me—the holiest of hermits—are always Chinese products. Here, look at this, a plastic container of rock candy made in China. I got this for advice on the best auspicious day for a wedding!"

Lasker took the object. It was a plastic candy dish. He put it down. "I am sorry things are so hard for you."

"Bah—I manage." The hermit grinned. "And now, tell me, where have you been since I last saw you, and what's happening?"

Lasker unfolded the story of his arduous trip out of Tibet last year. He told of his giving the wish-fulfilling gems that he had stolen from the Bonpo to the Dalai Lama. Then he related how he stayed on at the Tibetan exile Capitol at Dhramsala and pursued the study of traditional Tibetan medicine.

"Have you made friends with your other self, Lasker-la?"

"Well," Lasker admitted, "not exactly. But Raspahloh has been—useful."

"You really should, Lasker-la. Raspahloh was not such a bad fellow. Full of rage, and thirsty for revenge, but not such a bad fellow. Remember, he *was* you, long ago. Be generous. Make friends."

"He wants my body."

"Really?" The hermit smirked.

Lasker smiled. "Aw, you know what I mean!"

145

The hermit tsk-tsked. "You nevertheless must make friends with your previous incarnation, or there will be trouble. Now, what is it you want from me? I assume you came here before heading to the cave of the Dancing Dead for advice?"

"Welllll . . . more than advice."

"Oh, I see. You want predictions? No, let me guess—you want me to give you more power."

"Yes. Help me if you can. In your mystic way."

"First, I tell you again, Lasker. Be the Mystic Rebel. You must follow your inner light—follow your instincts—and if you do so you will have power. You should have Raspahloh as an ally, not an adversary."

"I will try to do this—but—"

"Ah, you want material help? Well then, we will use Cultivator technology to help you."

"Cultivator technology?"

"Yes!" The hermit got up. "Come! We will use the highest of all technology. Science that dwarfs your feeble western machines—you will see, *hee hee*. Come."

Chapter 20

The hermit led Lasker halfway back along the snaking corridor and then pressed against the rock wall at waist level.

"Let me show you something. I found a hidden door and—ah, here it is." There was a humming noise. "Follow me," the hermit said. "Now, I push this wall just right . . ."

A panel slid open in the rock, and they stepped through the portal into a smooth blue-illuminated, spherical cave. The hermit said, "Lasker-la, see the walls? They are all covered with picture writing. Do you recognize the style?"

"Looks like Inca."

"Inca? Yes—I see what you mean. But more like Dakini writing to me."

"What's it say?"

"I translated it as 'This room is the transviewer.'"

"What?"

"It is a transceiver. Oh, you have something similar— What do they call it in the West? Oh, yes, television. Only the Cultivators' television is total. Come, I will give you a demonstration Lasker-la.

Just sit down here on this viewers' platform and think of something pleasant."

Lasker looked around and didn't see anything like a video screen in the bare room. Then he went with anticipation to the raised square platform. It was made of a translucent substance and was a solid block about a foot high. He sat cross-legged. The hermit placed what looked like a Walkman headset on Lasker's temples. It tingled a bit. "What do I look at?"

"There isn't any screen; just stare ahead of you, and *think.*"

Lasker sat and said, "What do I think about?"

"Might as well be something you wish to see, something pleasant for this first try."

Lasker started to daydream about his childhood. He thought of the cold winters when he sat in the window seat of his mother's Ohio farmhouse and watched the patterns of ice crystals forming on the window panes: Jack Frost's winter paint brush strokes. And he envisioned his mother bringing him hot biscuits.

She was suddenly there, right before his eyes. As real as the hermit. "Snacktime." She smiled. "Go get Gerard."

She never called his brother Jerry, but Gerard. It was her. Lasker reached out to touch the biscuits on the tray, but his hand went through them.

The hermit laughed. "No, Lasker-la, it is an illusion; that is all. You can't eat it!"

"It's so overwhelmingly real!"

"Try moving."

Lasker envisioned himself getting up, and he ran

out of the kitchen and threw open the back door. "Gerard, come and have biscuits," Lasker shouted in his child's voice. Then he saw Gerard—like he was when he was five; his brother who had died in Vietnam—and he couldn't take it. He pulled off the headset. The image dissolved.

The hermit touched him on his shoulder. "Nothing but an image. Don't think it's real, just an illusion."

"I saw my mother and my brother, too. It was real! I want to go back. I *must*—" He fumbled for the headset, but the hermit snatched it away.

"You must not. Control yourself!"

Lasker shook his head, again reaching for the headset, and the hermit pulled him bodily up, off the platform.

"That's enough for now! Why, you are a regular couch potato. You got lost in the illusions immediately. What would you do if I wasn't here? Watch it forever?"

Lasker rubbed his eyes. "Sorry—it seemed so real. I just—"

"You would not have been the first victim of this Cultivators' TV. See over there? In that dark corner?"

Lasker followed his pointed finger and was taken aback to see a skeleton in the dark corner.

"I found this skeleton," the hermit said, "on the platform. He probably sat there and slowly starved or dehydrated to death absorbed in illusion. A long time ago—maybe fifth or sixth century of your era."

"Who was he?"

"Some wanderer who found this cave and

stumbled on this chamber. From his bone structure and teeth, I'd say he was Mongol. Proves beyond a doubt that TV is no good for you! Now, we will try using the transceiver correctly, by steering your consciousness. Sit down again, Lasker, and don't think of the past! Keep your mind clear, and perhaps we will find out something about this cave of the Dancing Dead and its contents."

"Really? Can this TV show real places as well as memories?"

"Yes, Lasker-la, if you don't let it sweep you away, if you control it, instead of letting it control you," the hermit said. "Concentrate; center your mind on your quests; visualize rising up and travelling north, high in the sky like a bird, and looking down and searching."

"But I wouldn't know where to look."

"The thought of what you want to find will lead you to it." He gave Lasker back the headset. He put it on and tried to do as the hermit said, clear his mind and soar.

Slowly, Bart was drawn upward in his mind's eye as the hermit had promised, and it was as if he were a giant Asian condor, full of power and grace, sweeping rapidly northward on the wind, searching for the Padmasambhava's cave.

He saw a great plain, some red sandstone hills, and at the far end of that a gulley, an object: the Rong-lam obelisk!

It was the seven-meter-high, symbol-covered obelisk that marked the beginning of the Tsurphu map—the first mystic signpost on his trek north. It was clearer to Lasker now how to find the obelisk.

The Terton map's ornate direction indicators now made good sense.

Lasker soared onward, past the obelisk, toward a set of snow-capped mountains. Over a dune desert in a flash to those lofty peaks, he soared at incredible speed, speed faster than the fastest jet. He travelled beyond a ring wall of conical grey peaks. And then his condor eyes zeroed in on one snow-capped peak amongst a dozen others. Its granite face had a coppery hue in the slanting sunlight. It was the copper mountain. It was as depicted on the map, soaring above timbered land of many pines. And there was the symbol on the mountain, a series of ledges that outlined a swastika in the slanting sun's light.

He was there, wheeling down from high above, flashing over the wild country for leagues around!

Lasker was low now, rocketing over the pine trees on the copper mountain's south slope, and beheld a sign: a rock drawing of a blue deity. There were offerings of flowers and butter cakes at this rock shrine. So this shrine was the "Blue Deity that points the way" on the Tsurphu map! Indeed, the blue figure's left hand pointed at the copper mountain, toward its snowy summit. Lasker flew up to the brilliant snow top and saw a cave entrance outlined in red dust. Maybe it was red chalk.

He whizzed inside the cave and beheld a thin human figure with a jade face. The jade man made a fearful sound and swung at the Lasker-bird.

Lasker shouted, "No!"

*   *   *

The hermit pulled off the headset and shook Bart's shoulder. "It's been an hour, you must stop!"

Lasker's eyes slowly focused on the old man. He gasped, "I saw the copper mountain! And the cave! It is so high! The escarpments look in the light of the setting sun like a swastika. And I saw a creature! It swung a weapon at me!"

"Really? That creature you must watch out for, then, when you go in actuality to the cave!"

"Hermit—what does the swastika mean? It's a bad symbol in the West."

"It is an old Tibetan holy symbol. It's not the Nazi symbol of death; they perverted its use and paid the penalty. It's the original benevolent symbol of the sun's light.

"Well, we have achieved something big! Your map hopefully will lead you to the obelisk, and when you get there, you will recognize where you are and go on with assurance."

"I hope I can get there. It's so far." Then Lasker asked, "Hermit master, could—mightn't—you just use your powers—or some of this Cultivator-technology to get the text for me? And save me real trouble?"

"Ah, I was waiting for that, Lasker. When I saw," said the hermit, "that look of cunning on your face just now, I knew what you would ask. You noticed that this device is just a viewer! Anything you touch will not have substance. I have not found any Cultivators' devices that will let you reach out over a distance and grab stuff! As for me using my considerable mystic powers to do such a thing; I can't do it, and I wouldn't if I could. I don't get into

152

trouble for other people's reasons. Not even yours, Lasker-la."

"But it would be so easy. You bring things from the other cave to this one by walking through the blue crystal," Lasker insisted, "so why can't you walk through space-time to the cave of the Dancing Dead? You can't do it, then? Can't you astral project yourself—or me—directly there, and pick up the Padmasambhava's text?"

"It would be very dangerous to my karma to do so, even if one could. One can't go and lightly ignore the rules of the game, Lasker. Life is a game in some ways. To cheat it risks insanity and worse. The karmic debt would be enormous. Believe me, it would be a thousand times harder on you to try to get Padmasambhava's text by magic, than to go there and get it by—what you call reality. You Westerners are always trying to find the short cut, the easy way. The easy way can be harder in the long run. Haven't you heard the Zen Buddhist admonition: 'After you eat, wash the bowl'? Alas, Lasker-la, the hard way is the only way for you this time around."

"This time around?"

"In this lifetime."

"Swell. I'll do it the hard way, then. But I'll do it!"

Chapter 21

The hermit and Lasker left the transceiver room and headed back to the statue's chamber for some more tea and discussion.

After each of them had a cup, the hermit said, "There are some more things we can do now to help you. We can see if we can find more information on this cave you seek in the Cultivators' index book. Specifically you wish to know who the Dancing Dead are, and what their powers are."

"Index book?"

"Would you go get it? It's over there, in the drawer under the Peaceful Deity's statue. I suspect that Padmasambhava's prophesy text is a Cultivators' predictive book, or at least a translation of one. For even such as Padmasambhava do not have the power to delve into the Akashic record and find out what the future holds."

Lasker got up and slid open the hidden drawer. He saw a glowing rectangle inside, a foot long by two feet wide. The index book.

Hesitantly he lifted it. Despite its size, it was as light as a feather. He brought it to the hermit, who started flipping its thin shimmering pages. "This index book tells what was in the Cultivators' crashed spaceship's library. Let's see if this predictive text you are after is mentioned."

"It's supposed to be," Lasker said, "something Padmasambhava wrote about the future of mankind—way up to A.D. 3,000. I thought Padmasambhava just tapped into this stuff with his meditative powers."

"Hmmmph. Possible—but more likely he stumbled upon one of the Cultivators' librarys! Let's see, humanzak, huragams, ah here it is: humankind."

Lasker peered over the hermit's scrawny shoulder. He saw the book's print move and shimmer. It was in symbols Lasker couldn't understand or even identify. He reached to touch the page. It was gossamer soft, and it felt like his hand sank in.

"Don't lose my page!" the hermit said, slapping Bart's hand away. "Let me read. Hmmmm. It says here there is a book about the future of mankind. Earth people are, as you know, an offspring of the Cultivator race and the primitive pre-human creatures that they mated. The Cultivators were interested in what would become of the children race—us. So they delved into space-time in their unfathomable way and took a peek ahead and wrote it down."

"Yes, you told me that," Bart said skeptically. "But go on."

"Hmm . . . yes, a book like this is mentioned. It's cross-referenced to another part of the index. Let's see . . . Duncecap Caverns . . . Demigods' Realm

". . . ah yes! Here it is, Dancing Dead Cave. Indeed it is mentioned!" The hermit flipped more pages. They didn't turn, they sort of floated to the side until he got to a place where he stopped again. "Ah—here! It says . . . hmmm . . . that Padmasambhava, in the eighth century, your era, found the Cultivators' North Tibetan repository and was able to translate some of its books. He went on to form a successful sect of Tibetan Buddhism."

"Does the index say what the Dancing Dead are? Was that figure I saw with the jade face one of the Dancing Dead?"

"This book just says the library is also a—untranslatable—*Zmp* repository! Perhaps Padmasambhava put some jade-faced spirits there to keep the cave sacrosanct. Or . . ."

"What?"

"Well, it could be some tricks of your enemies, the Bonpo!"

Lasker groaned. "I never thought of that."

"In the north, Lasker-la, the Bonpo are still active. Their evil practices are still done; they still control some remote areas. The people in that wilderness are hardly peaceful Buddhists. If the Dancing Dead are Bonpo forces, you must call upon all your skills—including Demonic skills—to defeat them."

"Great! You've told me enough to make me turn around. What can you do for me?"

"Lasker-la, it is time for you to have a Yidam—like all Tibetan practitioners of the Great Short Path."

"Yidam? Oh yes, a guardian spirit."

"Much more than that, Lasker-la. You must learn

to visualize a Yidam protector perfectly, down to every detail. A deep meditation is called for to begin your visualization practice. I will show you how. Then, when you are able to visualize it perfectly, you will make yourself the Yidam and achieve Yidam's power. We will begin right away a visualization meditation to raise your Yidam. But first, I must decide what powerful deity it should be. Hmmmm, the Bonpo's Yamantalai has a lot of powerful children, perhaps—"

"No! No Bonpo Yidam for me. I've had enough Bonpo."

"But they are already connected to Raspahloh."

Lasker glared.

"Oh, very well . . ." The hermit scratched his chin under his beard for a while, staring up at the ceiling. Then he said, "I can't off-hand think of any Yidams powerful enough and available."

"Yidams are real?"

The hermit laughed. "Real-schmiel. What is real? There is a place, a world, an alternate universe if you will, where what is real here on earth is a phantasm!"

The hermit went back to his cushion, sat down and snapped, "Go into Vipassna meditation now, while I look up a Yidam."

Lasker took to his cushion and crossed his legs, aligned his spine vertically and began to sink into the quiet state he had learned to create at will in Dhramsala's meditation hall.

The hermit flipped through the glowing soft pages murmuring to himself. . . . A half hour later, he exclaimed, "Ah, here it is Lasker! He's perfect! One of the Yamantalai's demon children was converted

157

in the seventeenth century after attending a *puja* by force of a great Rimpoche. He is now a Buddhist protector. He knows Raspahloh; he is called Mampa. He will be your Yidam."

"What does Mampa look like?"

The hermit got up and went to a dark corner of the cave. Lasker heard drawers opening and shutting. Then the hermit reappeared holding a dusty woodblock print. Mampa was horrible beyond belief, all glowing red eyes and werewolflike teeth and claws.

"I don't much like the way Mampa looks, hermit. He scares me."

"Good! He will be horrible enough to unnerve your opponents, too. You can't send an angel to fight a demon, Lasker-la. This Mampa is an emanation of Mahaka, the deity of mirrors. You will stare into a mirror as I describe the colors and shapes of this image—until you feel Mampa is real, until you see him move."

"Like hypnotism?"

"Not hypnotism! We are dealing with powers from another plane than mundane reality. If you wish to defend yourself against the Bonpo, you must have a Yidam. You came to me for help. *Trust* me."

Reluctantly, Bart agreed to the visualization practice. He sat down. The hermit blew out some candles and placed a steel mirror before him, held in place by a pillow. The hermit began softly chanting: "Mampa rides a fierce snow lion, baring his many blood-drenched fangs. His wings are of leather, like a bat's, and his five heads have ten red eyes each. On his neck are three skull necklaces . . ."

The practice went on all night, until Lasker could see Mampa in the mirror superimposed on his own face, until his reflected image *was* Mampa and when he moved it moved.

"God . . ." Bart gasped, "it's real! He's—me."

"Very good." The hermit laughed. "Now we sleep."

In two days it was time for Lasker to leave. The hermit whisked Bart through the blue crystal, back to the cave at the Gayarong Pass. He stood with Lasker at the entrance to the cave, squinting in the sunrise. "Lasker-la, you are a good student. I don't want you to die just yet. I gave you spiritual help; now go get some physical help. Your friends the Snow Lions will be in nearby Yarang soon. Go there and get some of them—Tsering, Rinchen—the toughest ones—to accompany you as far as the Rong-lam obelisk. Once past Rong-lam, go on to the copper mountain by yourself," the hermit cautioned. "No delays. Now, I am sure you will find your horse is still grazing not far down the mountain. Don't tarry in your enormous task."

Lasker was choked up at the thought of again leaving his master, the man who had again given him so much. "Hermit," he whispered, "I will come back to you."

"You will," the hermit encouraged. "Don't forget—more cookies."

"I won't forget."

Chapter 22

Tse Ling's agent came to Yarang disguised as a brown-robed Tarapa Sect monk. He gave his name as Dewap, ostensibly travelling in the area to make offerings of sandlewood incense and mountain flowers at the small shrines scattered in the hills. This he explained when he made his way to Rinchen's uncle's bar. Of course, Rinchen's sour-faced uncle just nodded and set a chang (Tibetan beer) on the counter before Dewap.

Forgoing his great desire for the liquor, Dewap demurred and accepted some spring water. He sat down at one of the crude scattered tables inside the dark and dusty place.

"No, just water, kind sir, that is all I require."

Rinchen's uncle smiled and returned with a pitcher of water and some food. "Here are some unworthy vegetable buns—if you wish, Lama."

"Thank you." Dewap muttered something incomprehensible and low—a mantra or a blessing. The barkeeper went away to wait on some of his regulars, an unsavory-looking trio of customers who had just arrived from the trail, mean and hungry, and most of all thirsty for chang.

Dewap eyed the three nomads with apprehension. They were twice his size, scarred and dirty. They wore rough-hide coats and large copper earrings in their ears. They had odd headgear: hats made of what looked like black bear fur and sewn with occult witching objects; Chinese bottle caps, hounds teeth and—was it pieces of human skull?

Dewap listened intently to their discussion with the barkeep, but they talked only of breeding yaks and the best fodder areas in the mountain grasses and so on. Dewap soon tired of listening. These rurals were so crude. Dewap longed for a life of pleasure and luxury—western luxury which he had never experienced and could hardly understand, but had dreamed about anyway. If he could only succeed in this endeavor, Tse Ling would reward him well.

Another group of nomads came in noisily and snarled out something. The ersatz monk nearly dropped his bun. Evidently it appeared that the second three nomads to enter were saying they didn't like the cretin, stupid ass brother of one of the first three. Something then was shouted out about someone being cheated in a business deal. Then chang was splashed in one man's grimy face. It looked bad.

Then the fun began. Tables and chairs started flying, while fists met jaws and knives flashed. The melee rose in intensity. Dewap had to duck quickly under a table to avoid a thrown object. The barkeep was trying to protect his bottles of arak and Mou Tai with his body, with his life if need be. Fists flew;

furniture shattered. After a few minutes of rough and tumble clashes and curses, a pistol was raised by one nomad. The men all became sober suddenly.

The pistol holder snarled out, "Don't anybody move." But one did, jumping at him. The man fired and hit the other man's shoulder. It splashed an ugly red streak onto Dewap's shaven pate.

The shooter was then batted on the head by the barkeep with an immense bludgeon. He sprawled like a fallen bear, and the fight was over as quickly as it had erupted.

All the combatants seemed shocked by the injuries of each of their companions. One group went to the wounded man and quickly applied a compress to his bleeding shoulder, while the others carried out their unconscious bludgeoned friend.

Dewap followed the latter group, anxious to get out of the place. He watched as the bearers of the fighter threw him in the watering trough fifteen feet away. The man, shocked by the cold water, awoke. They lifted their staggering comrade and put him on his horse. Then the three rode away.

Trying to still his rapid breathing—he must not appear alarmed, for real monks are rather impassive—Dewap went back inside the inn and regained his seat. The barkeep was telling the remaining nomads where they could find a lama doctor, and they hefted their bleeding friend out the door. As the clatter of hoofbeats faded outside, the barkeep looked over at Dewap. "Are you all right, Lama?"

Dewap said calmly, "How terrible that was. The injury of one, the disgrace of another. I shall say many prayers to purify this place of the karma stain."

162

The barkeep prostrated before him three times, and said, "Thank you, thank you, fine lama."

After a long murmur of meaningless syllables of purification, Dewap asked, "What was the fight about? I didn't catch it."

"It was over a failure to deliver a paid-for yak."

"Yes—a yak. Well, never mind," said the fake monk. "Terrible things are happening everywhere nowadays."

"Eh?" sourface asked.

Dewap continued, "For instance, you have no idea what I have seen and heard up north. Such horrors."

"Please," said the barkeep, "do tell me."

"Well, maybe—" Dewap eyed the liquor. "Unfortunately, I have a lingering medical problem that needs arak. After long days on the trail, I develop an air-energy imbalance in my system."

"Yes, I understand," said the barkeep. He fetched the big bottle of powerful whiskey-like arak, then poured out some in a cup.

"Thank you. You understand, it is just for medicinal purposes. I will have just a few," he said and downed the first. Then he poured from the bottle into his empty water cup as he began tales of his extensive travels in the north, where he was, of course, visiting neglected holy shrines and placing fresh offerings.

He told of several recent Chinese atrocities. Dewap did not have to make these up, though he could have easily. In any case, rural Tibetans are always suckers for a well-told story—especially one filled with blood and mystery. Dewap, when he had his one-man audience spellbound, told the particular tale that Tse Ling wished him to plant at

Yarang: "After I witnessed the monks being buried alive, I was next in the valley they call the valley of the red mud. You know the place, north of Feng Tse?"

"Yes, I know! What happened, noble lama?" The barkeep poured him his third burning cup of arak.

"Well, there is a great gompa (temple) there called Mahaka Temple, and they worship Lord Mahaka— the god that lives on the other side of the mirrors and sees all evil in the world so that it may be recorded. Strange things are going on there."

The barkeep had a sudden fleeting look of shock on his face, "Yes, I heard of the great temple Mahaka and its guardian. Tell more!"

"Well, the monks there have such power that they have never been troubled by the Chinese-dog invaders—not even taxed by the Chinese! The monks there at Mahaka play such music that would chill the demons of hell on their human thigh-bone horns and skull drums!"

"I have heard," the barkeep gasped, "they have great power, sorcery enough to protect the valley below the temple."

"Ay," said the monk, as he leaned closer. "That is so. But there is a stranger among the monks now—a woman. And she brought trouble."

At that point in the story, the Snow Lions' hugest, meanest man, Rinchen, came into the bar. He thumped the counter at the other end. "Barkeep— arak!" Dewap noted the man had the hafts of a half-dozen blades sticking from belt, pockets, even his leg-scabbard.

The bar man rushed away and poured the

demanding Rinchen a cup of the liquor. The huge rebel swallowed it, and spat out, "More! More!" He rolled a brass coin down the cracked wood.

The lantern-jawed Rinchen downed two more cups of the near-lethal brew before turning. He leaned his huge elbows on the bar, giving a long loud burp in Dewap's direction. His keen brown eyes focused on the monk. "Who are you?"

Dewap, half cringing despite himself, answered, "I am Lama Dewap, a traveller from the north, doing holy services to the hill shrines."

"Izzat so?" Rinchen appeared dubious. He looked like he ate small men such as Dewap for breakfast.

"It is true," the barkeep assured, "and he has news of the Red Mud Valley—and the Mahaka Temple. He was just about to tell me of a strange woman visitor at the Mahaka Temple that brings trouble to them."

The big rebel's eyes flashed in recognition of Mahaka. He knew it was Dorjee the monk had news of. She was at the Mahaka Temple, in hiding there.

Soon Rinchen and the barkeep were huddled at the table of the monk as he explained the danger she brought to Mahaka.

"This Dorjee," said the monk, "is wanted by the Chinese authorities. I do not know what for. But the Mahaka monks keep her there for her own safety, and there she studies and prays. She is a woman of great beauty. And suddenly after a year's quiet, there is all this danger. Oh, such woe!"

"Oh, yeah? WHAT woe? Go on, monk." Rinchen demanded.

Dewap poured more medicinal arak for himself. He drank it down and whispered, "The Chinese general in the area found out about Dorjee. He wishes to seize this woman and has demanded that the monks give her up. They refused. The Chinese general has given them ten days to surrender this Dorjee. He has the monastery under seige and threatens to destroy it if they don't comply! Now there are but five days to go on his deadline!"

"What will the Chinese do with the woman?" the barkeep asked.

"I heard the Chinese officers talking at the local inn. They will hang her—right away. She will die for rebellion against the state, they said. For advocating an Independent Tibet—the worst capital crime!"

"The monks won't give her up. They are brave." Rinchen said flatly.

"Yes, brave," said the monk. Then he spat. "The Chinese are despicable. They will kill many to get her, destroy the temple! They talk of liberalization, and all we Tibetans get is more trouble."

The monk became too drunk to go on and was put to bed for a few hours. By dusk he was on his way again. For a few hours after he left, Rinchen sat and consulted with the barkeep.

Rinchen was aghast. And not knowing what to do about the plight of Dorjee, who Rinchen knew well as his American friend's lover, he took it as a sign that he should drink more than usual. "This bad news must be drowned," he muttered.

"Any excuse to drink," said the sour old uncle, "and you do so, tsk tsk. I hope your pockets are full."

Rinchen drank and drank, sitting alone by the

166

roaring fireplace. Others came in the bar, but in his black mood no one would dare engage him in talk; for surely it could soon turn into a murderous argument. Especially now that Rinchen's leg injury had made him miss the fall trek of his Snow Lion rebel compatriots.

Rinchen muttered and swallowed more arak—on the tab—and brooded. Dorjee was at Mahaka, in danger. So what? She was nothing to *him*. Was she? But Dorjee was the lover of that foreigner, the one that had caused so much ruckus the last time he was about. Lasker. He never liked Lasker. No. That wasn't true. Rinchen hadn't liked him at first, but Lasker was a close friend. Bah, who needs friends. Hmm, when Lasker participated in the Snow Lions' actions against the Chinese, he was brave. And Lasker got to be a great nemesis to the Chinese. Somehow, Lasker had been transformed into an almost supernatural, superpowerful foe of the Chinese. Rinchen had himself watched Lasker change. There was great karma there, a powerful attachment of this American's life-stream to the Tibetan cause. Lasker, in the brief time before he went back to India, somehow mastered the Tibetan language and customs completely. He had become strong, like himself, once removed from his lowland roots!

Lasker! If only he were here, he could do something about Dorjee's plight. *If* he were here. But he wasn't. How could Rinchen's rebel friends, with their few old rifles and revolvers, do anything about a whole platoon of Chinese beseiging Mahaka? No, the monks would have to give the girl

167

up—save themselves. No, that wouldn't do. His head spun.

Rinchen threw his cup in the fire. "It would be different," he yelled, "if I had a tank. With it, I would rescue her!" He pounded his chest, adding, "Of course, if I didn't have this injured leg, I would go right now and solve this problem without a tank!"

The barkeep moved back. Rinchen, in such a drunken state, was very dangerous. He could get one into his famous hammerlock and not let go for days! He could smash down walls, collapse the whole bar!

"No! I tell you!" Rinchen boasted, silhouetted in the light of the fireplace. "If Lasker-la were here—*burp*—we two would be capable of doing anything. Myself and Lasker—we would stop this."

He lifted up his nearly empty arak bottle and toasted to the fire, "My once enemy, now friend . . . Lasker." He sobbed. "How I long to see you once more!"

Rinchen drank down the rest of the arak and then threw the quart bottle into the fire and started to stomp-dance madly. He climbed up on a table, occasionally falling off and breaking a chair. The barkeep bided his time. He would wait till Rinchen was unconscious, then he would, Honam decided, take the price of the stuff Rinchen smashed out of his bag.

Chapter 23

In the first grey light of a bitter cold morning, Rinchen was standing at the animal watering trough outside the bar, smashing through the ice and throwing frigid water over his head. What a headache he had! Worse, he thought glumly, his pockets were nearly empty of renminbao. The price of arak liquor must have gone up! His binge had hurt his leg, too, inexplicably. Just when he thought it was healing! Now it hurt again. The nasty break and stiffness that Cheojey Lama had treated that summer was healed, but it felt sore all over anyway. What did he do last night to hurt it?

Rinchen hung around Uncle's drinking gobs and gobs of barley tea and pouring water over his head all morning, until the noon sun had made the day hot. He stripped his shirt off and lay against the still cool outside wall of the bar, in the shadow. He was muscular, and his skin showed many scars and bullet wounds, all of which he could explain in great detail when he was prompted. Especially when a comely woman asked. Speaking of comely women —he looked up and smiled as a group of five women

169

rushed by the bar. They were dressed in new rainbow-colored chubas, and their long hair was worn simply, in modern fashion—straight down and shiny. They each were holding several spools of brightly colored yarns.

"You are all looking very beautiful," he shouted.

They giggled, which he would have taken normally as a come-on. But who could think of womanly company with such a headache? His words had rung in his own head like a temple gong. No, like hoofbeats.

Or, were there real hoofbeats?

Rinchen looked up at the sound coming from the west. There were indeed five riders approaching, moving rapidly and stirring up a pall of dust. From the lead rider's face shot a glint of light. Rinchen smiled. That would be his friend Tsering, the leader of the group of rebel nomads that Rinchen usually rode with. He would have been with them the past month were it not for his stupid mending leg. The glint of light was from Tsering's copper-coin replacement for a right eye; a coin always kept shiny clean.

Rinchen bent down to pour one more splash of water on his head, then put down the wooden ladle and shook his head like a dog does to get dry. He swept his long thick, black hair back and tied it with his headband. He didn't want to look bleary eyed or dazed.

Soon Rinchen could recognize the other four riders, the youngest and toughest of the band aside from the leader and Rinchen himself. They were covered with trail dust; the horses were sweaty and all had bulging saddlebags. Rinchen hoped the bags were full of something valuable, that the group had a good trading trip. There would be money for Rinchen—his share. Those were the rules. No fault of his if—

The five riders pulled their horses up short and dismounted, shouting and coming over to their big friend. Rinchen hugged and shook the forearm of each man in turn. First, rugged one-eyed Tsering, wearing his raven-feather hat, with two intact huge wings on either side. The one good eye was bright with joy. The Snow Lions' acknowledged leader's grip was hard and indicated there'd soon be a challenge to arm wrestle. Thubten, their new member, afflicted with a deadly fever as a child, was, though merely twenty-five years old, bald as a monk. That and his circular loop Malacite earrings made him look strange indeed. Tseten Namgak, a cousin of Rinchen, was short legged and long armed. He had two, hundred-year-old, one-shot muskets jammed into his belt under a Levi denim jacket. Rolwag had slanted eyes and a small nose like many Chinese, but he was all Tibetan at heart. The last rider, Dondup, the best yak-train handler and rider of the bunch, had two thick braids with gold trinkets sewn in them.

It was good to see them all well, and with a glow of—was it—success?

"How's your leg?" asked Tsering.

"About as good as your bad eye!" Rinchen said.

"That bad? We will have Cheojey take a look."

"Never mind that. It was just a joke. It's fine! Where are the others? And how did the trades go?"

"We did well in Kemming, not so good in Larang and Becham. But all our wares are traded. Sad to say, we lost the old yak Bluenose. But that means there is much meat for feasting now."

"How much gold?" Rinchen asked impatiently.

"A good amount. And you will get some of that money. But let us not talk of that. There will be a settling of accounts meeting tonight, at the springs. Let us have a drink inside."

"Did you skewer any Chinese?" Rinchen asked as they entered the bar. "I certainly hope so!"

"No, Rinchen, you were not with us." Tsering laughed. "So we dared not take a chance."

Rinchen ordered arak. Sometimes, as Tibetans say, "a little dose of the yak that stepped on you is good for a hangover."

That evening Rinchen was at the Snow Lions' campfire at the edge of town where the other men of the band, and their women, had gathered with the goods and money they had collected on their trading rounds. Barley tea and cakes of butter and wheat, "chapati" vegetable pancakes with onion hot sauce, prepared by Lowan, their best cook, aided by Tenpa, Tsering's comely wife and her sister Dolwa, plus yak steak were devoured. Great fare!

Cheojey Lama, their eighty-year-old diminutive medical practitioner and spiritual advisor on the road was happy to see Rinchen. Rinchen was his most difficult case; the lantern-jawed rebel was dour and hostile most of the time, except when he was drunk. And Rinchen would sooner kill Chinese than say his mantras and burn incense before the Buddha. Still, he was, inconceivably, Cheojey's favorite rebel!

Cheojey, giggling as Rinchen complained, rolled up Rinchen's leggings and took a look at the leg he had treated with splints and ointments. "Ah yes, the bone is healed but the skin swollen. Did you use the lotion I gave you?"

"I forgot sometimes," Rinchen admitted, "and spilled some, so I ran out."

"Ah," Cheojey said knowingly. He untied one of the many small color-coded medical pouches from his robe's belt and opened it. Cheojey counted out ten small, hard, black pills and put them in Rinchen's ham-hock-sized palm.

"Take these. Crush them in your teeth or with a hammer, swallow them twice a day with boiled water."

"More of those gritty quartzite pills! What is the matter with me?"

"Nothing—if you stopped drinking."

"I do not like these pills. They are bitter," Rinchen complained.

"Still, they must be taken in the morning and before nightfall in hot steaming water." Cheojey explained, "The medicine I gave you worked well. I can see the leg is healed. You would be completely well if it were not for your drinking."

Then Cheojey took Rinchen's right wrist and took his pulses. There are dozens of pulses at the wrist, not just one. If one is trained to find and analyze energy pulses, it is possible to diagnose a person's disorder in that manner. Cheojey held the wrist,

173

lightly playing his fingertips over the veins.

"Yes, your pulses are better. Your circulation good! But alcohol weakens your leg."

"Hmmph! I am a man who drinks. Would you deny me my nature?"

"Would you deny yourself your leg, Rinchen? That is what will happen to it if you do not ease up."

Rinchen nodded—a great concession—and then got up and walked away muttering. Tsering had overheard, and when Rinchen reached in his saddlebag by the fire for a bottle of arak, he found nothing. Tsering winked his good eye and handed Rinchen a yak butter-tea in Rinchen's own cup.

Rinchen accepted it with a sigh. "I drink tea not arak for a while, because I do not want to stay in this godforsaken village anymore! I want to ride again, to trade, to track musk deer, to fight."

Rinchen drew Tsering away from the others at the fire. When they were out of earshot of the singing and partying men and women, he leaned over conspiratorially and whispered the story given him about what was happening at the Mahaka Monastery.

Tsering was stunned. "Dorjee is known to be there? Great Buddha, we must save her!"

"What can we do?" Rinchen lamented.

"We have to do something! We will ask Cheojey what to do."

Just then the aged medical lama came out of the darkness and said, "Ask me what?"

Rinchen told him about the siege at Mahaka, and Dorjee's danger.

The lama said, "My advice is to let our American

174

friend Bardum Tharpa decide what to do."

"Lasker? But he isn't here. He's in India," Tsering said.

"He is coming here. He is close already."

"Cheojey, how do you know?" asked Rinchen, feeling spooked. Rinchen did not like predictions, demon spirits, messages from the dead, miracles, and the like. Occult things, not men, were the only things that scared the big lug.

"I just know." Cheojey grinned. In the shadows of the rocks, the grin was all Rinchen could see. Spooky stuff!

Chapter 24

Lasker had found his horse where the hermit said it would be. He patted it, gave it some of the barley cakes from his pack, then he mounted up and headed straight toward the alluring light in the valley below. The brightest light was, he knew, the light pouring out into the night from Rinchen's uncle's bar. He always had thought of that bar as a way station in an empty universe. He was drawn like a moth to a flame.

First he'd ask about Dorjee. The last he had heard, a few months ago in Dhramsala, she was well and staying at a remote monastery. The word was third-hand from a refugee who had recently crossed over into India. The refugee had been told to get the brief message to Lasker, and he had. But Lasker now could find out more. Maybe—after he had the prophesy treasure—he could go to her . . . briefly. The thought made him nearly delirious.

He rode into Yarang, mindful that some Chinese might be around, but saw no vehicles save a few horse carts, and no Chinese flags. They were only up when a Chinese was about. In fact, there was a small

Tibetan flag decal glued to the moonlit bar's wall—a sure sign the place was devoid of a single occupying devil.

There were several nomads' horses—bristlemane short, hardy beasts—outside the building.

Lasker realized he needed supplies for his journey. If his Snow Lion friends could be found, well, he'd ask them to come along. But he would not linger long in Yarang. He wanted to get to the copper mountain before an early winter snow. He petted the horses, noticing one had a saddle with silver stirrups!

That could only be the mount of that Lone Ranger of Tibet. Rinchen! And there was a boisterous loud voice inside, shouting, "More tea!"

Lasker passed over the threshold and into a long shadow cast his way by the firelight. It was Rinchen's shadow.

Lasker touched the man's shoulder and found himself pinned to the wall by the man's massive fist.

"Easy, Rinchen. It's me!"

"Me?" Slowly, Rinchen recognized his old friend. "Lasker?"

"Yes, old friend. It is me. How are you? Strangle any good yaks lately?"

From out of the side room poured all of Lasker's Tibetan Freedom Fighter friends, shouting and laughing. "We knew you were coming! *Tashi delek!* Welcome!"

Even Cheojey Lama danced a robe-shaking brief jig that with his saffron robe's limitations made him look like a silkworm struggling in its cocoon.

They danced a wild impromptu dance of nomad

welcome for Lasker, bear-hugged him, even kissed him. Bart thought his E-Kung-hardened ribs might crack at the tight squeeze by Rinchen! Then he allowed Rinchen to pour arak for him.

Soon as was polite, after popping out a khatag for each of them, he began inquiring about all the relatives and friends and sons of each man—Tibetan etiquette. Only then Lasker asked about Dorjee.

"She is still alive and well, Lasker," Tsering said, adding mysteriously, "for now . . ."

Rinchen now passed on the news to Bart about Dorjee's hideout being besieged. "They are going to attack the Mahaka in four days!"

Lasker was staggered by the news. He sat down, and they all sat around him, waiting for his next words.

They were not long in coming. "I will go and rescue her!"

"And we will go with you," Tsering said gravely. "You again will lead us against the invaders. We will overcome all obstacles, if Buddha wills, and remedy this evil."

"You are always the leader," Lasker said. "But thanks, I do need you now."

Tsering pulled out a Chinese road map. "Lasker, here is the steaming lake, here the Red Mud Valley, and here is"—he slammed his index finger on a point on the map—"the Mahaka Monastery."

Lasker perused the map. The Mahaka was sort of on the way to the copper mountain. Not very far out of his way!

"We will need good weapons," Lasker said. "Not just old rifles. We need machine pistols, mortars even. But where—"

Tsering interrupted, "Wait a minute, Bardum Tharpa, I have a surprise for you."

He left briefly, going into the back room. He returned with a heavy sack. He put it on the table, and from it he pulled a Chinese-made AK-47 submachine gun. "We have six! We bought these from a group of Khempa tribesmen who removed the guns' owners from their worldly problems! Tibet is being reborn, Lasker. After the October 1988 protests in Lhasa, the movement for independence has new life. The world rallies behind us now. The dragon banner unfurls. It is time for a bold act. No more disappearing monks, no more can the Chinese hide the ugly nature of their occupation. It is war again!"

Snow Lions gathered around, each taking up one of the AK-47s. They raised their ancient cry, *"Lha Gyal Lo!*—Victory to the Buddha!"

Chapter 25

Careful plans were made. The Snow Lions and Lasker would keep to the high ground, avoid the areas of Chinese concentration. The ride to the besieged monastery was one hundred twenty rugged miles. There was no way to pretend they were traders. Traders have yaks, and yaks normally make only fourteen miles a day.

If the Snow Lions rode hard, they could easily make it in time. But they had never gone that way before. There were few trading posts in the Mahaka area, a dry part of Tibet notable only for its religious monuments and the great Mahaka Monastery. The first day out of Yarang, the dozen would-be rescuers including Tsering, Rinchen, Thubten, Rolwag, Cheojey and six more of Bart's old friends made good time. After the briefest sleep period—three hours—they rode on by night under a bright moon. They were halfway to their goal by noon the next day.

But now they were in high mountains, and there was only one pass to go through. It was supposed to be a deserted pass, but Tsering, peering through his battered binocs at the nude hillside snapped,

180

"There's some new Chinese garrison smack dab in our way!" He handed the binoculars to Lasker.

Bart focused on the squat stone-and-corrugated-metal structure ahead. "Yes . . ."

Tsering said, "My friend, it is bad news! Since the beginning of the new uprisings, they've been building these military outpost forts all over—even out here! They block the pass just to cut off the way north for rebels like us! If we go around, then we will arrive at Mahaka too late!"

"There is hope," Lasker said, engimatically. "I have an idea. If it works, we go right through the Chinese without trouble." Lasker explained his rather unusual plan in detail, and Tsering gave his begrudging approval.

Lasker left the group without his mount, heading toward the fort. He made sure he could fish out the papers saying he was Charles Grant without difficulty. There were lots of Westerners about Tibet now, he had reasoned. He would claim to be an archaeologist, as his papers said, but use some psychologist's tricks.

It wasn't long before the Chinese soldiers saw him coming down the slaggy slope. After all, he had on a bright maroon nylon parka and was waving and shouting. A jeep came out to meet Bart. His heart pounding like a tom tom, he showed his papers and explained in halting Chinese his alleged situation. He accepted their invitation at gun point and got in. The Chinese soldiers took him to the base to see their commander. Still part of the plan, but frightening nonetheless.

Lasker was ushered out of the harsh sun into the

main building. There he was taken to the office of the garrison's commander, who turned out to be an older, short, thin man with a narrow jaw. He puffed on a white porcelain pipe. An anemic Sherlock Holmes?

Lasker was offered a drink of water or Mou Tai. He took the water.

The officer examined his papers, then handed them back. "I am Major Hong. We don't get many tourists up this way. It is dangerous."

"I'm not a tourist," Lasker said. "See? It says archaeologist. I have been doing a study of this area's Buddhist ruins, and I'm sorry to say my Tibetan guide and his assistant deserted me, stole my money! They were supposed to bring me to Tarlang—"

"Tarlang?" The Chinese officer smiled. "Why, that is far north. They dropped you off in a dangerously unpopulated area. If you will give me their names," he said, picking up a fountain pen, "I will report them. You could have died out there in that wilderness. We will try to get your money back for you and punish them."

"Getting the money back would be sufficient," Lasker said. "In the meantime, I will wire Barclay's Bank to cancel those traveler's checks they took."

"You needn't do that! I can handle it. Just give me the numbers."

Lasker handed over a set of made-up numbers to the officer.

"Now there is no hurry—tell me . . ."

"Grant."

"Yes . . . what are you doing here?"

"I'm an archaeologist by profession and a hiker by hobby. I'm on an extensive work-vacation hunting for an obscure place called Gar-lum."

"Gar-lum . . . ah . . . I have not heard of such a place." The major appeared skeptical, one narrow eyebrow raised.

"It is a town that disappeared in the fifteenth century. I must say your English, Major Hong, is excellent."

"Thank you. The fifteenth century? That explains why I don't know the place. I see," the major said in an understanding manner. "That's why you are so far north, trying to find this lost town."

Lasker spoke on for another half hour on the subject of Gar-lum. He hoped the officer wouldn't be able to trip him up. Bart happened to know a lot about Gar-lum. Raspahloh had visited it once! The Chinese officer, it turned out, did know a lot about the subject. He asked many questions but appeared to be satisfied with Lasker's thoroughly correct answers.

The commander seemed taken in, and he was obviously an educated man. He seemed to warm to Lasker, and suddenly said, "You must see this." He showed Bart his good collection of Thanka paintings. Hong was quite an art and antiquities expert. "It grows late, my friend. There are showers and a place to sleep for you. I'm afraid you'll have to eat with the officers—say at eight P.M.? It is six now."

"Already? But it isn't dark yet."

The officer smiled. "Remember, all provinces are on one time standard. Same as Beijing."

Lasker nodded. "Of course. Very efficient. The

Chinese bring efficiency to this barbaric area—and many modern benefits."

"Yes," the officer agreed eagerly, "we Chinese are helping the peasants out of their backwardness, rebuilding their decaying culture in many ways."

"Yes, I know. I saw that all the monasteries down south are being rebuilt with Chinese assistance."

"Yes." The officer smiled. "What an unexpected pleasure to meet a fellow art connoisseur. My assistant will show you the facilities. Please honor me by being my guest at dinner. Eight. Set your watch."

Lasker did.

Lasker was almost dizzy with the irony: to be a freedom-fighter surrounded by one's enemies, exchanging pleasantries with these martial opponents!

The supper in the officer's mess was noodles and Chinese dumplings. It was good. What did the enlisted men eat, Lasker wondered. The ones who had picked him up looked gaunt. Lasker could hardly believe he was spending the night with a Chinese major, in the man's room yet.

He listened for a long while to Major Hong's soft snoring, then managed to relax enough to himself fall asleep.

After Lasker had morning tea and dumplings with the officer, he went to a window. From the window, he reflected the bright sun off his pocket mirror as a signal to Tsering in the hills: "Plan okay." He saw the faint glint back. "Message received."

So far, so good.

"Mr. Grant" was asked what his plans were, the major mildly suggesting to the western visitor that he not head farther north, but abandon temporarily his search for Gar-lum until another time.

There was a knock. "Sir," the tall lieutenant said in Chinese, "there is a small group of Tibetan riders arriving."

Hong explained the interruption in English. "I will have to see these people. There have been some unfortunate incidents lately, and we are looking for some bandits. We will see if they are just ordinary travelers."

Lasker nodded. He watched out the open window with bated breath as Tsering and his men rode into the courtyard. He knew their bulky garments held six machine pistols. All hell could break loose out there . . . or not. This was it.

The rider showed his papers, and the major appeared to treat the whole check routinely. Evidently he bought the story about the group being mourners joining relatives for a funeral in Steam-lake Valley. Then Lasker saw the riders being handed back their papers and faintly heard Tsering being told to move out the funeral party again.

Shit! That wasn't supposed to happen! The plan was—

But as the riders turned and started away, Major Hong wheeled on his heels. He shouted for the riders to come back. Bart listened for a while to his conversation with Tsering. And smiled.

The officer returned upstairs. "I think you're in

185

luck; these riders coming here is helpful. These crude nomads are safe enough to travel with, Mr. Grant, if you insist on going north. I will admonish them to take good care of you. But remember—always. The Tibetan race is not like us. They are inferior," said the officer. "All their life is superstition and ignorance and fear. Treat them accordingly."

The major took Lasker down to the courtyard and introduced Lasker to the group. Hong explained carefully to Tsering that Mr. Grant would be travelling with them as far as the provincial capital of Tharulun. Tsering seemed to have trouble digesting the Chinese words but finally said he understood.

Then Tsering protested, "It's somewhat out of our way."

The officer snapped, "How dare you talk back to an officer of the People's Liberation Army! I could have you shot. Obey the will of the people. Do as I order!" The major had his lieutenant rush upstairs and fetch his chop (the Chinese signature seal) and travel documents.

When he returned, the major took the chop and pressed it into a small lacquered box with smelly red cinnabar ink inside. He pressed the ideograph to several documents in Chinese.

"There. That will assure your quick delivery to Tharulun. These riders will not have to go the long way. These papers allow you all to pass right through this restricted valley. I am especially pleased that you, who love art, will see one of our preservation projects on the way."

Lasker took the documents and smiled. "Thank you."

The plan, as crazy as it was, had succeeded. They would travel on the short way toward Mahaka!

As they left the courtyard, the officer shouted, "Let the officials in Tharulun know if the caravaners don't treat you right."

When they were well on their way down the valley trail, Tsering muttered to Lasker, "I hate that major. I wanted to slit his throat."

"You looked like you were deferential. You're a good actor," Lasker complimented.

"I will get him someday for saying those things to me!"

Chapter 26

They continued on, feeling secure to go through the forbidden valley, armed with the documents from the major—all nice and official with his chop. Lasker could read a bit of Chinese, so he perused the document. It said to let the Britisher and the eleven Tibetans pass unencumbered, and uninspected, through the long valley.

There were four documents, all the same. One for each of the four checkpoints in the twenty-mile-long, dry-river valley.

At the first checkpoint, a mud-wall hut and a road block, they encountered three card-playing soldiers sitting on a blanket. The soldiers quickly put away the cards and picked up their rifles. Tsering, riding up in front of the group, held up the documents from the major, shouting in Chinese, "We have pass, Major Hong's pass!"

The guards were a bit suspicious of the group, but when they saw the official document and the chop impression, they were fairly groveling. They let them pass with smiles and good wishes.

And so it was for the next two checkpoints. The rebel nomads and Lasker were greeted suspiciously, AK-47s trained on them. Then the guards would check the document and all was sweetness.

The last checkpoint's guards were grimmer. Even after seeing the documents, they checked every Tibetan's papers. The reason for the delay their sergeant gave Lasker was "some secret construction ahead."

Lasker figured that must be the art preservation work Hong had spoken about. But why so *secret?*

Once away from the last barrier, Rinchen said, "At Mahaka the Chinese will pay for these insults! Imagine! We need passes to travel our own nation! I am sick at the thought! Why, I came within a half an inch of slamming my dagger"—he pulled its gleaming curved steel blade half out of its scabbard for emphasis—"into that last dog's gut when he asked me for my papers!"

"Glad you didn't, Rinchen," Lasker said.

"Bah! The day will come when we Tibetans will rule ourselves once more. That is the only way to end the oppression. Enough of this liberalization!"

"Rinchen is right to be angry," said Tsering. "Tibet must be free."

Soon Lasker and the others saw the valley ahead was a beehive of activity. A great one-hundred-foot-high statue carved on the cliffside, an exquisite deep-relief frieze depicting Boddhisattva seated, holding his hands palm up in his lap, his eyes half closed, was all scaffolded. The image was remarkable, an ancient monument of Egyptian scale, evidently being cut into sections. There were huge rock saws powered by diesel generators, cascades of running water cooling the blades. A hundred men and scaffolds and dust everywhere.

"It's being cut into truck-sized chunks," snapped

Tsering. "Why would the Chinese do this, Lasker? If they wish to destroy the statue—why this way?"

"I suspect," Lasker replied, "that the Boddhisattva's image is not being destroyed. It's being cut into chunks to be transported away, maybe to China. No wonder the local commander is an art expert."

Rolwag, reining his horse to a halt, spoke up. "They're preserving our culture in some museum in Beijing?" He started to open up his heavy coat to withdraw the AK-47 there. "Better to kill them here and now!"

It was all Tsering could do to dissuade Rolwag from shooting. Rolwag nearly weeping, they rode on down the valley beyond the disassembling statue and saw an army of laborers approaching. When Bart came within yards of the marching work gang, it became obvious that the laborers were not more Chinese soldiers, but monks, their frayed robes covered with white dust. Some wore just cloth tatters, and Bart could see fresh red whip marks on their backs. The whips of their escorting contingent of guards were out of sight now, however, probably because of them.

Cheojey whispered, "Some of the monks are those who disappeared after the Lhasa Prayer Festival riots. I recognize a monk named Talang. And there's Komel-Tsumpa, too!"

Lasker's heart sank. He had freed many prisoners a year earlier from Tse Ling's prison camp, but all over Tibet there were more such places of servitude and pain. Rinchen was right: only a free Tibet could solve this.

The prisoners were a sorry lot, thin and coughing,

their bloody feet swathed in pieces of cloth, not boots. There were a hundred of them, necks looped with rope; they were tied one to another, head to head, in five rows. Alongside the work gang, every one-hundred feet on their forced march, was a sullen SMG armed Chinese soldier.

Lasker, who was riding next to Rinchen, heard the distinct sound of a safety being clicked off. Rinchen's hidden snub AK-47!

The lantern-jawed giant had, unlike Rolwag, been unmoved at the Buddhist monument's dismantlement. But evidently the sight of these abused Tibetan monks was too much for him. He was, Lasker realized, about to kill a few dozen Chinese guards and thus get Lasker and the Snow Lions all killed. Lasker had to do something fast!

He stood up on his mount and plunged off. His shoulder slammed into Rinchen, knocking him off his saddle. Lasker grabbed at the AK-47's barrel, shoving it back into Rinchen's coat as they hit the dust.

Some of the Chinese soldiers watched them struggle, unaware of what had almost happened. Lasker shouted in Tibetan, "You call my mother a whore! I'll kill you, you bastard!"

Under his breath Lasker said, "Rinchen, you idiot, put away your anger for one day. We'll kill plenty of the Chinese bastards at Mahaka tomorrow."

Rinchen subsided. He said, "Tomorrow," between his teeth, and then aloud, "Son of a dog, let go of me!"

The crisis over, the two remounted and rode on, mumbling insults the Chinese soldiers understood well enough at one another.

Chapter 27

There was a brief stop after Monument Valley for yak butter tea and some tsampa, then a hard day of riding across the windswept lunarlike waste. When the rebel band camped for the night, Tsering said, "The moon will come up an hour before dawn. When it does, it will give light enough to ride by! We will get up then and ride some more."

The men all groaned save Lasker, who said, "Tsering is right—even though we are well ahead of the Chinese deadline. Once we arrive at Red Mud Valley, we need time to scout out their positions and gauge our response."

They bedded down beneath the starfields, so bright here at eighteen thousand-plus feet altitude that it felt as if they crushed down upon one's brow.

Lasker felt so close to Dorjee now, he could see her in the stars, her silken body outlined in the heavens like a new constellation. He could almost smell her jasmine perfume, run his starhands down her perfect copper body, kiss her. Needless to say, he couldn't sleep a wink, so he counted meteors. There were dozens per minute, like a welcoming fireworks' show.

Lasker, as was his preference, slept tonight a bit away from the others. So when he heard a noise, he sat up, knife quickly in hand. "Who goes there?"

A giggle.

It was Cheojey. "You were not sleeping, Lasker-la?"

"No."

Cheojey came closer and put down a thick blanket. "Then I will watch the dropping stars with you."

"Okay."

After a while Bart asked, "Cheojey-la, Tsering said everyone knew that I would come to Yarang last week. That you told them so. How did you know?"

"When we were on the last part of our trading route, several days before we Snow Lions arrived at Yarang, we stopped briefly by a small pond. It is known in the area as Vision Pond, and I went there to gather the floating aflara flowers which are useful for treating vomiting. I was at the pond in early morning, and there was no breeze. But still I saw a wave forming on the water, and then I saw what at first appeared to be a fish. A giant fish, I thought. But it wasn't. It was a naga!"

"A lake spirit?" asked Lasker. "I have heard they are horrible looking. Did he scare you?"

Cheojey giggled. "No, that pond has pleasant nagas. It was a lady naga as a matter of fact, with the beauty of a Dakini."

"What did she say?" Lasker asked, feeling skeptical.

"She just pointed and said, 'I have come a long way through the underworld waters, to tell you a prediction.'"

"What prediction did she give?"

"She pointed a radiant blue-white finger and then there was a great blackness on the pond's water, like I was staring into space, into a dark night sky without stars. Then, out of that darkness came an image . . . a temple besieged. It was the Mahaka Temple and then you, Lasker-la, coming on horseback. I saw Tsering and myself coming along, too, and there was fire in the sky and a wind. This the naga showed me. It said then, 'Do not be afraid.'"

"What then?"

"Then alas, Rinchen came along, and the naga wished to conceal herself from him—she was naked, you know. The naga whispered, 'The Mystic Rebel must look to the Dakinis for safety when he is in Mahaka. Only that will save the day.' Then she dived under. You cannot believe her voice. She had a voice like smoke!"

"What does her prediction mean? What Dakinis? Can you tell me more?"

"I'm not sure, Lasker-la, what she meant. But be mindful of her warning when we arrive at Mahaka."

In the light of the rising quarter moon, the rebels rose like sleeping rock demons from their blanket bags, and they saddled their horses. Once again, they rode toward their valley of destiny.

By dawn they were weary and half frozen. By midday their mounts' mouths were flecked with foam, their hides running with sweat. But they were heading up the last pass before Red Mud Valley.

With just hours to spare before the planned Chinese onslaught.

194

Chapter 28

The riders ascended the pass before Red Mud Valley. They rode between the towering peaks of Kaliwar and Ganesa mountains. At nightfall they crested the pass and saw the Mahaka Monastery, abode of the Mirror God, beyond and above the barren valley. In the shadow of the twin peaks the monastery was flickering with orange night torches. White prayer flags on tall poles snapped like ghosts trying to get free above the Mahaka's many roof's multitudinous, gold energy-drawing points. Unlike most other monasteries Lasker had seen in Tibet, this one had its full complement of ancient buildings: over a hundred white-washed, red-pillared two- and three-story structures set upon a multitude of escarpments. Access to the Mahaka's main temple—now catching the sun's last full rays and bursting into glorious golden color—was via short bridges from the other buildings. It was perched on its own jutting cliff, separate from the other structures.

"Ten thousand monks once lived there," Tsering said. "Now, there are a tenth of that number. The Chinese, though, have been mysteriously reluctant to deal with the monastery in their usual way. It has

195

never been shelled on a pretense, or even looted, according to what I've heard."

"But it's about to be." Lasker grimaced. He was looking through the binoculars at several Chinese mortar emplacements in the rolling hills before Mahaka. There were vehicles, too, their grey camouflaged presence unobtrusive in the rocks.

Tsering had a look, too, then asked for two scouts to go and survey those hills and report back. "No fires, no lights. Be quiet everyone," Tsering ordered. "We stay back here until our scouts return. There is still ample time to act."

Lasker couldn't take his eyes off the temple glowing in the sun. Which window, he thought. Which window was the one to Dorjee's room?

The scouts—Rolwag, and Tseten—came scrambling back through the boulders an hour later. They gasped out tales of many Chinese, well armed, and several armored vehicles laying hidden in camouflage in the hills. A couple of hundred soldiers. They scratched out a sand map of the area and made marks at every Chinese position.

"There were metal tubes pointed up here and here," Rolwag said, making Xs with his twig at three spots on the sand map. "Each tube about two feet long. Many sand bags around."

"Mortars," Lasker said. "They could devastate those buildings."

"Their weak spot," Tsering noted, "is that ridge to the south, and here." Tsering pointed at some crooked gulleys.

Lasker nodded. "You are right. I think we can

sneak through the middle gulley, avoid open ground, to get to the Mahaka. We have to," Bart insisted, "somehow get in and out of the monastery without them noticing. That would be the best way—maybe the only way—to rescue Dorjee. And once she's left, the monks could invite a Chinese inspection to prove she wasn't there."

"But how do we get into the monastery?" Tsering asked. "The gulley leads to the base of the monastery's cliff, to the long open ten-story stone staircase. In plain sight!"

"I don't know the answer," Bart lamented. "Maybe—a diversion?"

Cheojey had been sitting on a flat rock meditating. "Ah," he exclaimed suddenly, and rose. "There are secret ways into the Mahaka. See those cliffs, Lasker-la? I was wondering why they look so familiar. I meditated and saw through my mind's eye an old picture I once saw of this place. There are hermit tunnels in the lower cliffs, below the Mahaka monastery, on the right. I remembered just now."

"Are you sure?" Lasker asked.

"You can check for yourself. Take your binoculars. Look carefully. You should see the pattern of a dragon on the rocks. If I am correct."

In the field of the seven by fifty night-binocs Lasker saw what Cheojey was pointing at. "Yes, I see markings. . . . They look like a dragon. . . . So what? There are no entrances there. Just solid cliff."

"Not so," the monk said. "The drawing is definite indication that there are hermit tunnels in that cliff. There are bushes there, is that not so?"

Lasker nodded.

"Well, behind those bushes, then! The hermit

tunnels have access to the holy Mahaka itself. They wind upward in the cliff and come out in the monastery; of that I am rather sure. This type of tunnel was used by refugee monks from the monastery. Those who wished ultimate solitude. Yet they needed the tunnels—so they could be fed. And if they were sick, so they could be gotten to."

"Interesting," Rinchen complained. "But when was that? Ten centuries ago? If they aren't blocked off, how can we get up there on those cliffs to these alleged tunnels?"

"There are ravines—good cover—between here and the cliff tunnels," Cheojey explained.

Lasker and Tsering conferred on the side. Then Tsering went back over to his men and said, "I will take four raiders to the place of the tunnels. If we are—unsuccessful—if we do not return in two hours, then the rest of you will try another way. Do whatever Tseten tells you! Tseten—my friend, I am trusting you with the job of leading all the others if I fail."

Tseten replied sadly, "That means I am to be left behind—now. But I will do as you say. If you are caught I will come rescue you."

Everyone except Cheojey was amazed that Tsering wanted the monk along. Cheojey said, "Of course I go. You need me to find the way."

Lasker, Rinchen, Cheojey, Tsering and Thubten were to be the infiltration party. They set out for the gulley, Cheojey armed only with rope and pick axes, but the rest with short swords and SMGs.

*　　*　　*

An hour later, Lasker and the other raiders had worked their way along the snaking ravine to the base of the monastery cliffs. "We're just below the dragon figure," Cheojey whispered. "Now follow me. There should be some indentations in the rocks—steps for the ancient hermit monks to climb up. I know they are here somewhere." They edged along the gulley, keeping low, while Cheojey tried to find the way up.

"Bah, I don't see any steps," Rinchen complained after a while. "We should have found them by now."

"No," Cheojey whispered. "The steps are here—see? The first two steps—behind those birds' nests."

They crawled over the huge pile of intertwined twigs. The nests were of Asiatic stink birds—birds that use their excrement to keep the twigs and pebbles together. The nests were empty and crumbly—and smelly.

"If it were spring," Cheojey whispered, "the birds would be here and betray us."

"There had better be steps here," snarled Rinchen. "I can't breathe in this stench. It is killing me!"

Cheojey kept leading on. It was a hell of an effort, but Lasker lept across the nests and, following Cheojey's lead, grabbed a fingerhold on the cliff. He swung his foot into a niche that Cheojey said was the step, and then put the other foot on the second step.

"The stairs are here!"

Chapter 29

After a hair-raising, eighty-foot climb through the bramble-covered lower cliff, the climbers reached a tunnel entrance half filled with dry brush.

Cheojey squeezed through the thorny brambles first, with hardly a snag; then Lasker and the others, all of whom got some nasty cuts.

Cheojey, Lasker, Thubten, Tsering, and Rinchen wormed their way along in the dark on their knees, every pant and cough echoing in the low sinewy tunnel.

"It's heading up, I'm sure of it," Lasker gasped.

"You're right!" Tsering agreed. "But I wish we could stand up; the ceiling is so low!"

"Think how I feel," giant Rinchen complained.

Lasker realized he still had his pencil flashlight and turned it on. That was a bit better. The dying batteries still had some power. Lasker occasionally would try to get up on his haunches, and each time he did so he banged his head. Cheojey was getting far ahead of him, crawling rapidly, anxious to get into the monastery. And why not—it stunk to high heaven in the tunnel.

"Some bones here," Cheojey called back. "Watch yourself—some are broken and sharp!"

Indeed, they soon came out into a low circular chamber about thirty feet in diameter filled with chalky bones. Cheojey was on his haunches, examining what appeared to be a thigh bone—but from what animal? It was ten feet long if an inch!

"These look like dragon bones," Cheojey said, "very old—and very interesting. Maybe only a few hundred years old. Dragon bones have medicinal properties that are very powerful."

"A dragon died here?" Lasker gasped.

"No, they don't die, Lasker-la. They are immortal. The dragon merely shed his bones . . . like a snake sheds skin. The dragons do this only once every century." He saw a look of apprehension on Rinchen's hard face. "Ah, don't worry! There haven't been any dragons seen anywhere in Tibet for a dozen years."

That didn't stop Rinchen from shivering slightly.

Cheojey fished around and picked up a small bone, one about a foot long and weighing about ten pounds. He wrapped it in his robe.

"Leave it!" Lasker insisted.

"But the little finger bone of dragon is good for—"

"Leave it!"

"We can get it on the way back?" Cheojey asked.

"Maybe."

Reluctantly Cheojey left it. They crawled on again through a narrow, winding upward-inclined tunnel in single file. This time, they found no larger rooms, and a half hour later, Rinchen was at the end of his patience. "Bah! We are like rats in a maze, Cheojey.

My back is killing me! How tall were the stupid refuge monks? Were their backs all bent with age? Did they breathe?"

"Your discomfort will not last much longer," Cheojey promised. "I smell clean mountain air ahead—and incense!"

Eager to get out of the claustrophobic narrow tunnel, they crawled on until they came out into a wide chamber. Lasker played his light around.

"We are at an intersection of all the hermit tunnels."

"Now which way?" snarled Rinchen. "There are a dozen different tunnels going off this chamber. Which way?"

"This place is like swiss cheese," Lasker observed. "Are we lost, Cheojey?"

"Not exactly, but kind of," the monk said evasively.

A low groan from Rinchen. "I knew it. . . ."

"We must get creatively lost now in order to be found. I am not sure it will work,' Cheojey admitted, "but it's worth a try. Listen to me—forget trying to find our way. Let's just plunge on like madmen through the tunnels!"

"What good will that do?" Lasker asked. He wondered if Cheojey had lost his marbles. He was an eighty-year-old man. Perhaps the exertion . . .

"I am not insane, Lasker-la. I am only using logic. Only madmen can find the way, because these tunnels were carved by holy madmen! You lead— you have the light!"

They did as he said. Sticking together, they began rushing whichever way they guessed, banging their

202

heads, trying tunnel after tunnel, changing their minds and getting coated with the dust of centuries.

Just when he was utterly exhausted—and thoroughly lost, as Cheojey wanted—Lasker found a tunnel which ended in a huge wooden door with a handle!

"Hey," he called out. "Look at this! I found the exit, I think!"

Shortly, the others joined him, squeezing to take a look. It was stuffy here. A dead end with dead air.

Cheojey said, "That door surely leads to the monastery."

"Yeah," Lasker said. "And its handle is rusty. It might break! Maybe the door opens outward." He pushed against it hard. "Ug—door doesn't bend."

Rinchen pulled on the handle, and the huge rusty ring fell apart.

"What do we do now?" he whimpered.

Too late to leave Rinchen behind, Lasker was realizing that the giant brute had a fear of enclosed space. Rinchen was, evidently, a claustrophobic. His heavy breathing became fast, erratic and wheezing! He was about to have a panic attack.

"Pry the door loose! Here, try your hand with the pickax, Rinchen."

"I'll never get it open," Rinchen said. "We'll die here!"

But with Rinchen's panic-driven strength, the dry beams fell easily apart. The disintegrating door fell outward. They walked up a ramp into a huge dimly lit chamber. It was a shrine room, one of vast dimensions, lit by butter lamps.

In its center was a huge golden statue with a dozen

faces! The statue was covered with red and blue silk streamers.

Lasker's eyes adjusted with difficulty. He couldn't seem to get his bearings. Everywhere he looked, he saw the same statue, or was it? Were there dozens, hundreds, millions of the same strange red-painted statue?

No! He suddenly realized he was looking at reflections. They had come up in a huge mirror-covered room. That's why it had looked like there were an infinite number of statues.

"We are in the secret mirror god's domain," Cheojey gasped. He started doing several prostrations. Rinchen, groaning in fear of the occult vibes of the place, Lasker supposed, joined him.

Lasker just watched. "This is something—really something," he muttered. "It's like a Coney Island funhouse."

It was indeed a mirror maze. Ancient steel-backed-by-copper mirrors everywhere, and the statue of the Mirror God Mahaka illuminated by butter lamps reflected in each mirror, floor to ceiling, even above.

"Behold there," said Cheojey. "Mahaka, he who sees all the world through its mirrors. He can be in any mirror in the world, and Mahaka watches."

Rinchen mumbled mantras nervously.

Lasker inched forward, now anxious to get to Dorjee. But he had difficulty moving, for in the confusion of mirrors he constantly bumped against either a mirror, or a statue. He found there were many lesser god's statues around the big one! Which was the way to go? It was all bewildering. And most bewildering—why didn't he see his own image?

Adrenaline now shot through Lasker's veins. Yes, where in this mad maze was he? What was real here? Was he real?

Lasker heard a creak. One of the statues moved. He reached for but stayed his blade when he saw the source. It was a lone ochre-robed monk who had turned slightly from his seated meditation to face Lasker. Or did he? Was he an illusion? A statue maybe different than the rest?

Lasker stepped toward the monk and reached out. He touched his robe. Real enough skin, too.

This monk was too ugly to be a statue anyway!

"Welcome to Mahaka Temple," the slattern-eyed boil-faced monk said calmly. "I am Ngarod." He stared up at Lasker. "What is your wish, Mystic Rebel?"

Lasker wondered if the grotesque monk had been in a fire. "Why do you call me that?"

"You are foreign, tall, strong. You got in here. You are the Mystic Rebel therefore."

"Call me Lasker—I've come for Dorjee."

Lasker quickly explained their plan, ending with his belief that once Dorjee was out of there, the Chinese would leave this monastery alone.

The monk agreed. "It is a good plan. Our Kongtril Rimpoche, in his divine wisdom, divined that someone would come to do just that—remove her, and thus save the monastery. The Rimpoche believed the Mystic Rebel might find the tunnels and come in that way. I was sent here to keep watch for you! Follow me, and I will take you to this Dorjee. The woman is in the utmost room of the temple, in the cupola of gold."

The intruders followed the monk, climbing a set

of red ladders and then some winding stone stairs.

"Where are the other monks? I see no one," Lasker asked.

"They are out on the walls and battlements, with such weapons as we have: boiling oil, stones to rain down on them in case the Chinese try to scale the cliff. The stairway door is barred with a huge timber!"

Cheojey said, "I must speak to Kongtril Rimpoche!"

"Alas," said the ugly monk, "Kongtril is dead—his eminence passed on two days ago."

Cheojey was greatly disturbed. "I must then pay my respects to his earthly husk."

"We must not tarry," insisted the monk, hastening them up another flight of stairs. "First we must pass through the Rainbow Hall, then—"

"Nevertheless, I insist," demanded Cheojey. "Tell me which way to the corpse."

"The Rimpoche lies in state in the mourning room. See that doorway? Go down the long corridor, and you will see a red arch." The monk did not break step.

Cheojey said to Lasker, "Go on—go to your duty. I will join you all back in the Rainbow Hall when you come downstairs with Dorjee. I *must* see the Rimpoche!"

Lasker was loath for the team to split up, but he knew Cheojey. It must be an important, vital diversion that the medical lama was now taking. He could see no reason to argue about it.

*　　*　　*

Cheojey rushed away in the direction of the room where Kongtril Rimpoche lay in state. He was deeply worried about what the ugly monk said, and suspicious, too. For a good reason.

He found the mourning room without difficulty—and the Kongtril Rimpoche, propped up on his meditation pillow. He was very dead, but that didn't mean he shouldn't get respect! Cheojey prostrated three times and then lit incense and sat before the open-eyed dead man in the tall grey pea-pod hat. He started chanting *Kongtril cheno Kongtril cheno* (Kongtril come back), the customary plea for the high lama to return to earth for rebirth to continue his Boddhisattva activities to again teach the dharma.

Then he spoke to the dead lama. "Oh great Kongtril, son of noble birth, there is a strange thing. Your monk Ngarod said I couldn't speak to you, for you are dead. But surely even the lowest monk in Tibet knows that a high lama can be spoken to for the first three days after his death! I do not wish to disturb your Bardo meditation, but this is important, holy lama—"

The butter lamps all flared up. "Oh, how unusual!" Cheojey exclaimed. It meant the lama wanted to speak back to him, with his own lips, not through signs.

Cheojey did as is always done in such rare cases. He went to the black box at the corpse's feet, opened it, and took out the long dark brown Arphur, the leaves of life. "I hope I'm doing the right thing, that I have interpreted the sign correctly." Cheojey worried. To frivolously rouse a lama passing on to the

Bardo world is bad business, unless he so wishes.

Cheojey reached to the dry cracked lips, pried them open, and took the black death-pill out of the lama's lips. He broke the brown Arphur leaves under the lama's nose. Soon, red and white streams of liquid issued from the nostrils and ran down to the dead lama's dry lips.

Now the lama's stiff body began vibrating. He was exerting the utmost of his strength, trying to raise breath to tell Cheojey something.

Cheojey pressed his left ear to the dead lama's lips and heard the otherworldly whisper that the lama moaned out:

"Danger. Not—real—monks! Chinese. . . . They . . . killed me . . . maha—ka. . . . Monks—in walls of mi—rror hall hiding. Go there—they . . . will . . . help . . . now! Huuuu . . ." It was done.

Cheojey got up and abruptly bowed. "Thank you, holy one, I understand! *Kongtril cheno!* Come back to us soon!" He pressed the black pill back.

He had to find the others—now. Before it was too late!

Meanwhile, the fake monk led Lasker and the rest of the intruders to the main hall of Mahaka—a magnificent, cathedral-like space. For Tibetan architecture, it was unusual for its lack of pillars. Lasker wondered if the ancient Romans might have been here, and inspired this Roman arch, high-vaulted ceiling.

The Tibetan equivalent of stained glass—quartz crystals—hung in a hundred openings high above, catching the morning's first rays of sunlight, shooting multiple bright rainbows everywhere in the empty area. They were all suddenly bathed in rainbows.

"Beautiful," Lasker mumbled, "but there's no time to admire it! Lead on, Ngarod!"

The ugly monk led them out into the open center of the vaulted room for some reason.

Lasker noticed now that there was a balcony winding all around the Rainbow Hall, and to his surprise there were many ochre-robed monks moving on that balcony. And they were holding—what?

A voice shouted out, "Lasker! It's a trap!"

Lasker lifted his AK-47 just in time!

A huge robed man cradling a bludgeon swung down on a rope from the balcony, shouting something like Banzai! The man was heading straight at Bart, who swung up his SMG.

But before the big monk collided with him, Cheojey came swinging down from his own hiding place in the rafters at great velocity. His small feet slammed into the attacker's head, sending him tumbling to the side.

Cheojey kept to his arc and flashed out of sight in the confusing maze of rainbows.

The monks on the balcony shed their robes, revealing Chinese uniforms and waving clubs and swords, then started sliding down wires to the central hall's floor.

Thubten and Tsering had their guns up by now and with ear-rending blasts cut down the first wave of soldiers. As they fell, others dove from the balcony. One soldier tackled Lasker—it was now hand-to-hand.

Lasker realized that no one except his own side had fired guns. The Chinese were trying to take them alive! That made the overwhelming numbers of the Chinese seem a bit less formidable.

Bart brought his AK-47's butt onto the tackler's neck, and the man went limp. But others jumped on him, at least five, determined to crush him down under their sheer weight.

Lasker spun and shouted, building up what the Bonpo trainers called a Chi-wall. They fell like tenpins all about him. And now some firepower! Where the hell was that traitor monk Ngarod that had led them into this trap! He'd be first to receive lead.

Chapter 30

The traitor monk was nowhere to be seen! Just Chinese soldiers with their staves and clubs. A few more bursts of fire from Lasker and his friends eliminated baker's dozens of these fellows! Were they stupid?

As if in reply, Cheojey yelled, "These Chinese soldiers are here only to exhaust our ammunition! The *real* threat is yet to come!"

"Do you know where Dorjee is?" Lasker shouted.

"We get her later! Now we must go back downstairs!"

Lasker and his friends formed a close group and started backing away toward the door they had initially come out of. The Rainbow Hall was a pentagon. Each of its five sides had an oaken door. As they backed away to their door, every one of the other four doors burst open, and a horde of black-clad men came from each doorway.

These were not soldiers; they were all in black and had slit masks on. Wu Shu fighters! The Chinese martial arts experts carried weapons of a large variety: katamas, broadswords, pikes, even long-handled axes and curved scimitars. And they all looked like they could use them!

Firing some bursts to stave off pursuit, Lasker and the Tibetans rushed pell-mell down the staircase toward the mirror maze. At each step, Lasker felt a sense of failure, for they were heading away from the direction he wanted to go. They were getting farther away from Dorjee. But he trusted Cheojey to be aware of their objective. And in any case, they might shake off their mad Wu Shu pursuers in the maze of hallways and ladders.

Cheojey was leading them back down a different way—or he was lost.

Two levels down, they traversed a workshop where the monks of Mahaka had painted prayer flags. The whole room was crisscrossed—just about head-level—with these pennants. There were all colors and sizes, hung to dry perhaps. It reminded Lasker of backyard clotheslines.

Making for yet another doorway, they ran smack into more Chinese soldiers, all with SMGs levelled at them.

A Chinese officer with twin red stars on his cap stepped forward, holding a sten-gun. "I try to be nice," he said in English. "I try to not hurt you. But no more Mister Nice Guy. I am Major Trang. I order you and your commandos to surrender immediately —or die."

Lasker recognized Ngarod's boil-covered face under the major's hat. Ngarod was Trang!

Lasker had taken opportunity of the ugly man's

212

little speech to size up the pennants above them. And now Bart lept up, his sword slashing a huge hanging white-and-blue prayer flag from its holding rope. It fell down over the officer and most of his soldiers. They struggled wildly to extricate themselves but, in their eagerness, only tangled themselves more. And one-eyed Tsering was not idle while they did this. He lept at the two soldiers that hadn't been caught by the falling curtain as they tried to fire. He wrestled the guns away as Thubten slammed a drop kick at each of the Chinese with a Snow Lion rebel's double dropkick. Their necks jerked back with a resounding snap.

Lasker swept his flaming SMG right to left, peppering the trapped men in the white silk prayer flag until the white was full of smoking red holes.

Cheojey mumbled mantras; Rinchen slammed heads together, gleeful that Lasker's flag gamble had succeeded. But they all moved again pretty quickly when they heard running feet.

"More trouble," Lasker said. "Let's go!"

The first of the Wu Shu fighters had found them now and were dropping down ladders from both sides.

Lasker picked up a Chinese SMG and fired the whole clip at the black-clad Wu Shu on the right. The bullets were apparently explosive ones and made burning orange-sized holes in the fabric and flesh of the scimitar wielding men he hit.

Then he was taking return fire. Lasker rolled behind a huge meditation gong just ahead of a stitch-line of lead. The ancient call-to-prayer device resounded with a dozen bullet hits. The sound was such that his ear drums nearly burst. Tsering and Rinchen were firing now, with full-clipped Chinese weapons they had taken from the dead soldiers. Thubten crawled around, strangling the wounded Wu Shu, making sure.

Cheojey was handling the attackers in his own monkly way—in amazing fashion. He was a martial arts windmill, throwing the bastards, ducking, weaving; all circles and loops. And Cheojey was apologizing as he threw them! "Please don't hurt yourself," he said. "Please avoid injury! . . . So sorry you fell!"

Lasker couldn't believe the skill and power of the eighty-year-old man.

In between throws, Cheojey shouted, "We must get down to the Mirror god's realm!"

Lasker couldn't think of a better idea. He delivered a full clip of bullets up the left ladder hole, and Thubten did the same up the right one. Screams above. Blood spattered down the rungs. "That'll hold 'em awhile."

They rushed down two more flights of steep wooden stairs and plopped down facing the elaborate dragon-motif red arch leading to the Mirror Chamber. So Cheojey hadn't been lost!

They made a beeline for the open door, with the sound of pursuers clamoring behind, close again.

Lasker caught a glimpse behind his back of a dozen burly ax-and-pike armed men. They had shed their Wu Shu black shirts, and were all muscle and sinew and cold eyed, screaming what must be

Chinese for "Get them."

Quickly they rushed into the darkened mirror maze, instantly dazzled and confused by the multiplicity of reflections. Most of the butter lamps had been extinguished. Cheojey leading, they rushed to the trap door to the tunnel. It was sealed shut. Even their knives' edges and the pickax pry-side couldn't get into the crack. There was nothing to pry the trap door with.

"The escaping monks," Cheojey gasped, "must have used it and sealed it behind them! Follow me," he whispered. "There is a place in here where one can see clearly, so I'm told."

They were as good as blind in the maze of reflections, holding on to one another's jackets as they crouch-ran following Cheojey up. The medical lama inexplicably knew where to turn right or left at certain mirrors.

Suddenly Cheojey said, "We stop here; stay low. Look to the left—you will see the room as it is—no reflections from here. This is the dead-spot."

Lasker and the others were amazed. It seemed as if the mirrors had disappeared. Perhaps from here, they were all seen edge on. They saw clearly the thirty-odd Wu Shu and their leader inching forward, apparently confused. The burly leader called out, "Surrender dogs! Or we will fire everywhere. Everything will be destroyed, and you will be killed. I know you will want to avoid unnecessary destruction of this holy place. Surrender!"

Lasker was distressed at the idea of shooting up this magnificent ancient shrine room. Was there a choice?

215

Cheojey whispered, "No surrender. The Mirror god will protect this place, and us as well."

The Wu Shu spread out through the room and suddenly were gone.

"What's happening, Cheojey? Why can't we see them?"

"The dead spot moves, as the mirrors do. The trick is that this whole room slowly rotates. Or so I was told."

If Lasker was confused by a hundred shifting reflections the Wu Shu were, too. And everywhere there was a tinkling, the mirrors shifting in the breeze of even a breath on their perfect swivel mounts.

Tsering whispered, "Let's fire—"

"No," Cheojey whispered. "There is a secret passage leading out of here and up to the top of the temple. We can still get to Dorjee."

The Wu Shu chief evidently heard the whisper. He swung his SMG up and fired in a sweep—missing them but shattering some eye-level mirrors.

The mirrors fell in crashing crescendos. Lasker and the Tibetans kept low, weaving along behind Cheojey. Were they behind or in front of the main statue? Lasker could only trust Cheojey's uncanny direction ability.

The Wu Shu leader saw Lasker suddenly. He appeared to be standing right in front of him. He let loose a burst of fire, smashing a mirror, killing two of his own men who were standing behind it. Even worse for him, part of the mirror evidently wasn't glass—but steel. The bullets dented them, and then spun off, nicking the Wu Shu master himself in the left shoulder.

Other Chinese felt their way along the passages of mirrors, some suddenly falling through a mirror they pressed against, dropping into pits with razor-sharp three-foot-long spikes in them. Others found themselves in yet another mirror maze, completely turned around.

The toll of just trying to find the raiders was mounting.

Lasker sometimes saw himself in front of him, sometimes a mirror god, sometimes Cheojey or Tsering. What was real and what was illusion? Once his heart nearly stopped as he stood face to face with his main opponent. But when Bart struck out with his left fist, it clanged against reflective metal!

Occasionally, there were screams, or firing—from all directions. The Chinese had lost their cool and were shattering all the mirrors—and killing one another.

Suddenly there was only smoke, shattered glass and the two sides facing one another. Five against sixteen.

"Come on Raspahloh!" Lasker shouted. "Please, if you ever wanted to come out, now's the time to do it!"

Lasker felt himself dissolving; not his physical body, but his mind. There was an emptiness sucking him up and away and then a feeling of spinning down, down, deep. Suddenly Lasker was deep inside himself, an observer, not a participant anymore. The transformation, welcome this time, was easier. Bart

Lasker was still there, but only faintly. He was a small wave lost in the tide of a more powerful personality. He felt no panic, though there was another being in control of the body of Bart Lasker!

Bart tried to say something, to move. But it was not his voice, not his legs and arms to do anything with. He felt his lips curl into a sneer and felt drool come down out of his-not-his twisted lips. And he heard a voice, deeper, more gravelly than his own, coming forth from his diaphragm. It said, "Raspahloh is here!"

Visions flooded in the shared mind, the mind Bart now had only a niche in, flashing through his shared consciousness in a nano-second, in slow motion. Bart saw it, smelled it, felt it, yet he was but an observer.

He was Raspahloh, riding his black demon steed through the darkness of the Tibetan mountains. The whole area was burning with the fires he had set. Men and women were screaming, tearing their hair out, weeping. It was a war, a deadly war. His side was the Bonpo magician priests, versus the Chinese warlord Keng Tse's army. This was the fifteenth century, in the province of Amdo. Raspahloh was the champion of the Bonpo, their assassin of ultimate skill, their dark visitation. "Kill, kill Chinese," Raspahloh screamed.

In the demolished mirror maze, the shared eyes of Raspahloh-Lasker took in the situation as if the twentieth century was a figment of the imagination. Raspahloh saw it as a repeat of the same situation:

218

the Chinese warlord's forces pitted against himself. The puny Wu Shu leader was Keng Tse, someone to be annihilated with the awesome killing skills of a bloodthirsty Bonpo assassin.

Their shared face turned into a shaking distortion: the left side of Lasker's lips curled, the other didn't. The drooling mouth made horrible chewing noises. Raspahloh-Lasker no longer saw colors; all he saw was a redness, a blood-lust hatred that knew no bounds. Raspahloh was facing a Chinese enemy, an enemy he hated every bit as much as the Tantric Buddhists he had also fought in those centuries long ago. And he uttered the oath to Yamantalai, his dark lord, the invocation of power. *"Zom-hri!"*

The few candles still dimly illuminating the room went out.

The Wu Shu fighters fired where Lasker had been, but he wasn't there. The flashes of their gun barrels showed a strobe-like series of images: Lasker in the air to the left, slashing the head off their leader; Lasker to the right, his sword cleaving the brain of yet another black-clad attacker. Then he snarled out a challenge and lifted the bloody sword again, with a swiftness and certainty that was unstoppable. Lasker's peculiar stance, his snarls, bewildered his companions. What was going on? They had fully expected to die; the Chinese had much ammunition, they but a few rounds. There were sixteen black-clad killers facing them. And yet—the whole bunch of attackers seemed to be afraid. Afraid of what they saw in Lasker's face.

And so were his friends.

They dove for cover, reciting protective mantras

219

as their American friend, Bart Lasker, moved into lightning action. He was like a demon wielding a sword. Lasker continued a tremendously skilled, ultra-fast attack on the black-clad killers, his sword whooshing and slashing too fast for the eye to behold. They could see flashes of gunfire, see Lasker first here, then there, the glint of the blade, a blur of motion; no more.

There was no match. Raspahloh was death incarnate, ultimate killer of all times. His sword was a veritable Scythe of the Grim Reaper. Rinchen moaned. Way too much spooky stuff!

The Tibetans watched as again and again the Chinese raised their weapons to fire.

By comparison to Lasker's speed, they were like slugs trying to move quickly.

Lasker was in front of the enemy, behind them. . . . He cut bodies lengthwise, sideways, never stopping, and his fierce, deadly-aimed kicks cracked jaws and shoulders and necks.

The Wu Shu fighters' weapons clanked and sparked from time to time against Lasker's sword, then they were skewered, sliced, diced. Lasker's friends scrambled to grab their guns. They were afraid to fire, however, for fear of hitting Lasker. They backed off in the darkness until their backs pressed against Mahaka's base. Somehow, it seemed a safe haven.

The remaining enemy was utterly panicked, firing at one another, at shadows, but never hitting their real opponent.

It was over; Lasker suddenly had no one to fight.

Cheojey, now that the slaughter of the Chinese

was over, feared the next events! He saw great damage; there were bullet holes all over the Mahaka statue, piles of bodies everywhere—a horrible sight to a monk. But by far the most horrendous sight before him in the semi-darkness was a crazed-looking Bart Lasker slowly approaching Cheojey and the other Tibetans. Their friend was smirking and lifting his red-edged sword.

"Lasker-la, stop it! It is Cheojey. We are fr—"

"Now I kill Buddhists," the twisted lips of his American friend uttered.

"No . . ." Cheojey began to chant, *"Om."*

Tsering said, "Lasker— No! Stop! Don't make us shoot. What's gotten into you?"

But before what appeared to be inevitable murder, something happened.

A ray shot out from the Mirror god's forehead, and it hit right in the middle of Lasker's chest.

They watched in bewilderment as Lasker's body convulsed, as his face went through shivering permutations. Before their very eyes the evil sneer, the cold eyes were transforming back into Lasker's familiar countenance.

The upraised red-edged sword clattered to the floor, and Lasker, his eyes rolling upward, fell also. He fell like a stone. Just for a second Lasker saw his yidam standing over all.

Cheojey bent and felt his pulse. It was rapid, but slowing. "Lasker-la, Lasker-la . . . wake up!" He slapped his friend's face several times until a moan came from Lasker's lips.

In a moment, Lasker managed to sit up. Cheojey could tell it was Lasker again, not the supernatural ultra-killer that had been about to turn on his own friends. His American friend's eyes focused on him.

"We have to get—to—Dorjee," Lasker gasped out. Then he looked around him: bodies, pieces of arms and legs. "I did this?"

Cheojey said, "No time to discuss it! Come! I have found the secret panel. Come out, Rinchen! It's all right!"

Following Cheojey, they crawled under the Mahaka statue, and Cheojey found a recessed panel and pressed it. There was a hiss and a secret passage was revealed.

Chapter 31

After climbing six flights of winding stone stairs in utter darkness, they reached a wooden barrier. "This is the secret entrance to the visiting lama's room," Cheojey said. "It is surely the room that Dorjee is staying in. The monks would want a female visitor as far from them as possible."

"What are we waiting for? Let's get it open!" Lasker exclaimed.

Lasker was eager to press forward and smash it down with his shoulder, but Cheojey held him back. "No, it will open easily if I can find the catch." The lama felt around, and after a minute of fumbling said, "Ah."

The panel popped out, and they burst into the brightly sunlit room. It was a beautifully appointed chamber, filled with elaborate *thankas* and dark-stained, red-velvet, cushioned Mandarin-style furniture. A room suitable for the head of the sect, the great Khesung himself. No doubt about it—this ornate, circular room was the cupola room. Dorjee's room.

Lasker's keen brown eyes swept the premises. He saw a low, wide bed; its blanket was strewn half onto the floor. There was a dressing table with a small mirror hanging askew on the wall over it. On that dresser were some typical female possessions: an ivory-handled brush, a comb, a turquoise clasp for long hair. The carved-wood armoire to the side of the dresser was open. There were several clean and pressed chubas, and a western-style black dress hanging inside it. Dorjee's size. But no one was in the airy sunlit room.

"Dorjee—where are you?" Lasker shouted. He rushed to the terrace door and flung it open, and there he saw Dorjee.

She was turned away from him, staring out into the distant mountains, her long silken black hair blowing in the wind. There was no doubt in Bart's mind that the tall, thin-waisted woman with her back to him was Dorjee. He knew her too well to be mistaken.

She was wearing nothing but a thin white Chinese dressing gown. And she was putting one bare leg over the balcony rail, intending to jump!

Lasker leapt to stop the plunge, grabbing Dorjee around the waist and pulling her back onto the terrace. Then he helped her into the room. She moved languidly, like a sleepwalker. She was barefoot, and her skin was ice cold. Dorjee made no sound at all. Her eyes were vacant.

"Dorjee? Are you all right?"

No answer. She stood still, like a beautiful mannequin. Lasker shook her by the shoulders.

No reaction.

"Cheojey— What's the matter with Dorjee?"

Cheojey rushed over and lifted her right hand,

then pressed his small fingers on the wrist. After cocking his head for a second as if listening to something, Cheojey concluded, "She is drugged. Very powerful drug!"

"Can you get her out of her stupor, Cheojey?"

"No, Lasker-la, I haven't got my elixirs. But she will come out of it in an hour or two."

"Can she travel?"

"Oh, yes. I strongly suggest it. But let us find some warm clothes for her first."

Dressing Dorjee was like dressing a rag doll. Lasker rounded up some soft, red-leather monk boots, and he threw Dorjee on the bed and pulled the boots on, then got one of her chubas on over the gown, meeting no resistance but getting no help. Dorjee's blank almond eyes occasionally blinked; that was all. Her high cheekbones were red from the cold, and he noted for the first time several small dots on her aquiline nose. Dorjee's well-remembered smooth light-mocha complexion was also dotted with small almost imperceptible red specks.

"Cheojey," Lasker asked with alarm, "what's wrong with her face? See those red spots?"

"It is just a mild drug reaction; it will go away, Lasker-la. Just a strong numbing potion. Now hurry. We haven't much time."

There was indeed shouting and running footsteps below them on the secret staircase.

Lifting Dorjee into his arms, Lasker took the lead as his party rushed out of the room. They went to the staircase outside the cupola room and heard pounding footfalls below. More goddamned Chinese, no doubt!

"Quickly, then, up to the roof," Cheojey implored.

"The roof?" Lasker exclaimed. "What good will that be! We can't fly."

"There is often a ladder from a high roof of a monastery to a side building's roof."

Lasker didn't have any better ideas. They hastened up the windswept stairs toward the roof of the monastery.

They burst through an open door into the brilliant sunlight. Indeed, they were out on the highest roof of the temple; the view was spectacular of mountains far away and the reddish-hued valley below.

"What now?" Lasker noticed the others—especially Rinchen—made efforts to not be close to him. No wonder, after how he had acted.

"This way, Lasker," Cheojey was leading them toward the low wall to the side of the roof in search of a ladder exit.

As Lasker bounced along, carrying Dorjee in his arms, Dorjee started to smile, saying, "How—lovely the sunshine is!" She began making little cooing noises, totally oblivious of the terrible danger they were in, taking it all for granted.

They came to the side wall and saw a sheer drop of a hundred feet to the adjoining building's roof.

"What do we do? There's no ladder," Thubten said.

Lasker noticed Thubten was holding his left shoulder. Redness leaked between his fingers. Blood. Thubten was badly wounded from the shots in the mirror maze. Lasker's eyes swept the approximately hundred by hundred foot flat roof they were on. "Look! There's a raised wooden platform on the other side of this roof. It has some poles or—"

"Large kites!" Cheojey exclaimed. "Festival kites. We can maybe borrow their ropes for our descent!"

As they rushed toward the kite platform, there were flashes on the hills all around the monastery and then the booming reports of those flashes. "Artillery!" Tsering lamented. "It is the Chinese opening fire on the monastery!"

In a second or two they all knew the targets. The whistling Chinese shells streaked out toward the base of the cliff the monastery was seated upon. Lasker realized that they were firing at the hermit holes below them!

"The Chinese must be shooting at Mahaka monks escaping through the tunnels," Cheojey said. "Poor souls! And it was I that directed them to the hermit tunnels!"

"Nothing we can do about it," Rinchen snapped. "Let's get the ropes off the kites." They reached the wooden platform, climbed up the three steps and saw the elaborately decorated box-kites, and the heavy coils of ropes wound around four stanchions.

"Enough rope to lower all of us!" Rinchen exclaimed, pulling out his sword to cut the kites free of the ropes.

"Stop, Rinchen," Lasker shouted. "What happens when we get to the lower roof?" Lasker asked. "I saw no roof door. Without a way to unhitch the rope and use it again, we will be stranded, sitting there ready to be pounced upon."

"And even," Tsering added, "if we make it down

to the next roof and through the building, and get the tunnel door open, the Chinese are shelling the exit from the tunnel!"

"No good," Lasker agreed. "We have to find another way."

Something was ticking at the back of Lasker's mind as Rinchen poised his big blade over the ropes attached to the elaborate heavy-framed kites. What was it about the kites?

"Cheojey! The figures drawn on the kites—what are they?" Lasker demanded.

"Why ask such dumb questions now, Lasker?" Rinchen complained. "Put down your Dorjee and come help me cut and coil up this rope!"

Cheojey gasped, "No, Rinchen—Lasker is right. He remembers the naga's prediction that our safety depended upon looking to the Dakinis. The pictures painted on the kites are Dakinis!"

"Do you suppose," Lasker asked, "that we could get inside them and fly?"

"It is remotely possible, yes!" Cheojey said excitedly. "Sometimes I've seen monks in the great prayer festivals ride this type of Dakini kite up into the sky. But always tethered, and not very high."

"What the hell are you two slavering about," Rinchen complained. "Here, give me a hand, Thubten, Tsering!"

Evidently the big man had decided Lasker was Lasker again.

"No, Rinchen." Lasker ran his hands along the first eight-foot-high kite. It was heavy canvas cloth, and the stays were bronze piping, not wood. "Don't damage the ropes, Rinchen," he implored. "Listen to what I have to say!"

Rinchen threw up his hands. "Tell me quick!"

Lasker told, "Cheojey had a vision. A naga spirit told him that when we are in danger at Mahaka, we must look to the Dakinis to save us. These kites, I am sure, are those Dakinis. A way to save ourselves."

"Good, then the ropes are going to save us," Rinchen snapped.

"No, Rinchen," Cheojey said. "I remember the exact prediction. The Dakinis will raise us out of our problems! That's what the naga spirit said to me."

"Do you mean—how can a kite—" Rinchen stopped in mid-sentence. "Oh, no," he gasped. "You can't mean that we should fly?"

"Oh, yes," insisted Cheojey. "The kites are solidly built, there are even stirrups inside the lower frame to place one's feet."

"And there is a good wind rising," Thubten said, looking up at the shadows of dark clouds crossing the sun's disk. "The kites will fly! But I will not. I will launch you all!"

"No way! What if we get up into the sky? How do we escape?" Rinchen insisted.

Lasker said, "When we are high enough, Thubten cuts the lines, and we sail over the Chinese, across the valley, on the wind."

"You're mad!"

"Mad or not, Rinchen, it's your only chance!" Thubten demanded. "Now hurry while your friend Thubten has the strength."

"No."

"Yes, do it!" Thubten insisted. Grimacing in pain he said, "I know I can't make it any farther. I— lost—blood. I will stay here, and I will launch you! Now go!"

Chapter 32

"We can't leave without you, Thubten," Tsering insisted, joining Rinchen in objecting to Thubten's brave offer.

"No. You must go. Carry on the great independence fight for me." A half smile crossed Thubten's lips. "Cheojey will take my pulse now. And I know what he will find!"

Cheojey took Thubten's right wrist and played his fingertips over the veins. He looked greatly troubled. His lips twitched.

"It is the death pulse," Thubten stated flatly.

Cheojey nodded, looking very sad.

"Then let me die for something good, something worthwhile," Thubten said. "Let me die for my friends."

"Do as he says," Tsering said. "Now!"

Rinchen didn't budge, but Cheojey stepped up to the smallest kite. "I'm going to fly," he said determinedly. "I've never flown before—but our friend Lasker has. He knows how to fly, so he will go first and show us; there will be no problem."

Lasker groaned inwardly, but said, "Right!" He

adjusted Dorjee in his arms; she looked lovingly up at him, eyes dilated.

It was like a dream—the sky—the kites. Sheer fancy. Flying a twin engine Vickers with three hundred horse per engine was a lot different than jumping off a Tibetan monastery's roof in a canvas kite. No matter whose picture was on it.

There were shouts below them now on the stairs. The enemy was coming.

Blood trickled from the edge of Thubten's lip. "Yes—now!"

"The kites will take us to freedom," Cheojey said. "Get in, Rinchen! Lasker take the biggest kite with Dorjee."

Lasker found that he could fit into the contraption by holding Dorjee by the waist tightly. He felt some sharp object in a corner of the kite, low and near the foot-support bars. It was a stick of some sort. He moved it with his right foot and found that it changed the angle of the fabric panels slightly.

Dorjee looked at him, her nose rubbed against his eskimo style, and she said, "We go fly?"

"Yes. We go fly. Dorjee, step on the bar below your feet; stand there; hold me tight!"

She smiled. "We go someplace nice?"

Lasker was kind of glad she was out of it. How could he tell her that what they were about to do would more than likely kill them both!

Rinchen had reluctantly crawled through the opening between the upper and lower fabric panels on the second large kite and taken his place on the bronze foot bar. "I don't believe it will work," he shouted. "I am too heavy."

The wind was building and building now; lightning flashed and thunder rumbled. A sudden gust of wind brought golfball-like hailstones falling down upon them.

Even with Rinchen's weight in it, his kite lifted off the roof a foot or two, restrained only by its heavy coil of rope.

Cheojey and Tsering each got into the smaller two kites. Thubten shoved free the release on the coils of Lasker's kite's heavy rope. Then he pushed Lasker's kite along the platform and gave a shove—pushing them over the edge.

Lasker shouted, "Oh, shit!" as the kite he and Dorjee were compressed into dropped like a rock for fifty feet straight down, before suddenly being caught by the wind and snapping to the side . . . and then climbing!

"Goodbye my friends," Thubten yelled. "Give my regards to the sky guardians."

Thubten expertly guided first Lasker's kite, then the kites of Rinchen, Tsering, and Cheojey to a good take-off.

The kites waffled and wavered up on the icy wind.

Lasker's heart was in his throat. The kites climbed into the thundering darkness above, tossing and pitching wildly, but not losing altitude.

Lasker maneuvered the control stick carefully and succeeded in moving to the right and left, up and down.

"Dorjee," he said, his words barely audible in the wind, "I can control the kite."

"Yes." She smiled warmly. "Make love to me! Yes." She started kissing him, all over his cheeks and on his lips.

"Not now, Dorjee! Not now!"

Lasker thought he heard Rinchen. He was shouting out the world's loudest "Ommmmmm!"

Lasker managed to see the other kites through the slits in the fabric. His kite was out front, above the others. He saw Thubten running from one coil of rope to the other on the roof platform, freeing or holding back on the various taut ropes.

And Bart saw something else—a horde of Chinese rushing out of the monastery's stairwell, heading toward Thubten.

The heroic Thubten saw them, too, and he immediately took up his sword and hacked each of the kite ropes in half. Lasker saw the Tibetan give a quick wave of goodbye, then turn to face the overwhelming enemy. Lasker had no time for more observation even if he could stand it, for his kite, suddenly cut free of its ropes, flip-flopped wildly in the wind.

He managed to steady it and looked back and gasped. He was thousands of feet higher, and climbing! From the valley below, tracer bullets flew up into the air toward his kite, but the kite was not an easy target, weaving as it did.

Lasker saw another kite zip by him. Cheojey shouted, waved and then sailed onward.

They were all up there, all four kites rushing through the stormy sky like mad condors! Lasker felt an odd sensation of invincibility. He was flying he knew not where, with little chance of surviving a

233

landing, yet he felt elated, even when he heard the hiss of the tracer shells exploding like death's fireflies all around his kite.

He looked back at the monastery in the distance. Am I really here, he thought, or is it a dream? When suddenly he came within feet of hitting into Cheojey's kite, he expertly maneuvered the stick. For an instant he saw Cheojey's startled face, and then it was lost to the roiling clouds. He and Dorjee rocketed onward.

They slid on the current of the icy wind, faster and faster over the Red Mud Valley, and then over a series of grey hills to the west. Lasker could soon see the silvery thread of a river ahead between moving layers of clouds.

"Might as well get wet," he said. "It's softer in water than rock, Dorjee, and we've got to get down!"

He started to maneuver the stick and shift their weight to try to bring the kite slowly lower.

Chapter 33

Lasker managed to steer the kite by shifting their combined weight and using the bronze lever. He was coming down at about one hundred feet per second toward the valley with the sinuous silver river in it. The valley was heavily treed, but if he could get over the water, there might be a slim chance to land and not kill them both! The trick, Bart figured, was to come in fast and low over the water, horizontally, then sweep up and twist the kite so that they'd come down with no forward motion. A fine theory, but to put it in practice was another matter!

Problem: The wind was now shifting, as the storm dissipated, and was sweeping them away from the river a thousand feet below. Lasker managed to change the kite's direction back toward the water, and then, when they accomplished a stomach-wrenching nine hundred foot descent, they put the kite into a sudden vertical twist.

The change in direction carried them up and directly against the wind, cutting their speed to zero. They dropped like a huge rock into the icy silver waters. The shock of hitting the water was not as bad as its temperature! It was deep, and cold, and really moving, like most rivers in Tibet.

They submerged, but he held on to Dorjee and managed to surface with her still clutched to him, half out of the kite.

"Stop struggling!"

"I can't. My foot—" Dorjee shouted, "is caught!"

The look of alarm on Dorjee's face, and her loud cry, convinced Bart that she was out of her stupor. The icy water had brought her to her senses!

He stuck his head under water and saw her ankle was wrapped in the canvas, and with a tug, he broke it free. Then Bart grabbed onto Dorjee lifeguard-style and swam diagonally, not fighting the flow, through the swift cold waters toward shore.

"You okay?" He rubbed Dorjee.

She whispered, "So cold."

They were sitting, drenched, on the gravel shore of the rapids, pressed against one another, their hearts still racing. It still rained torrents, but no hail.

Suddenly there was an unearthly scream overhead. It was the voice of a banshee—and yet familiar!

"It's Rinchen!" Lasker exclaimed, as he looked up into the clouded sky to see the red Dakini kite of Rinchen as it rocketed by.

"Twist into the wind—over the water, Rinchen!"

Lasker didn't know if Rinchen heard him, or if the same thought had occurred to him. In any case, he saw Rinchen make an attempt at the same maneuver Lasker had done. He partially succeeded, but Rinchen was a lot higher when he twisted.

Lasker watched in horror as the big man's kite fell like a meteor for fifty feet, smashing into the waters. He had hit the river near the far shore—head first!

Lasker girded himself to jump in again, despite the cold, and swim to save Rinchen. Then he saw the Tibetan strongman come up, splashing wildly, making tremendous breast strokes to reach the other shore. Lasker watched Rinchen make land. The big guy even waved, after crawling up on the shore.

"Look," Dorjee said, "there's two more kites!"

Lasker searched the sky. The kites were there, high up, swirling back and forth like separate parts of a disassembled dragon. As the last of the storm winds subsided and a bit of bright sun peered from behind a towering cloud bank, the kites lost speed. They fluttered downward, their wild permutations back and forth, keeping them from a more rapid fall. Neither man had found the controls—or did but used them wrong. Good.

Both kites hit the beach one hundred yards down from Lasker and Dorjee, and Cheojey and Tsering tumbled out.

"Some ride!" Cheojey said as Lasker's strong arms helped him get up. For the first time in Lasker's memory, Cheojey was not at all cheery. He wore a sour expression.

"Are either of you hurt?" Lasker asked with concern, as Dorjee caught up to them.

"No," Cheojey stated, emphatically, "but flying does not agree with me!"

"Never again," Tsering said, really low.

All of their clothes dried within minutes. At

Tibet's altitude, there was no need to take them off. But it was now mere hours before sunset. They would have to make a shelter immediately—a fire.

And what of Rinchen, safe, but on the other side of the river? That question was answered forthwith, as the huge Tibetan crashed ashore one hundred yards farther along on a pair of tree trunks lashed together with vines. Rinchen's make-shift raft!

For a quick shelter, they bent down the lower branches of a conifer tree and secured them with heavy stones. Then they covered the quick-house with torn up tree branches of a wide-leafed tree. As Rinchen started fashioning arrows and a rudimentary bow, Lasker patched the holes from the shelter's inside, leaving enough space for the smoke of a fire to rise in the center. No one said a word about Thubten, just kept busy.

Cheojey's flint pack was the only one dry enough to start the fire in a pile of small twigs and pine needles. In its soon-emerging heat and cheer, they all huddled together in the small shelter. Dorjee stopped shivering.

Rinchen, Tsering and Cheojey, after absorbing quite a bit of the warmth, crawled out to get some air and reconnoiter. Bart and Dorjee were left alone in their snug place. In the red light of the small fire, they held one another and kissed.

Dorjee said, "What manner of man are you now, Bart? I have heard wild stories at Mahaka. Stories about your exploits as the Mystic Rebel. Your hair is streaked with white, and your eyes are different, as if they had stared into another world. What has

238

happened to you since I last saw you?"

"I am the same man," he said. "The man who loves you. Do not be frightened by the stories."

"I am just a bit frightened by you," she admitted, biting her lip. "And in awe of you. How can you do these things? How is it that we are alive? What happened to enable these wonders?"

Bart told her in brief what happened in the Bonpo Monastery—where his abductors had taken him. How he had been partly transformed into Raspahloh—and how her prayers had saved him.

Bart spoke of his arduous trek to India with the wish-fulfilling gems he stole from the Bonpo.

"You saw His Holiness?" she asked. Evidently that was more impressive to her than his wild tale of adventure and sorcery and mass slaughter. Or perhaps she thought he was exaggerating, as Tibetan men are frequently wont to do when telling their exploits to their women friends.

"Yes, I saw His Holiness!"

"The Chinese said he was dead," Dorjee explained, "when they invaded the Mahaka. But I am so happy he is still with us; I mean—still in this incarnation." She smiled. "And I am so glad to be with you, my giver of light!"

Bart wanted to make love; right here and now. He started slipping the bone buttons out of the loops on Dorjee's chuba.

"No. Just hold me for now, Bart. The others will soon return. We will wish to be away from their view—so we will be free to love."

"Later, then."

"Yes . . . soon!" she cooed.

239

Chapter 34

The three Tibetans climbed a nearby prominence to see where they were. They returned after a while.

"We are in the Kermeng Valley," Cheojey said. "Our friends will find us, if they can believe we are alive. They must have seen our kite escape."

"And what of the Chinese?" Dorjee asked. "Won't they find us, too?"

"The Chinese," Tsering said, "will surely think we have died."

"Were it not for the protection of the Great One, expressed through his naga," Cheojey said reverently, "we surely would have died. But our friends will believe. They will come here. We must wait."

Lasker thought now, for the first time since deciding to raid Mahaka, of his ultimate mission. He must get going again toward the Rong-lam obelisk, and then onward to the copper mountain and Padmasambhava's cave.

But his maps and the small amount of climbing equipment and survival gear he had brought along were back with Tseten and the others. He sighed. Nothing to do but follow Cheojey's advice to wait here—and hope the others came to them!

"I will set up a shrine," Cheojey said, "and make *puja*. This will help. The forest lords will guide Tseten to us."

"And I will hunt," Rinchen said. He had already carved out several arrows and fashioned a springy bow from a tree branch. "I need meat."

"No, don't. Instead help me gather the area's abundant food. Tomorrow," Cheojey said, "if you must hunt, do so. Look, already I have gathered a few nutritious tubers. Here." He placed the twisted dry roots before the carniverous Rinchen. "Here is supper!"

Lasker and Dorjee went off together. They ran through the wild-flower strewn fields like children and fell exhausted by a brook in a natural clearing. They leaned against a tree's huge twisting trunk and kissed.

She explained to Bart about her year of hiding at the Mahaka.

"At first," she said, making a garland for his neck while she talked, "there was nothing for me but study and meditation. I hardly saw the monks. You can imagine that a woman guest in a monastery is most unusual. I was apart, living in the gold room as they called the visiting high lama's room. I was treated well, but I was unhappy to be away from you."

"It was a beautiful room, Dorjee."

"Yes. I prayed for you every day Bart—that you were safe and that, if possible, you would return to me."

"I thought of you, prayed for you, too, in India."

She put the flower garland over his neck. "There! Bart." She looked wistfully in his eyes. "Bart?"

"Yes, Dorjee?"

"Make love to me now. It's been so long."

They slipped down onto the bed of deep green grass, and he helped her take off her chuba. Their restricting clothes were quickly and unceremoniously shed, and naked, they merged together.

It was like an electrical storm, the surge of a primeval tide against a welcoming shore. He had almost forgotten. At first, kisses, tentative touches, caresses. Then the passion.

Dorjee's hips rose again and again to meet his thrusts, to keep Bart in her whenever he drew back. Their dance was tentative at first, but soon they felt the rhythm that was the confirmation of their love for one another. They became as musical instruments in perfect time, pouring out a rising wail of celestial music. They became a symphony of motion, as if they had known each other's body for a thousand years.

As Bart moved in and out of Dorjee, shivering in the power of the rising tide of ecstasy, she rocked her head and moaned, muttering the names of diverse gods.

They came together, shuddering in multiple orgasms.

With a sigh of promise fulfilled, she subsided, limp in his arms. They lay there for a long time. Then Dorjee stirred and gently pushed from under him.

Bart rolled on his back, and tried to take her in his arms; but she shifted, and at first confused, now he knew Dorjee was going to do something else.

Her eager lips slid down his body, kissing his chest, his navel, and then moved even lower. As he shuddered and closed his eyes, her lips encompassed his again fully engorged member. Slowly she moved her tongue around, her lips tightened, slipping up and down tightly until Bart groaned and came again.

Life. Pain. The unexpected, longed for pleasure. These were the mysteries Bart thought of as they lay sated, together in the humming field of their love. No answers, just questions. But it didn't seem to matter.

The group of Dakini-kite riders made the most of their keen survival abilities. Fabric from the torn kites was used to patch their bower tent; they gathered the ample berries and nuts and roots and made stews and soups. Vegetarian delight-a-la-Cheojey, who preferred wild vegetables to any and all other foods anyway.

Rinchen looked unhappy with the fare and started fashioning a larger, deer-killing bow and arrow.

There was nothing to do but wait for the other Snow Lions. Seeking a constant privacy, Lasker and Dorjee made their own bower-and-stone home away from the others; and lived in it. A day and night passed; another. They took brief expeditions this way and that in the virgin woods, whose animals, rarely having seen a human being, came close, unafraid. Once they heard a whoosh then wild curses and a heavy thrashing through the under-brush. It was Rinchen. He had missed a three-point buck with his primitive arrow and cursed a blue streak as he retrieved the arrow from the tree trunk and plunged on into the woods. They almost wished he would continue to miss.

She made more flower garlands for Bart and herself, and they often sat by the river and spoke softly of their hoped-for future life together, especially at dusk.

Somehow, Bart and Dorjee knew that these future-together plans were fantasies; that fate would part them again for a long time—or forever. They therefore made the most of these halcyon sunny days.

Dorjee bathed Bart's many small wounds in the crystal waters; they made love many times. Before Dorjee, Bart realized, lovemaking had always been indoors. This was freer. More—natural.

"I will pray to the gods that this evil side of you—Raspahloh—will disappear," she promised, long after they had discussed the Bonpo-created problems Bart had.

"Don't be too hasty," Bart responded. "Raspahloh's power has come in handy. Pray that he makes friends with me, and aids me."

"I don't want to share you. But—if you—it's all too odd. You will make peace with him?" she queried.

"I suppose so," Lasker said. "It's hard to imagine either of us will accept the other."

"I will pray that you both are united in defense of the dharma. What you want I want."

Rinchen in all his hunts had managed to bag just

one rabbit. That was all. He was upset when, after he cooked it on a spit, no one wanted a bite. Even Lasker had firmly adopted the Tibetan abhorrence for eating any small sentient being.

Rinchen snorted out, "Bah, when I bag a deer, you will ask for venison! I shall eat my poor catch by myself."

Cheojey said, "No, Rinchen. No more hunting. We gather vegetables—wild roots. We do not kill—especially small animals. Bad enough to kill a large one and share with many."

"Gather the greens if you wish," said Rinchen, "but I, for one, am tired of grass and roots, Cheojey. I go to hunt!"

Another day passed: clear cool weather; cold nights. Surly Rinchen's rudimentary bow and arrows failed to produce more meat for his stomach. Grumpily, the lantern-jawed Tibetan rebel suffered with Cheojey's root stew.

As they ate their tenth or eleventh meager meal together, Rinchen suddenly said, "Shhh." The big man crept outside their bower shelter and put his left ear to the ground. Then he sniffed the air.

"What is it?" Tsering asked in a hushed tone.

Rinchen got up on his haunches and said, "Someone's coming—a party of men on horseback."

"Where are they?" Lasker asked.

"They are coming from the west—about a hundred yards away from us—in the forest. The hoofbeats grow louder, and that means they are headed this way."

Lasker had a sinking feeling in his gut, for if it were a Chinese horse patrol, the party had little defense. No guns at all. Sizing it up: Tsering and Rinchen had their knives yet, and then there was Rinchen's bow and arrows. A pretty meager defense.

Rinchen took his knife and from his scabbard and said, "I will go have a look."

"No, I will—" Tsering started to say, but Rinchen was already off, running in a low crouch toward the pine trees.

Soon all of them could hear what Rinchen's keen ears had detected earlier—the hoofbeats of about a half-dozen riders.

"They are Tibetan shod horses," Cheojey said, tension leaving his features. "I think we will live after all."

True enough to Cheojey's words, Rinchen came back out of the trees, running and shouting, "Come out! It's Tseten, Rolwag, and our other friends! They have found us after all!"

There was a lot of hugging and back slapping—a gleeful reunion marred only by Tseten and the others learning of Thubten's death. Tseten reported there were no Chinese around.

Then they sat around in the clearing and built a large campfire. They shared the chang that the arriving party had brought, and generous bowls of tsampa, laced with strips of venison. Tseten explained that they had shot the deer on the trek to find the kite escapees, and welcomed dimunition of that karmic stain by sharing the meat with all.

Rinchen, alone, consumed an enormous amount of the barrel of chang and half their store of deer meat. He said, "Flying makes one hungry!"

Rinchen, once he had downed more than a few changs, was vehement and expansive. He explained how he had "personally" killed "hundreds" of Chinese, and how, once his "raiders" were trapped on the monastery roof, he had managed to convince the others to take the deadly gamble of riding the Dakini kites to safety.

The rebels gathered around the "Lone Ranger of Tibet," as each felt his bicep muscles and dutifully observed the torn frames of the kites that Rinchen showed them.

Dorjee whispered to Lasker, as this was going on, "Rinchen is in good form today—exaggerating! Or was it really like that?"

"It is far more interesting a tale the way this big fellow tells it," Lasker lied. "The Chinese didn't give us much trouble."

Lasker managed to cut into Rinchen's dialogue long enough to make sure the lug acknowledged Thubten's part in the escape.

Tseten, once he had heard of Thubten's sacrifice, said, "Thubten died well. A good death in defense of friends."

"Greater love hath no man," Lasker muttered.

"Well, then why so gloomy?" Rinchen bellowed. "Let us toast brave Thubten the way he would have toasted us if we had died. And hope we die as bravely!"

Lasker and the others raised cups high over their heads—in the Far East, one does not toast half-heartedly. They quickly finished off the huge containers of chang that the Snow Lions had bought at the Red Mud Valley's inn. Then it was time to knock off for the night.

Once Rinchen lay down to sleep it off, Lasker drew Tseten aside and asked, "What of the monastery? Did the Chinese shell it?"

"No, I have good news. The Mahaka monks are back in their monastery. Some had made their way to the local government office. Ming Anh, the Chinese general of this province, is not as bad as many. Because this particular officer once had a vision in the monastery."

"A vision? What sort of vision?"

"They say an ancestor of the general appeared to him and warned him not to harm the Mahaka. In any case, Ming told the monks that the siege and occupation for the monastery had not been cleared with him. And that the besieger—Major Trang— had probably acted for a foreign reactionary influence!

"We ourselves have knowledge from underground sources in Lhasa that Trang was suspected of being more in allegiance with the disgraced Tse Ling than with the Beijing regime."

"Tse Ling? Yes," Lasker said. "I have heard she made it out of Tibet and joined up with the head of an international crime organization run by a Dr. Woo in Hong Kong." In his mind flashed a picture of Tse Ling, naked, desiring him—or was it Raspahloh whom she had desired. "So the whole siege of Mahaka was Tse Ling's operation!" Lasker looked sad. "Then I suspect it was all done to capture me. Dr. Woo and Tse Ling, too, evidently want me dead more than anything."

"Why?"

"For what I did to his nuclear operation here in Tibet. And I have caused you to lose a friend again," Lasker lamented.

"No. You have again helped us rise in defense of our country—and triumph. The world will soon hear how a few rebels defeated a whole company of Chinese."

"The Mahaka Monastery's leader, Kongtril Rimpoche, was killed by the Chinese. My fault!"

"Rimpoches don't die. The monks are back where they belong. They await the reincarnation of their great Kongtril Rimpoche."

Tsering came out to join the conversation, and they got onto another matter. "Dorjee must not go back," Tsering stated. "This General Ming now knows of her, and he would wish to seize Dorjee and question her."

"Then," Lasker said, "we must think of an alternative place for her."

In the twilight Lasker and the two rebels walked for a while along the dark waters without words.

"You know Dorjee will not agree to leaving Tibet," Lasker said finally. "Besides, I doubt I could get her out. In any case, I must leave her with you for now, and go on to find Padmasambhava's cave. I hope you have the maps and my gear, Tseten!"

"Rest assured Lasker-la," Tseten said, putting his arm over Lasker's shoulder. "I have safe guarded your things as if they were my own. I know the importance of what you are seeking. If His Holiness the Dalai Lama requested, then you must get on. As for Dorjee, I believe we can leave her at her cousin's village—Kemming. It is about a hundred li southwest of here, and not too far off our way back to Yarang."

When Dorjee heard from Lasker about his plan to split away from the group she protested, "I want to be with you, Bart. We can't part again so soon!"

"This must be, Dorjee, for now," Lasker said sadly. "Wait for me in Kemming, I will come back to you."

Chapter 35

Tse Ling was awakened at five A.M. by her maid servant shaking her. She was about to slap Ming Star, for Tse Ling had told her never to awaken her so early. But before she could strike, the girl said, "Mistress! A call from Dr. Woo!"

Tse Ling slipped on her blue silk dressing gown, and without bothering with tying the belt, she rushed to the jadeite scramble phone in the living room.

It wasn't Woo himself on the line, but his personal secretary. Tse Ling was told that Dr. Woo wanted her at the mansion in a half hour.

That was barely enough time to throw something on and have her driver take her to the private tram, but she said, "I will be there," and hung up.

While she was on the phone, Ming Star had laid out an outfit for Tse Ling in the dressing room.

The imperious Chinese beauty, upon seeing the selection snapped, "Not a dark dress, you fool!" She slapped Ming Star and went to the wardrobe herself and pulled out a light peach cheong-som slit to the upper thigh.

"But the temperature is—" Ming Star began.

"I don't care. Here, help me zip up."

Tse Ling, once dressed and having dabbed on a bit of mascara, rushed to her private elevator and dropped the seventy stories to garage level. She surprised the dozing morning chauffeur, Andre. She snapped, "Take me to Victoria Peak—the tram to Palms mansion, with haste." She got in the rear door and slammed it. Andre started the engine and roared up the ramp into the cool fall morning's harsh light. Tse Ling lit up a pink gold-tipped cigarette and watched the streets slide by. Furious, she exhaled, then snapped, "Too slow! Do you want this job or not?"

Andre nodded, and the black limo's wheels screeched as he shot through a red light before it changed, horn blaring. He drove as if his life depended upon beating all records.

By the time they got to the peak, there were sirens closing in from behind.

Tse Ling opened the door herself and got in the tram as a pair of motorcycle policemen arrived. She watched them stride up to Andre, guns levelled as the tram started to ascend.

Four minutes later, not a minute late, Tse Ling was shown into Dr. Woo's office.

The head of the world's largest and most secret crime organization sat behind the broad mahogany desk facing the floor-to-ceiling window. She heard a slurping noise. Was Woo drinking something, or was that just his labored breathing?

The chair swivelled to face her, and Tse Ling was not happy that there was no screen to hide her employer's hideous disfigurement. The crime master's swollen right hand put down his glass-strawed drink.

She almost winced, but controlled it. Woo had dispensed with the mask. Between large bandages were squarish patches of what she guessed was transplanted skin on his high cheeks; his lips were swollen purple boils. His eyes were bloodshot and half closed under scarred eyelids. His hair was in patches, as if it were falling out.

Tse Ling eyed a chair to the left of the desk.

When he spoke, spittle drooled down his chin. Woo rattled, "Do not sit down, Tse Ling, you will not be here very long. . . ." He paused. Then he slammed down a swollen fist so hard the desk shook, startling her.

"You have failed me again, Tse Ling!"

"H-how?"

"I just received word from Tibet that Bart Lasker has escaped our trap. He and his friends killed over a hundred of Major Trang's men; Trang himself is dead. His second in command called. I was also informed that the failure was due to your orders to capture Lasker alive. I gave no such order. I wanted him dead!"

"I thought—"

"Wrongly." The radiation-sick man finished for her. He drummed swollen fingers on the desk, staring at her a long time. She took it.

Finally, he said, "I had plans for you, to move you up in the organization. Now . . . I will have to see."

"Could I say a wor—"

"No! Now go, and think over your failure. I shall let you know, Tse Ling, if you will continue in your current position! Perhaps I can find something more fitting for you to do . . . lower down in your organization. All the way down!"

"But"—she blanched—"my side of the Jade Octagon is prostitution. And the bottom—"

"Precisely." He drooled. "Now go, and maybe I will forgive you, maybe not."

She knew enough to say no more and turned and left.

On the tram heading back down, Tse Ling shuddered uncontrollably, smoking cigarette after cigarette. She would run away. No—Woo had all her money under tight control. She'd be penniless. She would be found. There was no way to leave the organization, alive anyway; she knew that. And there was no refusing any post Woo decided to put one in within the organization.

Tears streaming down her face, Tse Ling decided: She would kill herself if she had to be a bar girl. No man would satisfy his lust in her body—ever.

Chapter 36

The reunited Snow Lion rebels broke their Kermeng Valley camp and headed west. They rode toward the last spot delineated on the Tsurphu map—the obelisk at Rong-lam. It was a two-day ride.

When nightfall came, and the aurora flickered its multicolored curtain in the north, they camped in the shadow of a stand of giant pine trees. Lasker sat at the campfire with Tsering and spoke of the things that united them: the adventures they shared, the good times, the bad. "I have grown used to life in Tibet again," Lasker admitted, sipping on the hot boiled Tibetan black tea, thick with yak butter and salt. "I am happy to be with my Tibetan friends, at peace in the beauty of this land. If it were up to me, I would stay with you all, ride with you for the cause."

"But for your karma," the one-eyed rebel leader said softly, staring into the fire, "that would be so. But your karma is that we will have to part again. This is not something we mortals can control."

Lasker said, "I think that is true."

On the afternoon of the second day of the ride

from Kermeng Valley, they came to three ochre barren hills which were clearly delineated on the Tsurphu map. The riders turned to the right on Lasker's call and headed north by northwest coming down a slope into a dry curving arroyo. There they came upon the Rong-lam obelisk.

It wasn't a very spectacular sight. The obelisk was a pitted and wind-scarred structure barely the height of a man, though it was probably at least twice that height buried underground. It was a steep pyramid of black basalt rock. Its surface was carved with many vertical lines of strange writing.

"I have heard of this holy monument," Tsering stated, "but I thought I would never see it. No one knew where it was. I suppose that's best. If anyone did know, it would wind up in a damned Beijing museum."

Cheojey was the first to dismount, curious to see the writings firsthand. He ran his fingers down the obelisk, top to bottom, right to left, peering closely at the writing.

"Can you translate it, Cheojey?" Lasker asked.

"No. I believe it is a very old language. Not Tibetan, not Sanskrit based. I think it is from before we Tibetans were here in these mountains. I cannot understand a word, though I pride myself in a knowledge of ancient tongues."

"Is it Dakini writing?" Tsering asked.

"No," Cheojey stated flatly. "This was written by men, not by holy spirits; I can say that for sure."

"It's not necessary to know what it says," Lasker explained. "The Terton discovery explained it was a marker with directions to the cave of Padmasambhava. The Terton map is based upon those directions, translated in ancient times, when the obelisk could still be read."

Lasker moved his horse over to Tsering, and they clasped their hands around each other's forearms just below the elbow. "From here," Lasker said, "I must go on alone."

"You head north, am I right?" his Tibetan friend inquired. "That will take you into the Taka Matan Desert."

"Yes." Lasker replied gravely.

"Do you know what those words Taka Matan mean, Lasker-la?"

"They're not Tibetan words."

"They are old Mongolian," Tsering stated. "Taka Matan means, 'You enter but don't leave.'"

"I will enter and leave. I will get across it and come back." Lasker tried to sound supremely certain for the benfit of Tsering.

"I know you will. Here," Tsering said, untying his sword and scabbard from his belt. "Take this as a symbol of my confidence. We will wait for you at Kemming for as long as we are able."

"Your sword? I couldn't."

"Take it. Do not refuse the gift of a man of Kham. You wish to insult me? Is my gift unworthy?" Tsering smiled. He had Lasker there. To refuse this sword would be a killing insult. Tsering held it out with both hands, as Tibetans do when they give you something valuable, and Lasker took it. He said nothing, all choked up. He knew the sword had been in Tsering's clan since time immemorial.

Rinchen rode over and said, "Friend, we will wait

for you as long as possible in Kemming. Bring me back a souvenir!" He leaned over and shook forearms. "I will want to drink with you when you come back, and you must tell me the whole story."

Saying farewell to Dorjee was next—and hardest. When Lasker pulled his mount alongside hers, he found Dorjee was holding back tears. But she gave a smile for his benefit. Bart asked her to dismount, and he did as well. They went behind some rock outcroppings, and he kissed her wet cheeks, her lips. "I have to go now, Dorjee. But I'm coming back for you."

Her eyes shined toward his, and she said, "I understand in America they say, 'So long,' not 'Goodbye' when friends are going to meet again. So I will say 'So long.' Come back to me, Bart."

"Yes. I promise."

Cheojey and the others in turn solemnly bade a farewell and good luck to him.

Bart rode off swiftly after that, not looking back as the cry, *"Lha Gyal Lo,"* resounded in the canyon.

There was no Taka Matan Desert at first, just a day's swift travel across a flat plain dotted with plants and brush.

Lasker camped in a beautiful valley, the first landmark on the Tsurphu map. It was every bit as beautiful as the valley that they had landed their kites in. He camped by a quiescent lake and made fortifying Tibetan barley tea, starting the fire with his tinder and flint. He could almost do that as fast as light a western-style match now. Dorjee's face swam on the sparkling waters in the starlight that night.

The next day he travelled along the wide slow river that the Tsurphu map called, enigmatically, "The Dying River." It was the first of ten markers on the Tsurphu map. A flock of white swans—or at least they looked like swans—landed in the still waters. They swam slowly toward some reeds.

The whole scene was tranquility itself—beyond words. He paused just to gaze at the sparkling water and the swans gliding on it. Then Bart heard a ripple of water. From out of the tall reeds, a magnificently crested red swan, much larger than the whites, was swimming to meet them. Bart thought how nice, like some ballet— Until the red swan, close enough to attack, suddenly leapt from the waters. Its razor beak slashed at the lead white swan and tore it to pieces. Then the red swan seemed to swallow its victim whole.

The rest of the white swans had by now flown off screeching madly. So much for beauty and tranquility. Unnerved by the sudden violence, Bart rode away from The Dying River. He knew what the words meant now.

The terrain became rolling hills, and occasionally there were gulleys that his horse had a hard time traversing, for they were full of shifting fragmented shale. Lasker kept his direction by the sun and the small compass. The terrain let up on horse and rider, again becoming a rolling grass plain. One day of hard riding passed, and a second. Bart felt he was making good progress; if his guesstimates were accurate he was nearly halfway from the obelisk to the copper mountain.

On the fourth day out, though, he became anxious. According to his estimates, he should have already seen the next signpost on the road to the cave. But he hadn't. Where were the so-called Balancing Heads? And what were they? He kept on in the direction the map indicated—straight north. And he began to wonder—was it magnetic north or true north indicated on the map?

At dusk, he was greatly relieved to see several bulbous protrusions on the horizon—boulders. Those must be the Balancing Heads. He took up the binoculars and was amazed at what he saw. The boulders, each about fifty feet high, appeared to be carved with faces. One of them, its face turned his way, was outlined in the harsh light of the sunset. A hideous face, fangs and large fierce eyes. He saw the profile of another face with a flattened nose. Surely the others were carved as heads also. There was something familiar about the faces. The heavy-browed eyes and long flat noses. . . .

When he rode closer, he saw that the boulders had three faces, not one. Each gruesome likeness had fanged teeth, and one face out of three had a half-dozen eyes. Lasker recognized the many-eyed version: These were the faces of Yamantalai, the Death god of his Bonpo enemies.

Somehow he sensed that this did not bode well for the rest of his journey. He had been planning to camp here until dawn, but now Bart didn't want to stick around. He remembered the dream-place of the Bonpo and the danger it had posed to him.

The map said these faces were the last signpost

before the Taka Matan Desert itself. Bart decided to ride through the field of boulder faces onward. It was still a half hour until darkness.

Lasker guided his skittish horse between the highest two faces. His mount's hoofbeats echoed between their towering presences. Just as he passed between the two towering heads, which sat atop high tumulus bases, the earth shook. It was an earthquake, Bart realized. Small rocks started to shake loose on the tumulus piles and came skittering his way. Worse, the boulder faces themselves began to wobble. Lasker was nearly thrown from the saddle as the horse, frenzied with fear, reared up, and then bolted. He hung on tight and tried to get the horse to head away from danger.

He whipped his horse savagely with the leather reins, but frightened by the rolling rocks, it made circles between the heads. The earth shaking increased, and the huge Yamantalai heads were unseated, tumbled over and started rolling down the hills that supported them. Rolling down toward Lasker like avenging demons, their cruel features were lit by flashes of red lightning from the cloud-boiling sky.

If ever a rider and horse made speed, it was now. Lasker got the horse pointed north and whipped at it, shouting "Go! Go!" The tumbling Yamantalai heads crushing everything in their path, got closer and closer, bearing down like they wanted to hit Lasker, to crush him like a bug. They even changed course and began to bounce after him, and then they met in a titanic encounter that sent shockwaves for fifty miles.

With less than a yard to spare, Lasker had escaped the clashing heads of death.

The danger was not over, though, for the heads fragmented into a million spearlike shards of granite. Just at that second, the horse stumbled on the loose moraine, throwing Lasker. The horse then was pierced by several of the two-foot-long rock shafts. But its body shielded Lasker from those shards.

Bart crawled away, his ear drums numb from the concussion of the collision, his forehead bleeding, his hands cut. He crawled through a dust-filled world of devastation, as the earthquake slowly subsided.

Slowly the rock powder settled, and he sat on the ground half numb. He couldn't believe it; he was alive. But for how long?

The fading light on the western horizon told the story: Soon it would be night, and cold. Very cold. Perhaps he would live another day, and the following night. But out here in the uncharted Tibetan wilderness, without a horse, there was only death to look forward to. Death by exposure, or starvation, or thirst. A lonely death.

Lasker made his way back to the bloody carcass of the horse and pulled his belongings free. The blanket roll and survival tent were wet to the touch. With warm blood. He could barely see, but there was a moon—a quarter moon's worth of light. He nearly panicked, crawling around looking for his sword. Then he found it, half-buried in rock fragments. Relieved, Lasker limped away from the death site. He got as far away as he could before collapsing. He set up the little tent, crawled into the drying bedroll and lay there thinking, feeling sorry for himself. Despairing. Then he shouted, "No, I will not die. I will go on!"

After a time, exhaustion claimed him.

He awoke coughing out dust, with his hands and feet dead numb. As the sun crawled upward, he jumped up and down on his bedroll, slamming his hands against his body until he could feel tingles in them. He had avoided frostbite!

And now—a walk for survival.

Chapter 37

"Alas poor country afraid to know itself. It cannot be called our mother, but our grave; where nothing but who knows nothing, is once seen to smile; where sighs and groans, and shrieks that rend the air, are made, not mark'd; where violent sorrow seems a modern ecstasy.

The dead man's knell is there scarce ask'd for who; and good men's lives expire before the flowers in their caps, dying or ere they sicken . . ."

—William Shakespeare, *Macbeth*

The land Lasker now traversed was utterly dead—and forboding. It had a blasted, incinerated look, as if hell had poured forth its furies here long ago and said that not a thing shall be alive here again. But something was—Bart Lasker, the Mystic Rebel.

This had to be, he thought, that evil place the hermit had told him about, the ground zero of ancient times, wherein one of the Cultivators' awesome mega-weapons was used. On the Tsurphu map it was called simply the "War Plain." He moved on over a smooth, fused, green glasslike surface. Curious circular stones, perhaps tektites hurled up from their meteoric graves deep under the earth, were everywhere.

How many forlorn miles he traversed, he knew not, but eventually, Lasker saw some vegetation—but the manner of vegetation led Bart almost to prefer the barrenness. There were no regular plants and flowers, but instead foul-smelling pale blastulas, sickly sea-anemone-looking things that clung to twisted fragments of rock. One squirted grey puss, not nectar, when Bart stepped upon it. He couldn't stand the smell of the foul liquid. He scraped his boot off in sand until the substance was worn off.

There was another plant with large red leaves that seemed to attract flies. When these black wasplike things sat down to suck its sticky juice, the leaves instantly snapped closed upon them. It was more rapid than the eye could see, unlike the slow movement of a venus flytrap. More like the snapping jaws of a tiger.

Also, on the gritty dry soil, there were some spiky plants—like cactus. Bart wondered if they were edible or possibly contained water in their swollen stems. His canteens were near empty. He was about to stoop down and cut one stem open when he saw a large, lace-winged, blue dragonfly alight on one of the spiky brown petals. Immediately the spikes snapped into it, piercing the creature, pinning it in place. The swollen stem opened, and the leaf bent to feed the dragonfly in the mouth-like opening. Bart decided that nothing that deadly was worth trying to

265

eat, and moved on.

He finally found grass, then a small bubbling brook. With relief he drank its cool fresh waters and filled the canteen. He soaked a bandanna and tied it around his forehead.

By late afternoon he had reached the first of the Taka Matan's sand dunes. It was a tall job—about a hundred feet high. Lasker climbed it and groaned. He saw an endless series of dunes to the north, fading into misty conical-shaped mountains—the barrier mountains.

How far was it to those mountains? A hundred miles? Two hundred? Again he despaired at the lack of distance indicators on the Terton map. But beyond those conical peaks was the copper mountain.

A spiraling dust devil crawled across the distant dunes. Great! Run into one of those jobs and he'd get sucked up into the stratosphere, but there was nothing to do but head on. There would be water in those mountains—and probably food, too. At least some roots.

The Taka Matan was a small desert, not a Saraha for sure, but big enough for a man on foot.

It was murderous going. His feet and ankles were pitted against the sucking sands. But it wasn't hot, strangely enough. He looked up to see why the sun was dim and saw a double rainbow arcing around its pale disk: diffraction circles caused, no doubt, by windblown sand obscuring its rays.

He walked on and found it increasingly bitter-cold going. He wore his blanket over his parka, his fur hat's flaps down. He had on everything he could wear. Still, his hands and feet became numb despite the exertion.

And what of tonight? The thought dogged his every step.

In the late afternoon he saw something: a caravan, a row of camels and riders. The camels were dromedaries—Asian camels with one hump—the riders and those walking along beside the heavily laden beasts were Mongolian traders. He heard them, though they were yet some distance away: the camels braying and the traders joking amongst themselves; the sound of bells. Bart decided he would risk going to them, for he doubted he could go on much longer. He'd have to hope they wouldn't turn him in to the Chinese—or kill him.

As he rushed forward across the sands, the camels rose up in the air. Everything did. The camels and men broke apart into several thin floating layers suspended in midair, then vanished.

A mirage.

Bart sat down and stared into the sandy distance. A mirage. One with sound yet. He had heard these illusions of the desert were realistic, but who would have believed one could hear them!

He continued up and down the dunes, at the summit of each catching sight of the still distant mountains, evidently not an iota closer. He was exhausted, and he figured he was nowhere near a fifth of the way across the desert. How would he make it?

At dusk, in the cobalt sky, huge Asian black

vultures circled high up. They sensed someone in trouble down here, and were waiting for him to die. That infuriated Lasker. It seemed that their cries were a challenge, that they dared him to go on. And he would.

As the last rays of sun shafted up from the west, Bart sat down to rest. He pulled off his pack which seemed to weigh two tons and took a drink of his precious water. One thing about the cold, it had cut his consumption of liquid. He was startled to see his dim shadow suddenly brighten and move.

He looked up, and a glowing object whooshed by his head. At first he thought it was a white bird, but then another glowing globe flashed past him as swiftly and silently as the first. Then a third flashed by. All glowed and were translucent, like dandelion's floss. His eyes tracked them floating slower and rising. The glowing things were about a foot across, completely circular. They had no substance, were just blue-white lights of no weight. The objects flew in a long slow line toward a nearby sand hummock as if driven on an eddy of the wind. Only there was no wind.

Lasker watched the three lights whizzing around and around the dune's top. Maybe it wasn't a good idea, he thought, but nevertheless he stood up and walked toward them. The objects had a sort of friendly glow that attracted him. Bart thought he heard a hiss in the air, a very low sound, also pleasant.

Bart climbed up the hundred-foot-high dune, stood on its top, and watched the light dance around him, less than ten feet away. There definitely was a soft hiss. Then the lights started coming closer to him, spiralling in. He was drawn to touch one as it swung by at head level.

When he made contact with his right index finger, the object gave off a hissing noise and gave him a mild shock, like static electricity. It changed shape, its blue-white light spreading over his body, suffusing him with its glow, giving its light to him. Lasker was permeated with a pleasant tingly sensation. Then the blue-white light separated from him and reformed as a globe in the air. All three lights shot off toward the distant mountains at incredible speed.

He stood there on the hillock and watched his hand and body glow for a few seconds. Bart wasn't afraid; it hadn't hurt, quite the opposite. Soon the light faded from his body. Only then did he see that his charred sky-object pendant had been restored to its silvery lustre.

Chapter 38

That night was colder than the day, and there was a slight wind; but the survival tent and the sleeping bag sufficed for a night's rest in the midst of the desert.

In the sullen morning, the sun rose higher and higher, but the warmth never came. Again there was a haze of ice particles shielding the Taka Matan from warmth. A wind from the north began to beat against Bart. By noon, it became obvious that with the added agony of the windblown sand, and the temperature dropping, things looked grave. Lasker, exhausted and without food, was going to die. He might not last till the night. Hoping for some shelter, he peered through the binoculars and dimly saw a knob in the endless dunes to the northeast.

Some rocks! He would try to make it that far, take shelter there—a faint hope.

He staggered on for hours, even though it was just a few miles, and finally fell, half blind from sand in his eyes, among the rocks as the sun hung low. Every minute brought a numbing drop in temperature. The boulders were partial cover from the wind, but it was not enough.

Why not die. . . . No! Never. Delusion. Talking to himself. Why not? Why not die?

No.

The crescent moon came out behind a thick veil of icy clouds. Only the brightest stars winked on as the daylight faded. Perhaps this was it, the end of his long road. Better luck next life. . . .

Beyond the boulders there was a low hillock of volcanic slag sticking out from the sands. He crawled onto it, grit eating into his face, his eyes. For what reason he crawled there, he didn't know. No! There was a reason. Perhaps he was delirious, but he saw a glow—a faint glow at the top of the low cinder hill. Bart thought it was an hallucination, but as the sky got darker, the light got brighter.

He sat up and shouted out, "Here! Help me!" He was sure it was a nomad setting a lantern outside his tent for the night. No answer. Was it really there at all?

So what if it wasn't real, it was something to strive for, something to hope for before eternal night closed in on him. He remembered a line by Dylan Thomas: *Rage, rage, against the night.*

The reddish light got brighter and brighter as he crawled up the hill. It beamed upward like a searchlight, only much smaller—could it be a flashlight beam?

"Hello!" he shouted. *"Tashi Delek!"*

No answer!

Blindly Bart tried to push himself up, but he couldn't get to his feet. He settled for crawling, hands and knees again. His hands were raw meat now. They were cut on the slag and the cracks, oozing. Blindly, he scrambled up the last fifty feet to the top of the grit hill with a last burst of effort. Ten feet from the top, the light moved.

"No! Don't go!" he shouted.

Then he realized the light wasn't moving, but rather he was leaning right and left on his weakening arms. He continued slowly upward, upward. An inch was a million cold, cold miles.

Just a little more, a little farther he told his screaming muscles. Then suddenly he crested the hillock, and he was staring down into a five-foot-wide, circular depression—a small volcanic pit. And there it was—the source of the light.

Was it fire? No not a fire. He tried to focus his frozen grit-filled eyeballs on the warming reddish glow. It was undulating in brightness—like hot coals, but more white than red. Had—to—rub his eyes. Pain. Pain. There! He could see!

In the small crater, only a few feet deep, he saw what he had only heard of as legend before. He saw the exquisite five-petalled fire blossom, the rarest flower in the world, unknown anywhere else in the world, except Tibet.

He crawled down into the six-foot-wide crater's warmth, laughing and babbling. The mysterious hot blossom was exuding heat as well as light. Like a stove! Bart crawled in a fetal position bending his icy limbs around the foot-wide blossom, careful not to brush it. It was almost too bright to look at now. The five six-inch-long petals were like those of a mountain laurel blossom.

"So, so beautiful," he cried. He already felt his fingers and toes thawing. He lay thawing, while uttering, "Thank you, thank you . . . the beauty . . . beauty."

This was the fire blossom, the mystic blooming essence of the mysterious underworld, the sacred flower of Shambhala.

Legend told that it bloomed only once every hundred years, the result of a long tuber root sending its flower up hundreds of feet from caves far below the earth. It was a cave plant that pushed just one blossom to the surface to open for only one night, producing radiant heat and light once each century.

A miracle.

In the morning light he awoke to see the blossom was shriveled and turned black, and without light or life. As he leaned forward to touch what was left of it, its dry brittle petals just blew away on the wind—and he cried. He beat the ground and dug for the root, but only found charred dust.

Crying for the beautiful, ephemeral thing that had saved him, Lasker moved on. There had to be a reason. He couldn't die now. But he was so thirsty, so hungry.

It became somewhat warmer, the ice clouds no longer obscuring the life-giving rays. Soon he was able to tie his parka on his backpack again.

He was alive, and somehow he had to go on. Providence, the gods, chance—for whatever reason —had let him go on!

But which way? He was turned around, and where he looked for the mountains, he saw just dark mist where the compass pointed—north—and dunes in the other directions.

The mountains were obviously in the direction of

the mists, or were they? The compass needle started wavering as he stared at it, and then reversed itself! He sighed, closed it up and put it back in his pocket. He'd head toward the black smear on the horizon.

In a half hour the dark mist seemed a lot closer and a lot less like a mist. The wind was again picking up—hot wind, not cold—and he realized that the dark mist had a yellow tinge. It was another sandstorm heading his way! Was there no end to the brutal tricks of the Taka Matan?

The sandstorm hit Bart like a brick wall, toppling him, the grit quickly building a sand hammock over him. He had to keep moving now, for the sand threatened to bury him if he lay still more than a moment.

He despaired, for soon he could barely breathe. Might as well use the last water. Maybe some water . . . maybe. He sat up and opened the canteen, poured the last of his water over his kerchief and tied it around his face so he could suck air through it.

It was dark now because of the sun-obscuring sand cloud, and he staggered on. The wind went on for hours, he fell and crawled like a worm, making a trail like a worm—a mark, he supposed, of his obscurity, his meaninglessness.

"Can't die now?" the wind mocked. "Why not?"

Then he heard a tinkle off in the sand clouds. It sounded like a yak's bell! Was it just some trick of the wind? No, he heard it again. A bell? Was it a bell?

The winds were dying down at last, and he could hear more clearly. He wiped sand from his eyes, peering right and left.

And then the most awful sound—halfway between a bellow of a charging ox and the cry of a Snow Lion—came echoing on the wind.

There was something large and monstrous-shaped coming. A ten-foot-tall, long-necked figure floating toward him over the sands. It became clear.

A camel and a rider. The bell on the camel's neck tinnkled and the camel brayed.

He laughed. Another mirage, the Taka Matan kind—stereo mirage! Nevertheless, Bart stood up and ran forward. "Hey here! Here!" He fell down again. He was trying to intersect the rider's diagonal path. Bart managed to collapse at the camel's feet. Its sheet-wrapped rider jumped down, and Bart felt a dagger placed to his throat. A real dagger. No illusion.

Lasker had no strength to resist. He couldn't and didn't care if he was killed or not. But he was just the tiniest bit curious who this desert traveller was. He rolled over and looked up as the brown cloth was unwrapped from the face.

It was a familiar face! "Tinley?" he breathed out—"is that—you?"

"Lasker-la!" Tinley exclaimed. "I have found you after all!"

Lasker felt the Tibetan youth's copper canteen's lip pressed to his lips and drank warm butter tea. Thirstily. Pieces of burned barley tasted like the finest steak. Food.

It was Tinley, his thirteen-year-old friend and translator from his last time in Tibet.

The boy's dark eyes sparkled, as he told Bart, "It will be all right now, Lasker-la."

"But how—?"

"I will tell you. But let us get comfortable first. I will set up my nomad tent and cook some stew!"

Tinley quickly set up a large nomad tent in the lee of the camel. Tinley, once they had gotten inside, lay Lasker down and dabbed his eyes and mouth clear with ample water. Soon he smelled the cooking of Tibetan stew: yak meat, leeks, some barley. They supped upon the hearty, chunky stew, and Lasker succinctly told his story: the trip from India, the raid on the Mahaka Monastery, and subsequent events. Events all leading to his near death in the desert.

Tinley explained how he had left Dallek after his uncle's death to try to rejoin the Snow Lions. Once in Yarang, the teenager had heard of Lasker's joining Tsering and the band for a raid on the Mahaka from Tenpa, Tsering's wife. He followed, and in Red Mud Valley, Tinley heard garbled versions of the events at Mahaka Monastery. He headed west—the direction the Dakini kites were said to have flown. He came upon a mountain recluse who had seen the Snow Lions and Lasker head from the west to the desert.

At the end of his story, Tinley laughed, his black eyes twinkling. "I found a group of Chinese archaeologists and borrowed one of their pack camels, and I found you. There are, in the camel's pack, lots of tins of pork from China, and all sorts of supplies—even mountaineering gear."

"Tinley, I can't get over your being here. It's another miracle! But you must go back. It is too dangerous."

"You're not going back, are you, Lasker-la? We

276

go on together; it is better and safer for me—and also safer for you, if we go together—"

Lasker said, "No. It will be a hard climb up the copper mountain—if I find it. And then if I do find the cave, there is the Dancing Dead to contend with."

"Are they demons?"

Lasker explained that Losang believed that the Dancing Dead were guardian spirits put in the cave by Padmasambhava's magic to protect the prophet's text against the Bonpo.

"But we are not Bonpo." Tinley smiled. "We will get in!"

Lasker thought it over quickly and decided. "Tinley, go as far as the copper mountain with me. You keep a base camp, tend the camel, and go for help if I'm not back in—say—"

"No. That is ridiculous. I have climbing equipment and much more experience than you, Lasker-la. Remember, too, I am a Sherpa. Born to climb. No matter if I wasn't, it would still be safer to climb with two."

Tinley won the argument on the merit of his reason.

After the storm, they set off together on the camel. Soon they saw signs of vegetation again.

"We're still in the middle of the Taka Matan," Lasker said.

"Then this," Tinley stated, "is possibly an oasis."

"Yes. The map says the desert holds an oasis, 'the place of the tall man with cool water,' whoever that is."

Chapter 39

The rolling dunes gave way to sparse vegetation. The travellers found themselves in a more level area with ankle-high, bluish grass tufts. Small birds and cricketlike insects darted between the clumps of grass. Each low hill their camel surmounted brought new surprises—lusher and lusher growth, and eventually even short palm trees. There was now a humid mist in the air.

"There are hot springs ahead for sure," Tinley said. Bart had the map out, and as the camel undulated along beneath them, he tried to find a spring or waterhole in the Taka Matan.

"There's no place marked 'hot springs' on my map, Tinley."

When they came over the next low rise, they could see a gushing Artesian spring of steaming water surrounded by tall palms. And more spectacularly, there were man-made constructions. Ruins. Odd, spired towers with no sign of openings in them.

"Is it a city, Lasker?"

"It was—a long time ago. What you see are the tops of tall towers, I believe."

They rode down the hill and then between the weathered granite towers. The six-sided buildings all stood at a thirty to forty-five degree slant, as if the earth had changed direction since they were built. Some were partly obscured by thick twisting vines.

As they rode onward toward the hot spring, Bart saw what lay beyond a large structure—a statue.

Only half of the magnificent carving was visible above the ground. The statue was of a noble-looking, elongated man, and also stood at a steep angle to the land around it. Though it could only be seen from the waist up, it was still fifty feet high.

Bart told Tinley, "Get us closer." When the camel rode under the head, Lasker looked up at the greenish granite face, the half-closed eyes, the high cheekbones. And he knew. "It's the statue of a Cultivator!" he exclaimed.

"A what?"

He sighed. "It's a long story, Tinley. The Cultivators are a race that existed a long time ago. Different from mankind."

The statue seemed to be made of the same green stone as the Peaceful Deity's statue in the hermit's cave. But in its forehead there was no diamond, nor any depression where anything had been removed.

"The wonder of it . . ." Lasker muttered. "I'm surprised that such a thing is not on my map."

"The sands shift," Tinley offered. "Perhaps this whole oasis was covered by sand when the map was drawn."

Lasker nodded. "This seems like a good place to camp for the night. If a wind picks up, there's shelter in the lee of these structures."

They camped for the night in the ruined city. It was warm, so they didn't set up a tent. Lasker explored a bit on his own in the brief minutes before dark, while Tinley found a place for the camel to graze. His initial impression that the spired buildings had no openings was confirmed. He was disappointed, having wanted to see inside.

Lasker lay his bedroll down some distance away from Tinley's. Trying, but unable to sleep, he tossed and turned.

Tinley had changed. He had become almost somber, and he hadn't asked Lasker to tell him any stories of America. He was nothing like the cut-up he once knew. What in one year had changed him so?

The question unsatisfied, faded eventually, and tiredness came. Lasker dreamed. He dreamed of the oasis as it had been a long time ago—when the statue was upright, and all around the then-cool spring was not desert, but lush farmland. In this dream he was Master Zun-lan, sitting in the master's lotus pose on an ornate low platform. At Lasker's feet was a young and eager student—the hermit—but not the present day one. It was the hermit in another incarnation.

Even in his dream, Bart had to laugh at the irony of karma. Everyone changes places sooner or later: lover, friend, parent, enemy. And even students and masters become reversed. In this dream memory of ancient times, Lasker was the master; the young hermit was the student.

The instant that Lasker had fallen asleep and begun to dream, Master Zun-lan had awakened and addressed the student before him.

Zun-lan smiled at the student and said, "Xirew, my son, this is a perplexion! I have just had a dream of another world, a vision that was this place, but yet *not*. I believe I saw the future."

"What did you see in the vision, master?" Xirew asked seriously.

"That I will be in this place, in this city, a hundred centuries from now, when all around is sand, when the city is a ruin, half covered up by the desert. When we are all gone, without barely a trace!"

"I don't understand," Xirew said, confusion wrinkling his young brow.

"Neither do I, Xirew," Zun-lan said. "Would you then please go and fetch the oracle."

Shortly thereafter, the oracle came sweeping into the vast windowless room in his long blue robe and gazelle-horn headdress. Upon Zun-lan's request, he lit up his long divination pipe and sucked upon it. He began a circles-and-swirls dance. After a time, the oracle blew the akasa smoke out of his nostrils and stopped dancing. He intoned, "Your vision is correct, master! You will be reborn in the far future. I tell you this: In that time to come, when the world has not a faint trace of our great civilization, your future soul will be in great danger here!"

The oracle came forward. He touched the wet stem of the long pipe to Zun-lan's forehead. The oracle said, "One day I will be a gazelle. Remember this touch in the time to come—and remember to be careful, for there are hidden demons about to strike!"

Lasker, gasping for air, sat bolt upright. He

touched his forehead. There was a wetness, and he remembered his just-now dream of warning.

A sudden noise. He spun to face it and saw a gazelle jump against the bright crescent moon. The moisture on his brow—had the gazelle licked his face?

The gazelle ran between the statue and one of the spires. It disappeared in the darkness.

"What was that?" Tinley cried out.

"Just a gazelle," Lasker said. "It is all right, go back to sleep."

But Lasker didn't sleep. What did the dream mean? Was there danger here? He tried to remember the dream—something about an ancient civilization where he was a high-ranking person. That wasn't the important part. He had a message that there was danger—that there were demons here!

Lasker's eyes searched through the lonely spires. He wanted to cry out to the gazelle, "Don't leave me—I'm so alone."

Eventually he fell asleep, more to escape that awful feeling of loss than from fatigue.

Lasker and Tinley shared the Chinese archaeologist's food and broke camp. The camel complained loudly as the terrain became dunes, steeper and steeper. But now they were within sight of the scrub-covered foothills of the Kumbun Mountains.

A mere three hours later, they were in those steep, sandstone hills, and the going for the camel was impossible.

Lasker and Tinley dismounted. Lasker scanned ahead with the seven by fifties at the tumulus cluttered, twisting gorges and ravines. "We can't climb much farther with the camel."

"What do we do—tether him?" Tinley asked.

"Yes, I suppose we have to. But we may not be back for a while—let him graze."

They unloaded the packs from the camel, and Lasker said, "If he's not here when we come back, we would be in trouble."

"No way back across the desert," Tinley said. "But I have faith, Lasker. Something has always turned up, hasn't it? If we die, we are reborn in the circumstance we created. So there is no problem."

They started half walking, half climbing, up a red sandstone rise. At about two hundred feet, Lasker sat down. He looked back.

"Tinley! The camel is gone!"

They climbed back down. Search as he might, Lasker could see no sign of the camel. "We have to find it." He scanned the distance. "God, where could he have gone?" he muttered.

Lasker and Tinley followed the footprints until Lasker saw the ancient bones half hidden in the sand: a ribcage, a long neck, cloven hoofs scarred by wind and worms. A sense of fear. Was it a camel's bones?

"Tinley," he said, "do you suppose this is our camel? Weird things have happened out here."

"No"—Tinley smiled—"the bones are not a camel's at all. A horse perhaps. How could it have died, decayed, all that?" Tinley laughed. "You don't know camels, Lasker-la, they are very superstitious. My guess is that the camel saw the bones and took off—"

"Maybe . . ." Lasker said, "but we passed this

way, and I swear these bones weren't here."

"They were probably an inch under the sand, and as we climbed, the wind picked up a bit, cleared the bones . . ."

"Yeah," Lasker said, not convinced that something very strange hadn't happened. "I guess we go on."

They again started the climb. The first hours were easy. They got to about five thousand feet above the desert floor and reached the last of the scraggly pine trees.

"Let's keep on going," Lasker said. "At least the camel didn't disappear until after we got all the gear." He was making light of the event, but he didn't like what he was feeling in his gut.

Gazelle . . . gazelle, what did the gazelle signify?

Chapter 40

A day later they were over the foothills and climbing real mountains. There were patches of snow and ice, and the wind howled in their flap-covered ears.

This wasn't the copper mountain. Not yet. It lay—according to the map and to Lasker's vision in the transceiver—beyond this ring of grey granite mountains. The grey mountain they now climbed with ease—it was all a moderate even slope—was one of the copper mountain's encircling rings.

They topped the summit of the prominence with barely the use of a pickax, and Bart beheld his goal for the first time: the mountain, all coppery in the afternoon's slanting light. He scanned it with the binoculars.

He tried to find the hole of Padmasambhava's cave near the summit, but there was nothing but a seemingly solid mass of ice and snow atop the magnificent peak. More summit snow by far than he had seen in the transceiver. The season was getting on.

How the hell could he find the cave if it was buried

by a dozen feet of ice?

Would he have to wait until spring? Impossible!

"Nothing to do but start to climb her," Lasker said with determination.

They crossed the small fir-tree filled valley and made a base camp at nightfall. Mists clouded the view up.

In the bright morning light, Bart stared up at the copper mountain they were about to challenge with trepidation. This close, it seemed unconquerable. He could see the ledges that, in side-light, outlined a crude swastika.

Tinley was as anxious as Bart was to take advantage of the beautiful, windless day to start the climb up the mountain.

It seemed an easy climb at first. They were halfway up by noon; they had barely used their pickaxes, just their boots with the crampons attached. But Lasker knew from what he had seen in the hermit's transceiver that the way from here on was an awesome endeavor. A bitch, as a matter of fact!

As they stopped to rest on a wide ledge that was the first lower bar of the swastika, Lasker used the binoculars to search ahead. After a while he said, "There's not a single way up that has anything approaching a decent access to the summit. Lots of sheer rock!"

"How about circling the mountain?"

"Tinley, it's a long story, but I *know* this is the best way up. I've seen this place."

286

"How? Have you been here?"

"In a . . . vision."

"Then it is a fact," Tinley said, "that you have not seen it. Visions can lie."

"Get out all the equipment, Tinley, this is the hard part."

Lasker went first, Tinley on the rope tether following twenty feet behind. They were soon heading vertically up the stone face, using pickax and hammering pitons into the solid granite. A thousand feet plus to the next ledge. If either of them fell, it would be up to the other to keep a hold of the rope and save his partner. Security. Trust.

They were moving smoothly if slowly upward, and the weather was holding. Bart felt exhilarated, excited, happy. At about eight hundred feet higher, he reached a small ledge and sat down, legs dangling, back resting against the rock face. He was suddenly aware of a problem. Bart's elation wasn't natural; he was hyperventilating from the exertion and extreme altitude. That could make him reckless and dizzy. Or—the worst thing on a climb—it could make him black out.

Bringing all his E-Kung Chi power to bear, Lasker managed to slow his fast breathing and take shallower inhales. That slowly did the trick. By the time Tinley reached the ledge, Bart was clearheaded and able to give a hand-up.

"How are you, Lasker-la?"

"Fine," Lasker said.

"Really?" Tinley looked somewhat skeptical. "Then let us go on. I'll lead this time."

Lasker nodded. The Sherpa boy didn't seem the

least bit winded; perhaps he should lead, like Sherpas always do.

They climbed and climbed, and the wind came. The icy wind howled louder, until it sounded like a pack of wolves in their frozen ears.

Three thousand feet more.

Immediately above them now was what would be the most difficult part—a softer rock face.

Tinley said, "We can't use your equipment on that—it's basalt rock. The pitons will just pull out. We will make hand- and foot-holds with our pickaxes; climb it clean."

Lasker nodded. "Yeah, climb it clean—the old fashioned way."

Tinley started up the sheer face. As Bart listened to the boy chip away at the soft rock, it seemed that all of the trek to the copper mountain might be in vain. They would need an awful lot of luck to get up the crumbly rock surface. An awful lot. Bart felt a bit unsteady, but shook it off.

Tinley made the first of many holds and moved on up. Lasker had the easy part. All he had to do was not let his fingers or feet weaken their hold in the chipped away rock as he followed. Tinley whistled as he worked, keeping to the windward of Lasker so that the scrapings wouldn't fall in his eyes.

Tinley at one point smiled a queer sort of mocking smile back at Bart, as if to ask, "How are you doing?" Lasker had his hands and feet full of rock and was thinking it out—how to get to the next foothold.

He didn't like Tinley's expression. He felt like he knew Tinley wanted him to fall and could almost

288

swear that Tinley's skin was turning green. Well, he's not going to outdo me! I can be just as green. Lasker picked up the pace.

They seated themselves to take off their crampons, which were no longer necessary. Irregular rock staircases—couloirs—were everywhere now. Their only enemies were time and the wind. And, of course, any lack in their abilities, or any altitude sickness.

They traversed the couloirs and were soon on what real climbers call a bench. It was a flat area a hundred yards wide, sloping slightly to the west. Then it fell away steeply to an impassable scree formation. At each side of the bench was a pinnacle about a few hundred feet higher than they were situated. The left one was the one they had mistaken for a spur of the main mountain. They had been wrong. Both were dead ends, sticking up into open air.

"So go back down a thousand feet and start up the other way—toward the south face," Tinley stated carelessly.

Lasker didn't like the kid's patronizing tone. "Right!" Tinley knew his stuff, but he needn't get so smug about it. Who was running this show anyway? Bart fumed, but kept his silence.

Now that they were headed down, Lasker had a good look at the scenery. There was no denying the view was spectacular. He could see the sand dune desert, the ruined city, the bowl valley and even make out the tumbled Yamantalai boulders. It was ridiculously high, too high to look at anything but the place he put his foot next. Lasker tore his eyes away from the distance and got practical. Got to keep up, show Tinley I'm tough!

They got to an open area, set up their ropes and rappelled the thousand feet back down to the second ledge. From there they again inserted wedges and pitons and crawled up naked rock for five hundred feet in the icy wind. They reached a crumbling escarpment that was invisible but a few feet away. It made an ideal place to rest and prepare for the challenge of the southwest face of the copper mountain. Damn! Tinley still wasn't breathing hard, but his own chest was heaving.

Lasker was relieved to see that there was no soft basalt above, just hard granite with those fine lines that meant good places to stick your pitons.

Tinley hardly let him rest, then he said, "Shall we go on?" He again wore that mocking smirk, or so Lasker thought. Maybe not . . . perhaps he was feeling the paranoia that sometimes irrationally comes up on a climb toward those who are better— or more reckless—than you are.

They used to advantage the little cracks, hammering the aluminum wedges and eyelets to anchor themselves well. Once, when Lasker slipped, he jerked the line so violently that one of the eyelets popped out. But the next one held.

Tinley looked back and smiled. "Good equipment." The teenage Sherpa's voice could hardly be heard in the whistling icy wind.

"Yeah," Lasker shouted out, "just keep climbing. Thanks for being glad I didn't fall!"

Two thousand feet to go—straight up.

Much of the rest of the climb was silent and, for

Bart, reflective. On such a climb, one can hear one's own grunts and breathing and the wind, but little else. One becomes aware, as in deep meditation, that each moment is unto itself a lifetime, and that the next moment could be the last.

Tinley, the Sherpa in him showing, got far ahead, and they had more and more line between them.

Lasker was pissed. If Tinley or he fell, the line would jerk too violently for the other to hold on. He shouted and cursed for Tinley to slow down, but either his words were lost on the wind or the bastard didn't give a damn! The boy moved on like a god-damned mountain goat. A demon climber, showing off.

Four hundred feet more?

At last they reached another ledge, an indentation really, just below the ice and snow summit. Tinley had already snapped his crampons back on when Lasker reached it. Tinley reached to help Lasker, who was panting madly.

Lasker said, "No thanks, show off," and managed himself.

There was another fifty feet to the snow cap, and they managed it handily enough. Time to stand. They could now walk up the steep snow slope.

One hundred fifty feet to summit. Who'll get there first? *Me.*

They walked this strange high road on the top of the world as if it were a steep path through an English garden.

Their crampon boots crunched in unison, crunch, crunch. For some reason the sound made Lasker angry.

They'd be on the summit in another few minutes.

Lasker expected Tinley, as was Buddhist custom, to unfurl some piece of cloth, call it a prayer flag and wave it around shouting mantras. But he didn't; he raced forward without a word, heading for a dark smudge in the snow a hundred yards higher. The cave? Lasker still had the binoculars, and he focused the ice-clogged lenses onto the smudge. No, Tinley was heading for a rock outcropping. Stupid Sherpa! Whose the smart one now?

Lasker swung the lenses around and found a circular dark spot. There was the cave!

Chapter 41

Lasker ran toward the darkness, toward the cave of the Dancing Dead.

Suddenly he heard a wind-blown shout: "Heeellllpp!" Tinley was in trouble!

"What is it? Are you hurt?" Lasker spun about and saw Tinley lying down in the snow, thirty yards away, flailing his arms. His hat had come off.

"Help me," the boy shouted.

Lasker started toward the boy. "What happened?"

"I got my foot caught in some roots." Tinley grimaced.

"Roots? Up here?" Lasker was ten yards away.

"Maybe a fissure," Tinley yelled. "Come on—it hurts!"

Lasker crunched up to Tinley and wiped the ice from his eyelashes to examine the boy's trapped ankle.

"What the hell?" Bart exclaimed, seeing the boy's left leg was inside some sort of paper and stick contraption, a thing with red symbols and mantras drawn all over it.

"Someone put that there. That's no fissure."

"It's an animal trap, then," Tinley complained. "Never mind what it is, help me pull my leg out."

"Sure." And then, as Lasker reached for Tinley's leg, he hesitated. The foot was just inside the center of the paper square, not held at all—no steel jaws of death, no animal trap, nothing but flimsy paper and wood.

"What is this—a joke, Tinley?" Bart said angrily. "Pull it out yourself!"

"I'm telling you, I can't! Help me, for god's sake." There was an odd green fire in the Sherpa boy's eyes that Lasker didn't like. Tinley's lips were twisted in a strange grimace.

"Why can't you just lift your leg out?" Bart asked suspiciously.

"Lasker! You're altitude sick. Imagining things. Please, for god's sake, I'm in pain! Help me!" Tinley pleaded.

Lasker studied the trap's weird decorations. The thing looked familiar. Where had he seen this sort of thing before?

"Come on, Lasker-la, just a tug to help me?" The boy's face seemed expanded, swollen. Greener. No hallucination, the boy was green. Lasker stepped back. Where had he seen that paper construction before? Then he remembered!

"This is a paper demon trap," Bart exclaimed. "You yourself showed me one on a hill near Gayarong Pass last year! You told me, Tinley, that they are set up by the yak herders, to trap demons!"

"No! Please, don't be crazy. Help me!"

Lasker stepped another foot backward. "Tinley . . . these traps are harmless except to a demon!"

Tinley began anew to pull mightily on the trapped leg. The paper didn't tear. As he struggled, the boy was . . . changing! Tinley let out a low snarl, like a beast, then slowly began to metamophose into something unhuman. The more he struggled, the more distorted his features became.

Lasker stood in frozen amazement and watched the boy—the thing he had travelled with for days— change. Tinley was becoming a fanged, greenish being with a multitude of hideous green eyes. His hands twisted and deformed into paws with long razor-sharp claws in the place of fingernails. His huge jaws dripped a green slime. The Tinley-thing snarled and lashed out a paw at Lasker's leg. It managed to tear the fabric of his pants before Lasker could jump farther away.

He was Tinley no more; he was a hideous trapped demon! Lasker recognized the monster. It was one of Yamantalai's children, one of the scions of the Lord of Death, worshipped by the Bonpo!

Lasker sat down heavily in the snow and watched the raging demon struggle madly to get itself free. It was a sight to drive a man mad.

Within minutes the cries from hell itself faded, and so did the thing itself. Tinley was rapidly becoming discorporeal, fading, fading. . . . With a final supernatural howl, the demon thing was gone.

Without a trace.

The paper trap fluttered in the wind, undamaged. Its sacred mantras, the demon-dispelling words written upon it, had done their job.

Bart was extremely shaken. He had nearly led the

Bonpo creature to the treasure cave, nearly let the prophesy text of Padmasambhava fall into Bonpo claws.

The sun was a red ball sliding behind the far peaks before Lasker got up again. He picked up his rope and pickax, then staggered on, anxious to be away from this spot. He realized with each cold step how close he had come to being a victim of his own stupidity!

Tinley indeed! How foolish he had been to accept the unlikely encounter with the boy in the desert. To accept Tinley's wild story of following Bart north, stealing a camel, finding him in the vast Taka Matan desert! It had been a Bonpo demon that had found him, and probably it had used the convenient image of Tinley, taken no doubt from his own mind, to fool him! And he was fooled. Like some goddamned idiot!

The sun was giving up its last rays. He was over twenty-two thousand feet up, alone, and it was getting dark and cold. Too cold! The Tinley-thing must have held him in some sort of spell. It was colder than anyone could stand up here! Bart had to find shelter. Now. It was obvious that he would never survive up here on the mountain tonight, and he surely couldn't climb back down in the dark. The chances were, Lasker realized, that the demon had after all done its dirty work. He couldn't bring the Padmasambhava's text to India if he died tonight!

Nothing to do but get to the shadow under the ice hillock and hope it was the cave.

Darkness nearly upon him, he moved on, a mere dot on a white field of ice, atop a mountain in the most remote wilderness in the world, alone.

He could hardly see and wasn't sure if he was heading the right way. So close—but where? Where?

Then he found the round indentation in the snow-pack. His boot touched bare rock, and Lasker plunged with his last strength into a stygian darkness.

Chapter 42

Lasker, his hands, his feet, and his head numb, stumbled and fell face forward in the circular, dark snow tunnel. If this was just a snow tunnel, then this was it. With his last strength, Bart pushed himself up, dragged his frozen body on in the hole and fell six feet or so! A soft landing in a drift of blown snow.

How long Bart lay there, dimly perceiving wind swirls of snow, he didn't know. But at last he came around to a fuller consciousness and realized he was warm.

Rather than freezing to death, he was now too warm. He sat up and listened. Was there some sound besides the wind?

Yes! He heard trickling water; and there was a warm mist in the air. The cave must have a hot Artesian geyser in it. At last, he was in Padmasambhava's cave! Bart stood up. His clothes were damp to the touch; the caked snow on them was melting!

And something else. It was dim, not dark in the cave. He could see. There was some sort of illumination, a subdued bluish light. Radioactivity? If so, he could only hope it wasn't deadly. Leaving his backpack and gear, but taking his sword, he stepped deeper into the cave. There were drawings on the walls—pictographs—and the likeness of a lotus-seated thin man—Padmasambhava's likeness —in red chalk. His foot hit something hard. Bart looked down. There were clay pots with distinctively Peruvian-looking demon figures.

These pots and drawings were the find of the century for an archaeologist! But such artifacts were not what he was after.

Bart moved onward through a narrow twisting tunnel. The winding walls had the same blue glow.

He came out into a thirty-foot-wide chamber that was absolutely barren, and the blue illumination increased as if responding to his presence. Had he tripped some electric-eye-like detection device?

Then he heard shuffling feet.

His heart suddenly felt as if it were pierced by ice.

There—something forming. Greenish. Lasker lifted the sword Tsering had given him.

"Who are you? Come out!" Lasker demanded.

"Don't go in" came a muffled plea, and Bart strained his eyes to see the source of the meek voice. The form was solid now; some small creature from a dream. It was thin and humanoid, with a head a third the size of its thin red-robed body. Its head was green with many round yellow eyes. "Please, don't go in" came its muffled plea again. It seemed harmless enough but—

Bart swished the sword in warning. "Stay back!" He realized the creature was the one he had seen in the Cultivators' telescreen, the one who had struck out at him.

"Who are you?" Lasker squinted in the dark. "What are you?" He took a step forward, threatening it for a reply.

And then there was a hissing and a glow, and the figure with the green head disappeared, replaced by five swirling glowing vapors: blue, white, orange, red, and yellow. They grew in density, forming horrific images: teeth, claws, huge bodies throbbing with energy.

Bart heard an unearthly laugh. *"Hahahahaha-hahaha!"* the ten-eyed blueness cried out. "You have ignored the warning guard, now die!"

"Are you the Dancing Dead?" Lasker asked.

More laughter. "Irrelevant! How dare you defile the sanctuary of Padmasambhava!"

"I am sent by His Holiness."

"Nonsense!" the blue vapor being bellowed. It had a shape not unlike a genie only with claws. "You, the evil Bonpo enemy of Buddhists, would penetrate this cavern to steal the secret of the ages."

"I am not Bonpo!"

"We have searched your mind, your place in the Akashic Record—there is no mistake, intruder. You are Raspahloh, Bonpo assassin, enemy of the world."

"I am Bart Lasker—the Raspahloh part of me—let me explain!"

"No explanation," the hell-vision screeched. "You will die slowly, horribly, and your body will be skinned and spread out on a pole to warn others who would dare defile the sacred cave!" The blueness lunged forward with its curved sword.

Lasker's own weapon, raised in response, clanged

against it. Sparks flew.

The monster backed off and snarled out, "So? You have the sword of a Tibetan warrior, with magic mantra on its edge. How clever of you to steal such a thing! But no matter, you die anyway; only slowly, more horrible!"

Lasker beheld his opponents. It didn't look good, or fair. One human versus so many monsters wielding axes and swords and flaming torches!

The whiteness was a seven-foot-tall massively muscled man-thing in a white robe, carrying a large white metal Wu Shu fighting fan. The blue mist had become a blue-cast ogrelike thing; bald, with tight irridescent blue-fur body, carrying a huge adze.

The yellow vapor had coalesced into a two-headed being as wide as it was tall, swinging a heavy chain with an iron ball on the end. The redness was a red-skinned spiderlike creature with some sort of red-tipped hot metal torches. The orange mist was now an antlike thing with mandibles that opened and shut like steel vises—a crusher. They were all now apparently solid beings with weapons real enough to kill him.

Death five times over.

And as the five horrors confronted him, Lasker felt himself shivering, quaking all over. Not fear—but change. He felt the blood in his body accelerate; Lasker's muscles tensed and swelled—all the signs that he was rapidly becoming Raspahloh. He didn't fight it this time, for all of Lasker's skills as an E-Kung expert would be naught against these hell-beings.

Lasker's body was suffused with the evil Bonpo's

energy, with the demonic desire for blood that propelled Raspahloh against his enemies so effectively. Raspahloh's blood-lust, his highly trained instinct for murderous power, no one could match.

Or at least no earthly enemy could match.

The transformation from Lasker to Raspahloh continued very rapidly unopposed. Lasker felt his mind fading, going somewhere deep inside himself. He was still looking through his own eyes, but what he saw was in a red field of death potential. He was now an observer, not an active participant, and somewhat relieved.

"Ah, so you reveal yourself, Raspahloh," blueness challenged. "No more pretending to be sent by His Holiness, eh? You admit that you are a Bonpo killer sent to steal our prophesy treasure for the glory of your evil priest magicians!"

The voice that came in reply from Lasker's mouth, from lips set in a cruel sneer, was gravelly and loud. "Have it your way, puny thing. Now you face Raspahloh, who can defeat the gods themselves in mortal combat."

The blueness snarled, "Then let us begin, Raspahloh." The uncanny ten-eyed blue vision of hell crouched down. "Enough of your puny humor— and stalling. Fight! The sooner you are defeated, the sooner we eat your corpse." Blueness raised its gigantic sword.

"Why just one of you? Why don't you all come at me?" Raspahloh sneered. "I am up to it!"

"I doubt it! But in any case," growled blueness, "you and I first will have a little contest! I will try your skills first."

The blueness demon came at Raspahloh-Lasker, swishing his sword like a sushi chef after a piece of tuna, screaming a rib-vibrating "Killlll!"

Raspahloh-Lasker barely avoided the blade, throwing his body to the left.

Blueness came on again almost immediately, sweeping the enormous blue-glowing scimitar downward to rend its enemy in half. Raspahloh spun on a dime, using a rapid jerk of his hips to step aside, and grabbed the haft of the sword from the blue hand. Raspahloh pulled the enraged blue demon past him. In less than a thousandth of a second and before the blue thing could turn, Raspahloh plunged his own blade deep into the blue mass's neck. He heard the sound of its massive spine snapping.

The blueness screeched and howled in pain. Twisting, it collapsed to lay twitching on the floor of the cavern, gurgling blue puss.

But another enemy immediately charged at Raspahloh, before he could pull his sword free of the huge body.

Chapter 43

It was the red multi-armed spider thing this time. It wasted no time in coming at Raspahloh. Even before the blue thing fell, redness was upon him, giving no respite, no quarter. As Raspahloh drew his slimy sword from the back of the fallen blue creature and began to turn, redness was already swinging its multitude of flaming torches at him. And one hit.

The searing pain shot through Raspahloh's body, but he had steeled himself the instant the torch hit, driving a force of Chi energy through his veins and circulatory energy channels.

The blow from the red-hot, iron torch rod, which should have burned through his shoulder easily, merely singed the skin.

Using that pain as incentive, Raspahloh drove a steel-hard fist into the multi-rows of teeth of the red spider creature, his mighty blow sending bony sharp pieces up into its brain. Chi power focused with the force of a pile driver!

That took care of redness, which collapsed like a garish puppet with its many strings suddenly severed.

The two-headed yellow thing attacked next, swinging its nunchakulike chain. Raspahloh used his sword as a snag, and as the chain whipped forward with one ball end headed toward his head, Raspahloh ducked. The chain wrapped around his up-pointed blade. Then he had the yellow ogre creature.

Raspahloh pulled it off its feet and delivered the iron torch he had removed from a hand of the red thing into the right skull of the yellow creature, sending its puslike brain matter splashing up into the air. The left head was severed by a follow-up sword slash as it screamed in pain.

Stepping over yellow's crumpled body, lumbered the massive antlike orange creature, its mandibles snapping, its many-toothed jaw drooling a milky substance that Raspahloh in his ancient knowledge knew was a paralyzing liquid. An advantage hard to counter.

The orange thing backed Raspahloh into a wall, then charged forward with its huge bulk. Surprised by the sudden speed of the move, Raspahloh found himself in the grip of the viselike mandibles. They slowly closed around his waist.

He could feel the serrated edges of the mandibles tearing at his skin, and he shoved his mighty palms against the squeezers on either side. Slowly, ever so slowly, Raspahloh, strong man of the ancient world, forced them open, using all the Chi energy he could muster to stave off the liquid oozing from the slavering jaws, numbing him.

There was a sickening snap, and the mandibles were broken. The slavering orange ant creature slumped down to the cavern floor, screeching out a death song.

One opponent left. The white-robed man thing. It came at Raspahloh flashing its metal fighting fan open and shut. It was so fast, like an illusion, that Raspahloh couldn't figure out which one of the dozen images to jab at. They lunged and parried, lightning speed. The fan man was good, amazingly good. An illusionist of death. But he managed, by sheer luck, to deliver a sword thrust under the real fan, while blocking the same with a powerful forearm.

The wound to white thing was not deep enough to kill it. Raspahloh instantly pushed himself back off the metal fan and tumbled into a corner.

The white fan wielder was on him instantaneously, in one leap coming down, intending to rake its clawed feet upon Raspahloh's neck. But Raspahloh rolled away like a barrel, snapped to his feet and threw the sword as the fan thing turned. Anticipating that the white thing would raise his metal fan, blocking the sword, Raspahloh, a microsecond after it was in the air, threw the extra sword! The one he had wrested from the deceased blueness thing on the floor, just that instant!

His sword clanged off the fan shield, but then the second weapon stuck into the white man creature. Inklike blackness poured forth from the white-robed creature's wound, as the Wu Shu fan was lowered too late!

Raspahloh sprang for the kill, grabbing up and swishing his retrieved sword like a steel wind of death, severing the head of the wounded thing.

Raspahloh foolishly thought it was over, then a net fell from above and entangled him in its steel mesh death trap unleashed by an unseen hand.

At the same time the heavily weighted net fell, the blue creature, apparently playing dead all this time, shot forth its arm bearing a poison-tipped spear. The spear went in through the net and pierced the immobile prisoner inside it. But that prisoner was not Raspahloh. It was rather a body—the red spider's body!

"I'm over here," Raspahloh sneered as the blue creature turned, confused. "You speared the body of your friend. An example of my sorcery, until now unnecessary!"

Desperately, the wounded blue thing tried to extricate its spear from the tangle of the web and the body its poisoned barbed end was jammed into. But there was no time to do so.

Raspahloh dove feet first and drove home an E-Kung blow with his feet together. The blue thing's head smashed open and splashed putrescence upward as the skull caved in.

Raspahloh stood alone, triumphant. He had killed them all.

And now he felt the struggle. Lasker, the twentieth century incarnation, wanted to come out.

"No!" Raspahloh refused. "I am in control now. I am in utter possession of this body!"

Raspahloh was determined to take the cave's treasure—the Padmasambhava's text—for the Bonpo cause! He would return triumphant to their fortress aerie on Mt. Kailas with the prophesies that would give the Bonpo renewed power and dominion!

Lasker was struggling mightily for recontrol within himself. But Raspahloh laughed. "No use; it is mine now, this body. I have fought the unearthly powers, I have earned it. Thanks for bringing me here, for giving the Bonpo the power to destroy the Dalai Lama and all he stands for!"

Then there was a stirring all around the cave. And with one look at its cause, Raspahloh felt his triumph turning to sheer fear. A cold fear that he had never known.

All the dead color things were reassembling, all the puss and blood and guts spilled. All the severed heads and arms were crawling back into their places on the hideous bodies!

Now the five guardians of the cavern all stood up, and gathered around, surrounding Raspahloh.

"You—can't be alive—" he insisted.

"We can't be killed," the blue thing said. "Haha-hahahahaha!"

Together the things pressed forward, simply using their combined weight against the frightened Bonpo assassin. They were immune to his mighty blows; they held and knocked Raspahloh down. Then each separated in turn to get a large rock. One rock at a time, they began to pile them upon Raspahloh.

He heard the blue leader say, "The only way to kill a Bonpo warrior magician—pile rocks on him to bind him forever!"

Lasker felt Raspahloh's control fading away. A light going out! Was Raspahloh dying?

Suddenly, it was just Lasker, and the pain. He—couldn't—breathe! No wonder Raspahloh had left. Too—much—pain!

One last desperate hope: Maybe he could raise the visualization, the image to produce his Yidam, as the hermit had taught.

But Bart was scarcely breathing now, the weight of a thousand pounds upon him. His instinctive E-Kung Chi energy shield was the only thing that prevented him from being crushed. But he could not move.

He tried to conjure up the image of his Yidam, the way the hermit had taught him. But the pain was interfering, the awful lack of air. Rock after huge rock was slowly crushing him.

Summoning all his power of mind, all his strength of purpose, all his desire to live for the cause, for Dorjee, Bart visualized the Yidam intensely.

As Lasker's last breath came out of his mouth, the visualization succeeded.

Suddenly the Yidam was there, standing behind the preying color creatures. It grabbed out with huge clawed limbs, tore them away, and began unpiling the boulders.

The awful crushing boulders were lifted off him; Lasker sucked in a breath.

The guardian beings faced off against the fearsome twelve-foot Yidam. Its twelve-foot-high body had to crouch to avoid the cavern's roof as it fought the other monsters.

No contest: It tore them, broke them. Their weapons useless, bodies torn, snapped. In short order there was no doubt about it—they were utterly ineffective against Lasker's huge power being.

The Yidam fought with triple the power of Raspahloh, moving so fast it was as if the color things were in slow motion. Lasker lay there gasping for air and just watched, awed that it had worked.

It was inevitable that the vapor things should lose! They were soon strewn all over in bloody pieces, worse than before. The various parts of the cave's protectors again tried to reassemble, but the Yidam wouldn't let them. Rays of paralyzing light thought went out from its eyes, preventing any such thing.

Blueness got on his knees and begged, "Please let us live!"

The Yidam said, "Then admit surrender and kowtow to me, all of you." The rays from the Yidam's eyes faded; the cave creatures reassembled. Any more of this, Lasker thought, and I will surely go mad.

The blueness said, "We surrender, oh powerful and brave Yidam!" And all the cave creatures bowed down.

"Know now," said the Yidam, "that this intruder is not a Bonpo agent. He is truly in the service of His Holiness. Look at me! Do you not recognize Mampa, guardian of the faith?"

The blueness got up and said, "Forgive us! Mampa. We didn't know that he was telling the truth. You are truly sent from His Holiness, the Dalai Lama, or you would not have Mampa's protection. It is right that you remove the prophesy text; take it where you will."

The five vapor beings all vanished.

The Yidam snarled a goodbye also and faded away.

Struggling to maintain his basic sanity after all that had transpired, Lasker got up and, using his sword as a crutch, started to limp onward, deeper into the cave.

Chapter 44

As Lasker explored deeper into the cave of the Dancing Dead, the sound of water running grew louder. Soon he was in a vast open area with stalagtites and limestone rock formations. And before him was an acres-wide quiescent lake. The Pool of Light mentioned in the Terton text.

He threw a rock in its irridescent clear waters and watched it sink and sink—bottomless?

Bart skirted along the side of the hot water lake, hugging the wall. The footing was difficult, but he managed to circumnavigate safely enough, thanks to the brightness of the area.

He then proceeded down a gentle sloping path past gargoylelike foundations of rainbow-hued limestone.

Around a bend and through a narrow natural portal, Bart came out in another spacious chamber. One with heiroglyphic writings on the walls, stiff grey-brown sequence-scenes much like those he had seen in pictures of Egyptian tombs.

He stepped into the dimness, his footfalls echoing hollowly. This chamber was completely smooth and circular and suffused with a very dim, bluish light. There were six stylized sarcophagi spaced evenly around the chamber. No doubt about it; this was a tomb.

Lasker's heart pounded; he felt a cold chill despite the warmth. Whose coffins were they? Were these the coffins of the Dancing Dead? Was anyone inside those six sarcophagi?

Well, he would take a look. What horror could a decayed mummy be after all he'd seen?

He went over and jammed his sword blade under a dust covered stone lid and began to pry it up. With some effort it creaked open.

There was no mistake about it. The body wasn't decayed at all. Inside the sarcophagus was a perfectly preserved creature—humanlike but not human. It was seven feet long, clothed in a shiny blue one-piece outfit.

It was a Cultivator!

Bart was fascinated. The archaeological find of all time! The perfectly preserved body of an ancient space alien!

Should he touch it! Would it turn to dust? Or worse, would it awaken?

He stared down at the being's smooth leatherlike greenish-complexioned face, closed eyes. He stared at that body a long time.

Were there changes? Was it his imagination? Or very slow breathing?

Just a trick of his mind. This was a tomb; he was a bit spooked, that was all.

Lasker went through all the good reasons not to touch it: curiosity killed the cat; contamination.

He decided he had to do it.

He felt the creature's right wrist. It wasn't stiff—no rigor mortis, but no pulse either.

So the breathing he thought he had detected was an illusion.

He shut the cover, relieved that nothing bad had occurred, then turned to explore further.

Lasker, in the near-blindness of the dim blue light, walked toward a low object. When he reached it, he saw it was an obsidian statue of the Peaceful Deity. Just like the one in the hermit's cave, only black! A multi-faceted diamond in the middle of the statue's forehead glimmered intermittently with some strange internal light. The statue seemed to radiate a peacefulness, calming him.

Then he saw it. In the folded hands of this Peaceful Deity was a small replica of the Cultivators' sarcophagi around the room, only this cover was of clear substance. Under the glassine cover was a rectangular book. The long-sought book, obviously, for it occasionally sparkled with all the colors of the rainbow.

Surely this was his glimmering, shimmering prize: the Padmasambhava Prophesy Text.

Examining the clear cover, Lasker noted that there were several faintly glowing buttons—seven different colors: blue, white, red, yellow, green, orange, purple. He remembered the Terton Text's obscure admonition: *The prophesy text is there for the taking, but the wrong color sequence will end life.* Only now did he understand what that meant. These buttons would have to be pressed in the right order, and possibly not all of them should be pressed.

But what was the correct order to press? He kneeled there a long time, thinking. Did the color code have to do with the five guardians? Was it their colors, red, orange, yellow, white, blue? If so, in what order?

Nothing to really go on in making a life or death choice! Bart needed more information. Dimly he perceived a second portal. There were other chambers in the cavern. Perhaps the answer to the color sequence question lay in one of the other rooms.

He decided that he would explore further.

Lasker left the tomb and plunged onward into a natural cavern of tumbled rock falls and crystal amethyst formations.

Chapter 45

The exploration ended quickly and had no results. Evidently the Cultivators had carved out and modified certain parts of a natural cavern. He soon came to a dead end. No cave drawings, no information at all on what color buttons to press, in what order. What should he do now?

He traced his steps back to the tomb chamber and the prophesy texts that lay so inaccessible there.

He examined every inch of the circular smooth tomb chamber. He pried open all six coffins and found bodies identical to the first. Was six a clue? Was their green complexion a clue?

Which colors . . . which colors?

He knew sooner or later he would have to take a chance. The permutations were enormous—a thousand chances of being wrong, a thousand chances of dying. One chance of getting the sequence right.

Perhaps he could pry the cover? No, that would surely set off the unseen killer mechanism.

He crossed the chamber back to the Peaceful Deity statue and the text. A bright light came from his own chest. It was his sky-object, good-luck pendant! It had suddenly started glowing with a bright silvery beam. And it sent out a series of rays, one to each coffin.

Bart, expecting the worst, tried to cover the light, knowing it might do something to the bodies that he didn't want done.

But the light shone right through his blocking hand. He snatched the hand away—surprised that it didn't have a hole in it. The beams of light ceased. Winked out.

Then his deepest fear was realized. There was a creaking, and he saw all of the coffin covers lifting. The Cultivators' corpses were sitting up. They each opened huge yellow eyes like cats, and they turned their attention to him and started to climb out. First one foot and then the other came out of the sarcophagi.

They yawned, stretched and made strange dance-like stretching motions, extending long arms and legs.

The Dancing Dead!

They all looked at Lasker, and then they walked slowly toward him.

"Now, wait a minute," Bart said dry-mouthed. "I'm not an enemy of yours. Er, I was just leaving?" Lasker started to cross the tomb toward the exit.

An unseen door panel slid shut in his path, and as he darted for the second portal, another grey rock door slid tightly shut, barring that way of escape also.

Bart tried with all his might to dig his fingernails around the rock panel and force it open. No go.

The lights went out. He was in total darkness, sealed in an unearthly tomb full of menacing zombies from another galaxy.

316

Chapter 46

"Hey, Raspahloh, old buddy," Lasker whispered. "Hey, are you there?"

No reply, no stirring within. Just the darkness and deep, shallow breathing, the soft padding of large, six-toed feet, coming closer.

"Hold it!" he yelled, trying to muster a long-lost bravado. "Come no closer!"

Bart swung his sword, whooshing back and forth. A dim blue glow started to pour from the central statue's diamond forehead. He saw by that dim light he was still surrounded by the reanimated corpses, who stood just out of sword range. They had their yellow eyes open; their tongues darted in and out like reptiles. Their feet started moving again.

"Now listen," he said dry mouthed, "I mean you no harm, but *if* you force me!" He swooshed his puny sword one more time.

"Quiet." The voice was not in English. It was not even a word but rather a thought—and so powerful, so mind shattering a thought that Lasker screamed out. Clutching his head, writhing in pain, he fell to the smooth stone floor, dropping the sword.

The reanimated Cultivators hesitated in their

steps. Then a much softer but still loud thought throbbed through Lasker's brain: "Sorry, we did not know your capacity. We have no desire to harm you."

The pain went away as he regained his feet, and Bart saw that the corpses had begun to approach him again, holding their six-fingered, suction-cupped hands out toward him menacingly. They seemed all-powerful, but he would try to stop them. The closest one first—maybe a drop kick.

"We are reading your mind, so do not try it. We mean no harm. If you try to hurt us, we will destroy you. Please do not die. We welcome you here. You are our grandchild, and you have brought the message that our time has come—that our scout ships have returned to search for us. We sense your bewilderment. The lights that recharged your so-called sky-object pendant were automated search ships. Your sky-object is really a search-object, dropped by the automated searcher probes from our home planet Zag. After all these millenium that we have lay in suspended animation here, we are happy. We see you, the product of our experiments, and know it is a good experiment. Soon—at the end of our next sleep cycle, eight hundred of your years— we shall receive the rescue party. But for now, thank you for your message. Now we must enter second stage sleep. The final cycle. Farewell and thank you."

They slowly turned and started back to their coffins.

Lasker shouted, "No! Don't go to sleep yet. Tell me, how do I get the text out of its case? What is the

318

color combination?"

The taller Cultivator turned, and Lasker heard inside his head: That is easy; what colors make up all the others?"

"The primary colors!"

"Correct. Red, yellow, blue. Enjoy the book." The slide panels blocking the exits opened. As soon as the Cultivators were asleep in their coffins once more, Lasker went to the statue. Heart pounding wildly, he pressed the correct three buttons, and the cover on the prophesy text slid open.

He took out the almost weightless prophesy text and bolted for the entrance of the cave. He almost slipped edging around the bottomless lake, but didn't. He ran like an olympic champion, literally fell into the chillier outer chamber, picked up his backpack, and put the text in it. He donned his parka, then crawled up and into the ice tunnel.

The first rays of morning sun were shafting into the cave.

The day looked all right. He had a few days' food in his pack; there was water in the runoff streams below the mountain.

He looked back with a sense of wonder.

The cave entrance would be covered by the snows for the winter. Very soon. Perhaps never to be visible again. . . .

He had done it!

He had the prophesy text in his back pack!

He had accomplished the first part of his mission. Now to get back! At least it was bright clear weather. And he had no demon Tinley for deadly company, unlike when he climbed up. He started to descend, feeling elated.

Carefully, go carefully, he told himself. It was not just himself now—it was the awesome secrets of the ages that would be lost if he fell.

Lasker didn't know quite how he would manage the arduous return trip across the Taka Matan, and then through Chinese-occupied Tibet. But he felt a sense of confidence. As Malcolm Donnely, an old acquaintance would sometimes say, "A piece of cake!"